NEVER SURRENDER

NEVER SURRENDER

THE KURTHERIAN GAMBIT™ BOOK 16

MICHAEL ANDERLE

DISRUPTIVE IMAGINATION®

DON'T MISS OUR NEW RELEASES

Join the LMBPN email list to be notified of new releases and special promotions (which happen often) by following this link:

http://lmbpn.com/email/

LMBPN Publishing
PMB 196, 2540 South Maryland Pkwy
Las Vegas, NV 89109

Version 2.52 March 2023
eBook ISBN: 978-1-64971-583-8
Print ISBN: 978-1-64202-058-8

NEVER SURRENDER TEAM

Beta Editor / Readers
Bree Buras (Aussie Awesomeness)
Timothy Cox (The Myth)
Tom Dickerson (The man)
S Forbes (oh yeah!)
Dorene Johnson (US Navy (Ret) & DD)
Dorothy Lloyd (Teach you to ask...Teacher!)
Diane Velasquez (Chinchilla lady & DD)

JIT Beta Readers

Alex Wilson
Jed Moulton
John Findlay
Kimberly Boyer
Keith Verret
Sherry Foster
Hank Rothson
John Raisor
Ginger Sparkman

Bruce Loving
Micky Cocker

Thanks to our JIT Readers for this Version
Dave Hicks
Rachel Beckford
Peter Manis
Deb Mader
Diane L. Smith
Timothy Cox (the myth)
James Caplan
Veronica Stephan-Miller
Dorothy Lloyd
Kerry Mortimer

If I missed anyone, please let me know!

Earlier versions edited by
Stephen Russell
Kat Lind
Ellen Campbell

This version edited by
Lynne Stiegler

**Thank you to the following Special Consultants
for NEVER SURRENDER**

**Jeff Morris - US Army - Asst Professor Cyber-Warfare,
Nuclear Munitions (Active)**

*To Family, Friends and
Those Who Love
To Read.
May We All Enjoy Grace
To Live The Life We Are
Called.*

CHAPTER ONE

<u>Planet Yoll, Southwest Continent, Remote Canyon, Deadlands</u>

Due to the weather, it wasn't the best time to be flying. However, the Yollin Ber'knick was happy for the protection and opportunity it provided the smaller ship to hide from the humans' superior technology.

The ship had only two wings, and Ber'knick had to fight occasional gusts of wind as he stayed close to the ground. He worked to make sure the ship neither lifted high enough that it could be seen on radar, or went low enough to clip the occasional jagged rocks and peaks beneath it. Hitting the ground would result in loss of control and a nose-plant into the rocks below.

Captain Maek-ven yelled from the cargo hold behind him when Ber'knick had to violently jerk to the left to miss a peak that suddenly appeared in front of him—a peak the instruments hadn't shown was coming.

The pilot yelled over his shoulder, "Well, what do you expect, Captain? If you don't provide me a ship with decent instruments, we could all just end up flattened little pies against one of those rock faces out there."

The captain's four feet made their *click-click, click-click* sounds

1

as he headed to the front of the craft. When he stuck his head into the small cockpit, he grumbled, "If I had known that the humans wouldn't be able to track us I would have used our ship, but with limited understanding of their technology, I'm not willing to bet they can't find us. Who knows…the human who's waiting for us might be quite willing to cheat us."

Ber'knick risked a quick glance back at the captain before returning his gaze out the windows. He could see the lightning off to the east and veered a little bit more to the west. It might add a few minutes to their trip, but he really wanted to stay away from the sudden downdrafts a storm would bring. "Do you truly believe this human is on the up and up? Personally I find it curious that with all the humans supporting their leader, we found one who is willing to sell us the spice."

"Those humans who are willing to talk admit that this particular human likes the drink himself. Apparently he's prepared to provide the necessary ingredient for the rebellion's drink so he can purchase it when he comes to Yoll."

Ber'knick smiled. "If there is ever a person to trust, it's a junkie. They will do anything necessary to get their fix."

The captain knocked on the cockpit's door. "That's for good luck, and I have to agree with you. That was why I was willing to take this gig. Even those who had no reason to lie mentioned that this person was willing to do anything to get Pepsi. It wasn't even a very big secret on the base. They just don't believe it's much of a drug, these humans." The captain shrugged before working to turn around in the narrow passageway. He called over his shoulder, "However, we both know a drug is what you make of it. If this Pepsi is his drug, then I trust him as far as I can throw him, which is probably pretty far." The captain's chuckles reverberated off the decking as he walked back to the cargo hold.

"And I'm telling *you*," Ecaterina told Christina, "that I don't care if you can fight Aunt Bethany Anne to a standstill! You *will* change into your wolf form. I don't want these people knowing you are a human child."

Nathan looked around the area. He had selected this canyon since it had good defensive features. He had three different guns trained on the central location where they would accept the gems and money in exchange for the special spice necessary to make Pepsi.

It was pretty damned hilarious that Bethany Anne was using a drink she hated to fund some of their efforts. Using local currency—currency which had been cleaned through this effort —was pretty smart.

Trust Bethany Anne to use something she despised to further her plans.

"Follow the money," Nathan murmured.

Ecaterina walked up to him as she eyed their young daughter, who was now in her wolf form, run around the small canyon. "Follow what?"

Nathan reached out and put an arm around his mate. "One of Bethany Anne's quotes from way back. She always said to 'follow the money,' and now we are doing it again."

Ecaterina smiled. "I remember that. She said it all the time. Whenever you wanted to figure out something, or why someone was doing something you didn't understand, you just needed to follow the money."

"Right," Nathan agreed. "Now, we have the spice, and are about to trade it for currency that she needs—that we all need— to continue to build our base of operations here in the Yollin system. I find it funny as hell that Pepsi is the product that is helping her accomplish this and not Coca-Cola."

Ecaterina took two steps toward their daughter and yelled, "Christina Bethany Anne Lowell, get your furry tail over here! I did *not* say you could go that far away." There was a yip of acceptance, and their daughter started loping back toward the two of them. Ecaterina smirked at her mate. "I blame you for this."

Nathan chuckled. "You blame me for what, naming her 'Bethany Anne?' That's on you and Aunt Bethany Anne." He looked around for a second. "If she *is* taking after her name-sake..." Nathan pointed at himself, "don't blame me."

Ecaterina opened her mouth to argue but realized it was fruitless. Truth be told, Christina was acting just as much the independent young girl as Ecaterina had when she was a child.

However, neither Ecaterina's parents nor her brother had come with them through the Annex Gate, so there was no way for Nathan to confirm that Christina was acting like her mother.

The three Lowells heard the airship before they saw it come over the boulders and small hills in the distance. The pilot was keeping it fairly low to the ground, and Nathan smirked to himself. "That is some great flying, for all the good it's going to do him."

Ecaterina just nodded her agreement.

"The ship's scopes are showing three warm bodies at the landing zone, and three guns pointed at where we expect to land," Ber'knick told the captain over the intercom.

Captain Maek-ven weighed the information before pressing the button and asking, "Can you give me any more details on the three warm bodies?"

The answer from the pilot was quick. "Yes, two humanoid and bipedal. One animal, four legs. Much smaller than the two humanoids."

"Sounds like one of their dogs," the captain commented aloud.

Security Chief Ster-hel looked at him. "You mean like the ones that the Empress has with her most of the time? That white four-footed dog?"

The captain wanted to roll his eyes. Ster-hel was fascinated by those animals. No, not fascinated, he was mentally *unstable* about acquiring one. "I could not tell you if it is the same kind. I guess we will find out when we get there."

The ship's engines started to whine in a rising crescendo as their pilot slowed them down and directed more energy into gently landing the craft. For all the pilot's bitching, Captain Maek-ven felt the cost of the ship was appropriate. The technology on it might be a little old, but it did fly very well and was in good shape. He went to the hatch and slapped his hand on the button to open it. The ramp lowered to the ground as the pilot gave the all-clear over the intercom.

Ster-hel, weapon drawn, went out before the captain. In a meeting like this, no matter what species you were, you wanted to demonstrate trust and mutually-assured destruction.

There was no way the three little guns up in the rocks could harm the airship enough to keep it on the ground, but it could probably kill the captain, and that was enough. Now, Ster-hel could probably kill at least one if not both of the adults out there, but more than likely he and the captain would die too.

Ster-hel gave the all-clear, and Captain Maek-ven continued down the ramp and set foot on Yollin soil once more. He looked around at the location where the human had wished to meet.

He was impressed with the selection. It stopped any significantly larger ships from being able to land, and also offered plenty of locations to hide guns. The human had to understand that they would have enough technology to find additional bodies, should there be any here. So far, he seemed to be playing on the up and up.

Captain Maek-ven had paid attention to the information that was available on the humans, so he identified the other as a female of their species. Considering how close they were standing, they might be in a relationship.

It would be even better if both were junkies for this drink. Perhaps he could get spice he could plant, given enough time.

Unfortunately this exchange was for spice that would not sprout, although he would still take the product to a geneticist to see whether they could yank enough DNA out of the spice to propagate it.

It took Ster-hel and Captain Maek-ven another few minutes to make it over to the three humans. Well, two humans and...

"What is that?" Security Chief Ster-hel pointed toward the animal.

Captain Maek-ven wanted to palm his face in frustration. If his security chief blew this opportunity to purchase the drink's necessary ingredients, he would personally shoot one of his toes off.

Christina was enjoying running around in her four-footed form. She didn't mind being a wolf during this episode. It was rather fun when aliens mistook her for an ignorant beast.

For whatever reason she was advanced for her age, intellectually as well as in the ability to transform her body. Aunt Bethany Anne suspected her intelligence was a byproduct of the upgraded genetics from her parents and the nanocytes that had helped mold her body in her mother's womb.

Her ability to transform was most likely due to her mom's and dad's advanced nanocytes. Her parents were completely loyal to her aunt, the Empress, and had enjoyed the benefit of 'being turned up to eleven' after they had spent time in the Pod-doc.

Christina watched the ship land and had to agree that whoever the pilot was had done a good job. It took them but a moment to disengage the back landing ramp from the ship and lower it to the ground.

After a few seconds, someone came out with a weapon and

looked around. Christina watched as the Yollin carefully checked
out the area before heading a few feet in their direction and
looking around again—obviously a security person of some type.
He turned around and yelled back to the ship, and seconds after
that, another Yollin came out. This one looking like he was in
charge.

She sat on her haunches, tongue hanging out, as the two of
them headed in their direction. It wasn't long before the one in
front pointed at her and asked what she was. Christina turned to
look up at her parents, wondering what they would answer.

It annoyed Nathan that the first words out of their contact's
mouth sounded like a verbal attack on his daughter. "Nathan,"
Ecaterina gently whispered, "now is not the time to become an
overprotective daddy. We have an operation to complete, so you
need to keep your anger in check."

Nathan kept his voice down as well. "You wouldn't have to tell
me that right now if the two of you had stayed up on the *Meredith
Reynolds*."

"I am not spending the next twenty years of my life waiting
for you to come back from operations. Perhaps if you have to
keep your family in mind, you won't try too many risky
activities."

While technically true, allowing the family members to come
along on the operation wasn't a significant burden.

Christina's aunt had made sure that the little girl had incredible armor created just for her. Plus, she had a new type of repul-
sion harness around her chest that utilized gravity that,
according to Jean Dukes, would stop projectiles.

Nathan hoped they never had to test it, especially here in the
middle of nowhere.

"That—" Nathan pointed at his daughter, "is a small version of a wolf. It is an animal that comes from our home world." He nodded to the captain. "Now, if I have assuaged your curiosity, perhaps we can continue with our deal?"

For once, this whole operation looked like it was on the up and up.

From a security standpoint, Ster-hel thought this was great. The longer the human and his captain talked, the more time Ster-hel had to figure out the difference between the animal the Empress had with her and this one near the two humans. As far as he could tell, they weren't too dissimilar.

He had to have it.

He bided his time while the captain continued negotiating the deal, and within ten minutes or so the two shook hands. Ster-hel maintained situational awareness as he heard the whine of the antigravity pallet bring the payment from their own ship. Ster-hel noticed the hoverpad from the human ship made no noise whatsoever.

The male continued watching the two of them as the female replaced the spice from her pallet with the Yollins' payment.

Soon enough the Yollin captain nodded to the human, and the two pallets headed back to their respective ships. The captain nodded to Ster-hel as he passed him and continued walking toward the ship. Ster-hel kept the two humans in his view. As he took two steps backward he started to turn around, but then looked back at the humans.

"How much for the wolf?"

The male human shook his head. "She is not for sale."

Ster-hel chuckled. Everything was for sale.

He had been doing black-market forever, and it was only a matter of negotiation. Besides, they had a ship full of weapons and now the spice. He would get the animal one way or another.

He snickered, flipping on the arming button for his pistol. "Everything is for sale. I said, 'How much for the wolf?' How much is that little animal really worth to you? Is it enough to die over?"

Captain Maek-ven had made it approximately one-third of the way back to his ship when he heard his security chief ask how much the humans wanted for the wolf. He closed his eyes and hung his head as he walked another few steps.

This had *almost* gone well. He had turned to yell at his security chief to get his bony little ass back in the ship and stop harassing the humans when he saw the security chief flick off the safety on his pistol, activating it.

It was obvious that the weapon was armed, and he was using it to threaten the humans. If they were able to get out of this without a major altercation, he was gonna rip Ster-hel to shreds for such a breach of operational procedures.

The captain's eyes opened wide in alarm when the male changed forms.

One moment he was angry, but still human. The next he was towering above both his security chief and the female, who was trying to talk to him. The creature's roar shook the walls of the small canyon, and although his security chief tried to raise his weapon to fire it, only two shots hit the ground in front of him, throwing up dirt.

But it was too late.

The snarling creature yanked the pistol out of the security chief's hand and crushed it in his paw while reaching for his neck. His roar of a challenge reverberated through the canyon as Ster-hel screamed in pain.

The captain turned and ran toward the ship, yelling and waving his arms. "Dammit, Ber'knick, start those engines! Rev them to red, I don't give a shit! Get ready to blast us out of here!"

It took him but a moment for his feet to hit the metal of the landing ramp.

The ship's pilot had been monitoring what was going on, but it had gotten pretty boring after a little while. Apparently the human and his captain were getting along just fine; the security chief was keeping him up to date.

When they requested the money, the pilot directed the ship's computers to take the payment out on the pallet.

He started his preflight checklist, occasionally looking up at the video monitors to make sure nothing was going wrong. After a few more items, he looked up a second time. The captain was walking back, so he really focused on completing his checklist.

He had another four items crossed off when he heard the captain yelling for him to get ready to take off.

He started rushing through the checklist, skipping those things that he felt were unnecessary. He could hear the captain's running *click-click, click-click* through the ship, and his panicked yell reverberating down the hallway. "What the hell are we still doing on the ground, Ber'knick?"

The pilot tossed his checklist away and slammed his hand down on the emergency lift as he heard an unworldly beast screaming at them. Ber'knick asked Maek-ven, "What the hell is going on?"

The captain stopped right outside the cockpit. "That idiot decided he wanted the animal, and even though I told him to leave well enough alone he disobeyed orders. Now he's gone and pissed off one of those humans who can change into...something! Hurry up and take off."

"I've got to give it another fifteen..." A severed arm slammed into the cockpit's windshield, screeching downward as its carapace scraped in its journey and leaving a smear of blood down the glass.

The pilot, his mouth wide open, watched as it slid down the glass and spat the alien equivalent of "Fuck me!" He turned his head back to the controls, punched two buttons, and pulled on the yoke, and the ship rose quickly into the air.

CHAPTER TWO

Tabitha strode into her suite and called for her roommate. "Anne?"

She walked over to the kitchen table and dropped off her tablet. When she turned around, Anne was coming out of her room. The girl seemed in better spirits than when Bethany Anne had brought her to stay with Tabitha.

Sure enough, Jinx, one of Ashur's and Bellatrix's puppies, scooted out of Anne's room a moment later.

"Hey, R2, what's up?" Anne turned around and bent over with her arms held open, and Jinx jumped into them while Tabitha shook her head. Now that she was on the receiving end of playful nicknames—the kind she commonly gave Barnabas—she realized it could be quite annoying from someone much younger than oneself.

Saint Payback was *truly* a bitch.

Tabitha answered, "It's not 'R2,' it's not 'Ranger Two,' it's not 'Queen's Ranger Two,' and it's not just 'Two.' The name is 'Tabitha.' It's also not 'Tabby' with a 'y' or 'Tabbi' with an 'i.'"

She looked the young woman over.

"How about 'Tabbie' with an 'ie?'" Anne smiled, wondering what the Ranger would say next.

"If the Tontos and I didn't need to leave shortly, I would make you eat that question. Further, I don't think you have enough bruises on your body for the amount of workout time you've been spending." Tabitha raised an eyebrow as she checked the teenager out.

Anne quickly shook her head. "Nope, workout time won't be necessary. 'Tabitha' is what you want to be called, 'Tabitha' is what you will get. As for the bruises—" She waved a hand up and down her body, "Bethany Anne suggested that I needed to know self-defense as a researcher, but did not have to work out as hard as the rest of the team."

Tabitha drew her eyebrows together. "Is that the truth?"

Anne looked at her roommate and bit her lip, finally deciding to nod her head in the affirmative.

Bethany Anne?

What is it, Number Two?

Tabitha rolled her eyes before responding, *Is it true you told Anne she didn't need to work so hard on her physical training because she was going to be doing research?*

Have you ever known me to suggest such a thing?

No, I haven't, so you can imagine my surprise when your new Etheric Researcher suggested that this was exactly what you had said.

Huh, so my new Etheric Researcher is acting all teenagerish if I understand you correctly?

That's the way it appears.

Okay, since you have to go out with the Tontos on the slave issue, I'll make sure to take care of this with Peter. He will have some insights on how to get the best results from recalcitrant teenagers.

Very well, I will consider this a closed issue.

Bethany Anne added, *You can let Anne know Peter is going to have new instructions from me when she is due for her training session three hours from now.*

Will do, My Queen. Have a great one.

You, too. Go kick some pirate ass.

Tabitha smiled. *Oh, I intend to. This ought to be a hoot.*

Make sure you say hello to the twins for me.

Tweedledee and Tweedledum? I will.

Bethany Anne cut the connection between the two of them and Tabitha raised an eyebrow. "Bethany Anne says that Peter will have new instructions for your workout when you see him in three hours."

"Three hours!" Anne's face displayed shock. "I'm supposed to be meeting a couple friends in the library in three hours."

"I suggest that *next* time you do the workouts that you were told to do instead of trying to get out of them. I especially suggest..." Tabitha reached up and tapped the side of her head, "not lying to a Queen's Ranger who can talk to Bethany Anne directly."

Anne's eyes closed when she realized her mistake, and she turned around and kicked the air in the direction of the couch. "God, it was so much easier getting away with stuff when it was only my mom and dad."

Tabitha pursed her lips. "I understand you're doing well with your dad now, is that right?"

Anne turned back around to face her roommate. "Yes. We spoke a couple weeks ago, and he apologized for not intervening with Mom when she got so upset with me all the time. He says Mom is going to therapy sessions before she tries to connect with me again." Anne shrugged. "I'm okay with it all now, but it was pretty scary in the beginning when I thought I'd be on the outs with my parents."

Tabitha walked over to the young woman and put an arm around her shoulder, pulling her in for a hug. "You don't need to worry about that. Your parents will forgive you, no matter what the problems are. You might just have to give it some time. They love you, but your mom was under some incredible strain, and she broke. That's nothing against her, and really, it helped a whole lot. Now we understand that classes needed to be created for those of us who weren't coping as well as we had hoped once we left Earth. Some of us get so involved with the next goal, we forget that a lot of those who are supporting us might have their own troubles and difficulties."

Anne mumbled a response into Tabitha's chest. "Brgrlfllr-rrckraghen."

Tabitha pulled away and looked down at the teenager. "What did you say?"

Anne smiled. "I said, 'I can't breathe!'" Anne pulled Tabitha back in for another hug before releasing her. Anne continued, "I know that now, but it was pretty scary when the Queen emancipated me. I'm super-excited to be working on Etheric research, and it's kind of cool that I sometimes get to talk to my dad about it as well."

Tabitha turned and headed to her own room in the suite. "Well, he did all that work with that stupid black-ops shell company, so some of this is not that far out from what he was working on."

Tabitha's voice now came from her room. "So, who knows, maybe you and your father will be famous researchers into Etheric Travel!"

Tabitha didn't see the small tear that Anne reached up and wiped away as she waited for a moment to get her emotions in order. "Maybe. That would be pretty rad."

Tabitha's voice called, "Hey, so, while I go on this operation, what you going to be doing?"

Anne walked to Tabitha's door and leaned against the opening, crossing her arms. "I've been told that I will get my own small suite in about three or four days, so when you get back you won't have a roomie anymore."

Tabitha looked up from the little gym bag of extra supplies she was taking with her. "Really?" Tabitha looked around her room. "God, it will be so good not to have to be so clean all the time."

Anne looked at her with surprise and annoyance on her face. "What? Are you saying you're not naturally this clean?" She pointed to all the areas around the room that were spotless.

Tabitha chuckled. "Hell, no. I'm only this clean because I have a teenager here sharing my suite all the time. I had to set a good example. If you weren't here, I would have been messy. When I know somebody is coming over, I will throw it all into a basket and stick it somewhere in the back of the closet. I'm not *that* much older than you, for Pete's sake."

Anne continued looking at her roomie, and finally she threw up her hands and turned around. "I'll bet you I'm cleaner than you are unless you put in the extra effort."

Tabitha smiled as the young woman walked away.

It wasn't that Tabitha was a very messy person. It was just that she was a very busy person, and whatever she was working on had her attention. Slowing down to do something like…oh, cleaning up dirty clothes, never seemed to have the highest priority.

She finished adding the extra supplies she wanted to her go-bag, and after stepping back into her closet she laid her work clothes out on the bed. She was going in her synthetic black leather outfit this time, with the extra armor Jean had supplied.

She walked back to her closet and started pulling out different boxes labeled with symbols that she had created. They represented the different tools and tricks that she enjoyed using as a Ranger.

She made three more trips to the closet, setting boxes on the bed after each. She looked at what she had laid out so far and considered what she still wanted from the closet, and spoke aloud. "Achronyx?"

Her personal EI spoke from her tablet on the dresser. "Yes?"

"Do me a favor and order a transfer cart to the suite. I've got too much stuff to move myself. And then take it down to the ship in Bay 212. I understand that bay has the ship we are using for our trip."

Her EI responded, "Request taken care of."

Tabitha raised an eyebrow. This was the easiest Achronyx had been in the last three days.

Normally he was a pain in the ass. If she'd had time, she would have had ADAM take a look at her EI and find out what was wrong with him. However, it was one of those cases where she either didn't have enough time, or didn't think about it when she did.

He had to be the most recalcitrant EI that she had ever dealt with. If she didn't know any better, she would swear Achronyx was made up of a bunch of IBM PC Juniors all strung together.

Tabitha exited her room and crossed the suite toward Anne's. She was going to give the teenager one more hug goodbye.

Just to make sure the young girl was doing okay.

QBBS *Meredith Reynolds*

Giannini walked into the little kitchenette she shared with Sia. It was a nice two-bedroom, two-bath suite often referred to as a 'roommate plan' on Earth. The kitchen, living room, and dining room were situated between the two bedrooms.

She had the room without the en suite bath, since she was the neater of the two women and would keep it cleaner for guests. Giannini opened the little refrigerator—which had technology for cooling she was completely in awe of—and snagged a bottle of beer.

She looked at the little label All Guns Blazing had placed on the bottle and raised an eyebrow. It said that it had a hint of berry in it. She reached to her right and opened a drawer, grabbing a bottle opener to pop off the cap, then tossed the cap into a bag with the others. She would take all the bottle caps back to the guys when the bag was full.

She walked into the living room, sat on the couch and grabbed a tablet to turn on the news. When she took a sip of her beer, she had to admit it did have a nice hint of berries. She turned the beer bottle around to look at the label again and reviewed the ingredients.

It was raspberry that they had used in this recipe, or at least that was what they claimed on the label. Knowing Bobcat, William, and Marcus, it could be anything. As long as it tasted like berries to Bobcat, that was what the label said.

She picked the tablet back up and scrolled through the different channels available, both the internal options and those from the Yollin networks which would be translated. Although she could ask the entertainment EI to choose a station, she preferred to review the information in text form and pick one herself.

Giannini noticed that one of her favorite Yollin newscasters had a special on and asked the EI to turn on channel twenty-two. The suite's projector turned on, and a nice forty-eight-inch picture appeared on the wall opposite her.

She took another sip of her beer as she watched the breaking news about another public riot on the television.

R'Chkoklet, Planet Yoll

The young female Yollin reporter turned to view the camera. "Hello, this is Pehl-eck, and I am reporting from the town of R'Chkoklet in the Upper Caste Business Zone. There is a mob of protesters throwing stones at the building and shouting slogans at those inside. There was a violent outburst here just hours ago. Some of the upper-caste Yollins have refused to accept the edicts coming from the Etheric Empire. When a traditionally lower-caste member refused the commands of three previously upper-caste members in a small breakfast shop this morning, they grabbed him and pulled him out into the street."

The video showed some b-roll of the other location and people milling around as the reporter continued speaking over the clip. "It's reported that they then kicked him repeatedly, leaving him severely injured. I understand others called in medical support, who were able to provide him care.

"The lower-caste member suffered multiple head wounds and cracks throughout the carapace on his chest and arms as he tried to protect himself. These upper-caste members were protesting the actions of the alien Empress Bethany Anne, who challenged and defeated our Kurtherian-infested former king mere weeks ago.

"The whole revolution has upended our religious and societal understandings; many at the top are contending that the video of the king was faked. They are also accusing those of us in the news of supporting the overthrow, and are critical of us giving our support to the aliens. There has been a lot of strain between the various castes as all Yollins seek new equilibrium in our relationships with each other."

Pehl-eck ducked her head when a large explosion reverberated down the street from the building behind her. She gasped in shock when she saw the destruction wrought by those inside the building. It appeared that they used military weapons on the rioters surrounding the building, who were chanting at them for hurting the low-caste Yollin.

There were now bodies lying in the street, and screams of pain and fright could be heard from her location some distance away.

She put a hand up to her mouth and continued reporting, "Oh my gods! The upper-caste members have attacked the rioters around their building! This is no longer merely an angry group of people yelling insults and throwing stones at each other. This is now a war zone!"

Pehl-eck turned back to the camera. "We all know that changes in society can be hard. However, what will be done to those who refuse the edicts coming down upon us? That is an open question I would like to ask the Empress of the humans. What are you going to do to those members of the upper castes who refuse to accept that all Yollins are equal?"

Pehl-eck waved a hand, the gesture encompassing the building and the dead and injured people behind her. "Will there be any justice for these people, or is this something that we Yollins will have to figure out ourselves?"

CHAPTER THREE

Spaceport Outside Minor City, One Hour from Planetary Capital

"I see you're not drinking that new revolutionary stuff," Ghyr-lihk asked Captain Maek-ven as he slid into the booth the Yollin occupied. The lights were low in this spaceport bar, which was the haven of captains and higher-ranked officers.

Ghyr-lihk had fully expected to find Maek-ven here after the operation to get the spice.

Maek-ven glanced up and gave Ghyr-lihk a small smile, and he reached out and pushed the half-empty amber liquor bottle toward him. He pointed. "You might want to drink a bit of that. Considering how the operation went, we need to toast a fallen comrade. It's the least we can do."

Ghyr-lihk raised an eyebrow. "Don't mind if I do, although if the rumors about him were true Ster-hel was an asshole. I'm not sure if I will be drinking to his demise or toasting the fact I don't have to deal with him again."

Captain Maek-ven nodded in agreement. "Yep. He ignored orders one too many times, confident he had the ability to call upon the ship's armament to save his ass. This time it didn't happen."

Ghyr-lihk uncapped the bottle and held it beneath his nose, nodding his appreciation at the fine aroma. He raised the bottle in salute to the captain before pouring his glass a quarter full, then recapped the bottle and set it back in the middle of the table with a thump. "Did you pay for the good stuff to honor the missing?"

Maek-ven chuckled dryly in response to the question.

"That's what I thought. So why *are* you paying for the good stuff, Maek-ven?"

Captain Maek-ven looked around the bar, which was mostly empty. There were the two others: a waitress who was drying glasses behind the bar, and the barkeep, who was off to the side half-asleep. He turned back to his friend. "Every once in a while, you get sent on an operation where you see enough bad shit to appreciate *living* again."

Ghyr-lihk's mandibles clicked in confusion. "From a human? I've seen a few of them; they don't look like much. What happened to get you all messed up like this?"

Maek-ven reached forward and grabbed his glass, swirling the liquid before raising it and taking a sip. He lowered his glass and eyed his friend. "Let's just say, there are apparently some humans you don't want to piss off."

Ghyr-lihk waved a hand. "Come on. There's got to be more to it than that. Ber'knick has already said that Ster-hel was ripped apart, if you believe him."

Captain Maek-ven chuckled once more and set his drink down on the table. "You see the bottle right there, Ghyr-lihk? The one that's half empty?" Ghyr-lihk nodded. "I cracked that bottle just a few hours ago when I was finally able to release the built-up tension from the operation."

"Did the human try to cheat you?" Ghyr-lihk asked.

Maek-ven shook his head. "No. In fact, I would say he was the most up-and-up druggie I've ever dealt with."

Ghyr-lihk frowned, trying to understand the situation "Is that why you trusted him? He's a druggie?"

Maek-ven's mandibles clicked twice in agreement. "Yes. I know the power of drugs, and he wants a drink that's created from these ingredients—one his leader has banned. If he can get us to make the beverage, everyone is blessed and he gets to come down here and have the drink he wants. I can understand that motivation, and I can even *agree* with it." Maek-ven met Ghyr-lihk's eyes. "But let me tell you something. Don't ever, and I mean *ever*, try to buy his animal if he says no."

Captain Maek-ven's hand started to tremble as he finished his thought. "Just leave well enough alone."

QBBS Meredith Reynolds

"My point," Bethany Anne told the Yollin representatives, "is that the planet is poorly utilized. You were told that you needed to expand into space without *any* justification."

"That is just not true," Chr-taleen replied. "We have the calculations to support why we needed to go into space."

If Bethany Anne had known she was going to have to help rebuild the planet, she might have been tempted to just let the king live.

It had not taken long, with the help of an artificial intelligence such as ADAM and an understanding of the Kurtherian mindset compliments of TOM, to understand what King Yoll had accomplished on the planet.

Using machinations over generations, he encouraged the Yollins to believe they had outgrown their world. Then he used religious texts—which he had written—to further support efforts to take over other planets and enslave their people.

If you wanted to be strictly analytical about it, she could

appreciate his plan. Unfortunately for King Yoll, she wasn't analytical enough.

"Chr-taleen, I will give you a thousand pages of scientific documentation that proves—if you are willing to pay attention to facts—that this planet is only thirty percent utilized. That includes twenty-seven percent for foodstuffs, thirty-six percent of arable land, and seventeen percent for cities and communal areas. In fact, we could bring back every single one of the Yollins who are presently off-world and still only be at forty-seven percent utilization of this planet. If I have to get one of your religious bibles and beat you around the head with it until you understand, I will!"

Bethany Anne's eyes flashed red, reminding the Yollin just who he was speaking to.

Chr-taleen sat back in his chair, his mandibles grating against each other. "How much time do I have to review these documents?"

"You have three turns of your time to make a decision as to what you will or won't believe. If you choose not to believe, I will allow you one opportunity to make your case. If you cannot scientifically argue—and win—your position, your choices will be stepping down, stepping aside, believing the new information to be true, or being ejected off of a spaceship going toward the sun. Your pick."

Chr-taleen's mandibles stopped moving. "I do hope that is multiple choice, even if I choose not to believe the information provided me?"

Bethany Anne chuckled. "You'll only be ejected from a spaceship if you really, really tick me off. I don't mind a logical argument, but I abhor someone being obstinate just for the sake of being obstinate. Should you choose not to believe this information and you have no good reason why, I would suggest you retire from your job early."

>>**Bethany Anne?**<<

Yes, ADAM?

>>We are receiving information that there is an uprising in one of the smaller outlying towns. Started by those previously of the second-level caste, there are now injuries and potentially deaths on the scene. More of the press are heading in that direction. My interpretation is this is going to require force.<<

Bethany Anne put a finger up to stop the communication directed at her. "I apologize. There is an issue on the planet that I urgently need to review." Bethany Anne picked up her tablet, on which ADAM had already queued up the necessary news report for her. He piped the information straight into her ears, so she could watch the video but no one else would hear the video playback.

As she continued watching, those at the table noticed that her eyes were growing red. It was obvious something on her tablet was causing her to become angry.

A moment later one of her security men walked into the room. Chr-taleen recognized him due to his size as the one called 'John Grimes.' As he spoke to the human leader, her eyes went dim and then returned to their normal color.

She nodded sharply, and her security guard left the meeting room.

A moment later she was ready to continue their conversation, and Chr-taleen took the opportunity to ask a question. "What has happened?" He pointed around the table. "We saw that something upset you." He pointed to his eyes. "Your eyes started to grow red again."

Bethany Anne smiled in a way that Chr-taleen recognized was not meant to be pleasant when she answered, "There has been an uprising which has hurt Yollins. Those in the upper castes are not pleased with me abolishing the old system, and are upset that they must now pull their own weight. Some of those who are upset decided to try their hand at violent responses.

Had I gone down there, I would have had to restrain my reaction."

Chr-taleen was confused. "If you had gone down there you would've had to restrain your reaction? How would you have preferred to react?"

"I have no patience for those who resort to violence when upset. We can have conversations without it. As the leader of the humans who have annexed Yoll, I would have had to be nice or risk creating a larger issue with my reputation. If I had reacted as I personally wished, my reputation might have been manipulated in the press." She nodded toward the door through which her guard had left. "Now that John has gone down there?" She looked at those around the table.

"Their lives aren't worth *shit*."

CHAPTER FOUR

E'Kolorn, defense minister under King Yoll, reviewed the book in his hands for a moment, clicked his mandibles twice in annoyance, and threw the book across the cell. He barely noticed the loud *slap* and then *fwhomp* as it hit the hard rock floor as he thought about his life.

His life had been a *lie*.

He glanced at the religious text and the pages he had ripped out over the weeks he had been here in isolation as his mind ran through past scenes of him working for the king.

For a damned Kurtherian!

It took a moment for his mind to register the *click-click-click-click* of someone walking down the hallway. He glanced up from the couch where he was resting, and over toward the opening in the metal door where he might see a face.

Any face.

When the footsteps continued past he looked back down, ignoring whatever was going to happen to someone else in this cell block. No one was going to come looking for the false king's defense minister.

It didn't matter that his efforts had been for his people, his world. Even at the end, he had made a decision that ignored the king's commands and maneuvered the king into accepting the challenge.

His mandibles opened and paused there before they slowly closed.

E'Kolorn supposed that if he were honest with himself he had played a small part in the demise of that rotten royal bastard. If it wouldn't have messed up his little cell, he would have spat at the mere thought of that Kurtherian puppet.

Kurtherian… What a kick between the back set of legs that was.

A female voice called out louder, and E'Kolorn wondered if he could rip his sheet apart and use it for ear plugs.

He didn't want to listen to anyone enjoying a conjugal visit.

It took another couple shouts before he looked up, realization dawning on his face. "Rea-behk?"

"It's about time you recognized your wife's voice!" she answered. "Can I come in?"

E'Kolorn looked around his cell, thanking whoever was escorting her for the thoughtful act of not letting her see immediately into his cell. He got up from the couch and went to his bed, laying the sheets out nicely. "One second."

He kicked the false bible under his bunk, and grabbed three crumpled pages and dropped them into the trash can. Thank his ancestors he had at least kept himself presentable.

"You can come in now!" he called. He stood by the back wall, which was proper anytime the guards opened the door. The viewing window in the door slid open. He recognized one of the two guards, who nodded to E'Kolorn to confirm his position and opened the door.

It was but a second before his wife darted in, and they met in the middle of the cell.

He never heard the door clang softly shut behind her.

Nor did he know that there was a human with the guard, making sure this meeting occurred and it was respectful.

It had taken Kael-ven five weeks to ascertain the state of the former defense minister's mind and confirm his activities during the battle for the Yollin system. How he had acted and whether properly, and under whose orders.

It had taken Bethany Anne about five minutes to decide they needed him.

If he could be trusted.

After the hallway door had closed, Eric nodded his appreciation to the security guard. "I'll be back here to escort her safely up to her quarters on Space Station Rig-turrik." He handed the officer a small device. "If they have a spat or something, just click that and I'll return to take her back early."

Wut-ven looked down at the device and back to the human. "You expect them to finish early?"

Eric shrugged. "I couldn't tell you enough about Yollin relationships to answer that. I'm just basing it on human relationships, and I can tell you from recent experience that one small comment, even if meant in the nicest possible way, can upset a female in the most illogical manner."

The guard clicked his mandibles twice in agreement and pocketed the device.

Some foibles of relationships, Eric decided, crossed species boundaries just fine.

Personal Ship *Powerdrive*, Exiting Commercial Gate Five, Yollin System, Ring Three

Shi-tan engaged the autopilot. He was surprised by how efficiently the Yollin space traffic control was operating, considering they had been taken over by a foreign power not too long ago.

His ship, which could hold him easily and one other semipleasantly, was not capable of making interstellar jumps by itself.

Therefore, he had to transfer between solar systems using the transfer Gates. While he waited for the controllers to provide his ship with instructions, he reviewed the documents and information he could find related to traffic coming into the system.

It seemed that, surprisingly enough, these humans had increased the commercial traffic into the Yollin system, not decreased it.

He stood up from the pilot's seat and stretched his seven-foot-tall frame. As the Scion of a great warrior line, it was embarrassing for him to be categorized as a mere bounty hunter.

However, it beat becoming a mercenary in his book.

Fortunately, or unfortunately, depending on your viewpoint, his race was known for their hot tempers and quick violence. While he was a little better controlled than most, it wouldn't take much for his anger to inflame, and the spikes in his face to slide out of his skin, letting anyone who knew what was happening realize how close they were to being broken in half.

He reached up to his right ear and unhooked both his earrings. Fingering the larger of the two, he sighed and reached down to the pilot's chair, opening a small compartment and dropping them in. He closed the compartment and turned to walk toward the small stateroom on his ship.

He had more than enough money in the cross solar system banks to continue this chase. Furthermore, it provided him an opportunity to get to see these new humans up close.

Who knew? It might provide an opportunity to test his martial abilities against them.

Third Outer Ring - Yollin System Space Control

Third Shift, First Class Ships' Controller Yri-Keva took another look at the ship's information displayed on her registry for inbound craft. Her four legs still wrapped under her couch, she turned her torso to the right. "Turrel?"

"Huh?" he grunted. He was going through the ships in this area of space, handing one of the larger commercial ships over to the second ring. The ship was slowing down as it made its way toward Space Station One. They didn't care about the names of the stations here in Space Control. You got a number and you were good.

Except for the humans. Their station was the *Meredith Reynolds*, or just the *Reynolds* if you were short of breath.

"Check out Ship One-One-Six coming in from Commercial Gate Three," she told him.

Turrel confirmed his ship was passed off to Ring Two and flipped a screen, punching up Yri-Keva's area of responsibility. It took a second for him to recognize what she was pointing out to him. "A bounty hunter?" He punched another couple of buttons on his controller. "A good bounty hunter. A Shrillexian." Turrel reached up and scratched his right mandible.

A tic, Yri-Keva had figured out. It wasn't because he itched, but rather because he was thinking and he felt it provided an excuse not to talk.

Finally, he turned toward her. "I don't think the humans have any rules against a bounty hunter in our system." His right hand tapped his monitor. "I'd say send him the rules, and then notify the Empress' representative what we have."

"Yes." Yri-Keva turned back to her screen and moved her controller around. "That is a good point. I wish I were a small insect on the wall of his ship when he receives the rules."

The beep from the cockpit alerted Shi-tan that the ship had received instructions moments before he felt the artificial gravity make changes as they veered from their previous course and aligned on the new one. He looked up at the slaved monitor in his room and was happy to see his requested space station had been approved.

Then his eyes narrowed as a little red flag caught his attention.

He had received additional instructions. The red flag notified him they included rules not to break on pain of death.

Shi-tan slowly wiped his hands dry, then confirmed the sutures holding closed the slice in his chest were helping him heal properly.

They weren't caused by his quarry, but rather a random barfight he had been in during his last night at his previous stop. He hadn't started the fight, and once the video confirmed he hadn't escalated the violence when he was attacked with a bladed weapon, they had absolved him of the bar repair bills and the hospitalization charges.

He looked in the mirror and smiled, his many sharp teeth lending an air of menace to what was, he thought, a *very* welcoming face.

He winked to himself and tossed the towel over the holder as he made his way out of the room and up to the cockpit.

Time to see what new rules the leaders in this sector of space had for him.

Christina Bethany Anne Lowell hopped out of the Executive Pod and made a beeline for the bay's exit. At the moment, her parents weren't any fun to be around. She could tell they were frustrated and angry with each other as a result of how the operation had gone, and it had nothing to do with the success.

They had received the money, and they had traded the nanocyte-infested spices to the Yollins. However, Dad had gotten mighty upset when that maggot-ridden tapeworm had tried to buy her.

Personally she had thought it was funny, and she'd be happy when she was old enough to get away with using some of the creative language being around Aunt Bethany Anne was teaching her.

However, Mama had told her to go find whoever was working in All Guns Blazing and stay with them for a few minutes while her parents had "*a talk*."

That was good enough for her. They had the best root beer in that place.

Ecaterina closed her eyes, willing herself to remain calm. Opening them, she turned to her mate. "I understand that it upset you when the security person tried to buy our daughter. In the future, we will probably find this funny. And I know that he pulled a gun and armed it when both our daughter and myself were in the vicinity."

Nathan, his teeth grinding, worked to keep his anger out of his voice. "No, Ecaterina, I don't think you do understand. I had a family before, and I lost them. That was incredibly painful for me. And while I don't wish to bring up previous relationships, I want you to know that if something happens to the two of you, I doubt I will survive it."

Ecaterina stepped forward and placed a hand on his arm. "I get that, Nathan, but you need to understand *we* are doing operations. I don't want our daughter left up here. If it becomes too dangerous, then we will all quit."

Nathan turned to Ecaterina. "Too dangerous? How are we going to know what is too dangerous until it happens?"

"Perhaps that will be your responsibility? Make sure that we don't get into something that's too dangerous, right?"

Nathan faced forward, then slowly beat his head against the seat headrest one time for each word. "You. Don't. Under. Stand."

He stopped beating his head and turned to look at her. "Anything could happen, and we wouldn't be planning on it. We could be attacked just enjoying ourselves at supper sometime because we are known to be a part of this." He waved his hand. "You are exposing our daughter to danger."

"Our daughter is not a normal human, and she is one of the most protected young people in this area of space. Who is going to get to her through us—through you, for goodness sake? You just ripped off an arm and threw it against a spaceship, Nathan." Ecaterina chuckled a moment. "Okay, I hope the videotape shows that because it really was funny as hell. Our daughter can change shapes. She wears some of the most technologically advanced armor that Jean Dukes can provide for her. I would not risk our daughter if I didn't think she was safer with us than here."

Nathan turned on her like she had just lost the argument. "See, there!" He pointed at her. "She would be safer here on the *Meredith Reynolds* then down there with us."

Ecaterina's lips pressed together as she thought. She considered his arguments and had to finally agree. While she didn't want to admit it, her greatest fear at this second, was Nathan dying somewhere she couldn't help him. "I'll tell you what...each operation we can decide how dangerous it is. If at some time it only requires you, only you will go. If it is so dangerous that Christina and myself need to stay on the *Meredith Reynolds*? Then you and I will discuss whether or not it is necessary for *you* to go on the mission. Is that understood?"

Nathan nodded his head.

"Finally, I will bet you that she will do something that will amaze you, that will make you admit she is useful in an operation," she concluded.

Nathan stared at his mate for a moment. "You think she is going to be useful in an operation? Like, can she take care of herself or what?"

Ecaterina shrugged. "I don't know. I just feel she is going to surprise you. Hell, she'll probably surprise both of us. You've said yourself that she is the most advanced Wechselbalg that you have ever heard about."

When the two of them agreed on the bet, Ecaterina sure hoped that her mouth hadn't just run ahead of her gut feeling.

CHAPTER FIVE

"Scott, I am on my way to Jean's lab. I need you to cover Bethany Anne." John took a right down a corridor, heading there to get suited up. With Jean constantly talking about what they had accomplished in her group, he was aware there might be something new he could play with today.

And it seemed like this was his opportunity to have a little fun that wasn't in the schedule.

Provided the dumb fucks down on the planet didn't become wise and decide to throw down their arms.

His friend replied, "John, it's Scott. I'm inbound to Bethany Anne's position, ETA fifteen seconds. What's up?"

John took a left. "Hope I didn't take you away from anything, buddy. However, we have a situation down on the planet that is going to require some personal involvement. I told Bethany Anne I would go take care of it so she can continue the crap meeting she is in right now."

Scott chuckled. "You told her you would take care of it so that she didn't leave you stuck in her place in the meeting."

John smiled. "Well, I don't think they believe I'm qualified to run the meeting, but anything is possible. If I have to decide between Option A, which is staying up here and talking with a bunch of incredibly intelligent but charismatically lacking people or Option B, going down to the planet and potentially fucking up some people? I'll go with Option B."

"We would all choose Option B every damned time. Ok, I'm at the door, so have fun and see you back tonight?"

"You bet. Jean and I are looking forward to taking you and Cheryl Lynn out for dinner."

John arrived at the R&D facilities, typed in his security code, and pressed his hand against the wall. EI Meredith viewed him from seven different directions to make sure it was, in fact, John Grimes, then the door lock clicked and the two guards stepped aside to allow him to enter.

Planet Yoll, New Yollin Government Building

Kael-ven was sitting on his couch behind his desk going through different bits of information he needed to review as he and others worked to keep the lid on the planet.

He paused briefly to watch as Snow demolished her new chew toy, once again marveling at the strength in her jaws.

With all the upheaval due to the information that people were certain of, what everyone suspected, and what everyone was lying about, there were so many holes in the dam that he didn't have enough appendages to plug all of them.

Whoever said revolutions would be easy had never tried to accomplish one with a minimum amount of bloodshed.

He pulled up his tablet when it beeped and hit the button to speak. "Yes, ADAM?"

"Kael-ven, I have been asked by Bethany Anne to give you an update about a physical confrontation in the town of R'Chkoklet."

Kael-ven put his hand on his face and ground his mandibles together. He wiped his eyes and replied, "Okay, I'm going to assume it is upper-caste idiots again. However, if you're talking to me it must be more than what normally happens with these jackasses." He waved a hand across his desk. "There's activity in over a hundred and fifty different locations, right now."

ADAM responded, "Yes, this time there are deaths because advanced weapons were brought to bear. It is presently on the news, if you care to see a reporter's view."

Kael-ven's shoulders slumped. "Damn, I was hoping it wouldn't get to this. Okay, I will take a few minutes and view the newscasts—"

ADAM interrupted Kael-ven's reply. "John Grimes is preparing to come down and have a conversation with them."

Kael-ven jumped up off his couch and snagged his pistol, sliding it into the holster as he headed toward the door. He grabbed the small suitcase Jean had provided him to put on in the Pod. "Why didn't you tell me John was coming in the first place? Shit, man! Sorry, EI, AI—whatever acronym you are at the moment. John coming was the information I needed the most." Kael-ven pulled open the door and nodded to his two security guards, who stood outside. "We've got to go to a hotspot and try to talk some sense into some idiots."

He stopped as Snow barked from his feet. "You can come in the Pod, but you will need to stay there while I go talk to these morons."

Snow growled her displeasure.

Kael-ven waved her through the door. "I know you're brave and courageous, but you're growing faster than Bobcat can drink beer. That's why," he held up the case he was carrying, "you don't have any of Jean's armor. Once you stop growing so you'll be able to wear something for more than ten days before it's too small, we'll ask Jean to make you something. I care for you too much to have you hurt by some idiot who's too stupid to know he's dead if John has to 'talk' to him."

Snow's tail drooped as she went past her partner, but she

didn't voice any more objections. As much as she hated that he was right, getting shot wasn't part of her immediate plans.

One of the security guards shut the door and locked it behind them as they hustled to keep up with the Yollin leader.

The security people ahead of Kael-ven were notified, so every single door between Kael-ven's office and the Executive Pod Bethany Anne had provided him for rapid transit across the planet was open. The Pod was even warmed up, and lifted off the ground a foot as he and Snow strode across the tarmac and jumped in.

Four other security people were inside the Pod. The door shut behind them and it took off blindingly fast.

There were newscasters stationed around the building who noticed the speedy exit of the new Yollin leader. The fact that he was jetting somewhere blazed around the planet in mere seconds.

Most assumed he was going to the latest hotspot.

<u>Planet Yoll, R'Chkoklet</u>

Pehl-eck got the news that the Yollin planetary leader was most likely inbound, and she took a few moments to make sure she looked more than presentable. This could help her again.

She had already interviewed him once before, at the king's palace right after the Empress had killed the Kurtherian.

Kael-ven had kept his word and the Empress' word when they worked double-time to transform the palace into a museum. All the horrible and grotesque heads that had been on his walls had been buried with the plaque over them on the palace grounds, and each had a gravestone with their information.

Before they buried the heads, they had created videos of the palace to show people what it looked like before they took some of the furniture and other valuables out. However, you could find the video of exactly what the palace looked like when the king died. Bethany Anne had been very clear that it should all be there —both good and bad—for future generations.

It seemed but moments, even though it was thousands of miles from the Yollin leader's office to the small town. The commotion at the building three blocks away increased a little as everyone noticed the Executive Pod, which bore the emblem of the Yollin leadership next to the Etheric Empire symbol, coming out of the sky.

Pehl-eck was surprised that the idiots at the end of the street didn't try to shoot at the Pod. For all she knew, they assumed that they would be able to take it over and have their own transportation soon enough.

Pehl-eck wasn't willing to bet against these aliens, nor Kael-ven.

For a previously second-caste individual, he seemed to act very wisely and thoughtfully as he tried to support their people.

The rumor was that he had been a slave of the Etheric Empire's Queen for a total of seven years. However, a different story had it he had won back the punishment for his ship's crew, who had already been repatriated to their homes on the planet or the space stations up above.

She fluttered her mandibles in indecision as she considered whether she and her crew should get closer to the building, then surreptitiously she nodded toward the building and raised an eyebrow to her team. Her videographer shook his head in the negative.

She nodded and decided she would do the interview if they could get one with him from here.

When the Pod came down, she grimaced. They wouldn't get an interview. He was landing much too close to the building with the upper-caste fighters.

She looked at her videographer and whispered, "I hope you have a way to get the sound from here!"

Kael-ven had taken the short amount of time on their trip over to research what was going on here in the city.

Bethany Anne and her group had already placed multiple satellites around the planet, which provided more information than what was available even from the Yollin system. When this situation had blown up, they had even sent a small missile with nanites to get more information.

A request came from the front of the Pod. "Sir? We're being asked how close we wish to land to the building."

Kael-ven thought about it for a moment. "About a block and a half. That should be close enough to show that we don't fear them, and yet not so close that it incites them to shoot us right away."

He waited while the Pod landed. While it was under the control of one of the EIs, it required some input from those up front. As the ranking person on the ship, he had the ability to override the destination at any time by voice. However, most pilots didn't know this fact, and he had no desire to share it with them.

Upon landing, two of his security people stepped out and looked around before nodding for him to proceed. He hated this part. If he'd had his special armor from Bethany Anne he could've taken care of this by himself, but he had to be perceived as a political leader, not a military one.

That didn't mean that he didn't enjoy some special attention from Her Majesty.

Kael-ven stepped out of the Pod and looked down the street toward the five-story building which held the protesters. He ground his mandibles together in frustration as he noticed the blood and body parts littered in front of it. He whispered to his two security guards, "You two stay here. Snow, please remain here also, and keep these two out of mischief. I'm protected, and I don't want more deaths to happen due to these idiots."

Sej'hvek, the male on the left, asked him, "Are you sure, sir?" He nodded down the street. "It doesn't look very safe down there."

Snow growled at the male.

Kael-ven reached down to pet her. "It's okay," he told her. "He's not being disrespectful, just doing his job."

He then put a hand on the male's shoulder. "I'm sure. I doubt these idiots have anything with them that could harm me."

He stepped between his two security guards and continued walking down the street with the *click-click, click-click* of his feet sounding on the concrete.

Behind him, his two security guards looked at each other. "What protection does he have?"

Kael-ven made it to about fifty feet from the building before one of the windows opened and a voice called, "That's far enough! What do you want to say? You're the leader of the rebellion that changed Yoll, so why would we want to waste our lives listening to you?"

Another voice called from inside the building, "Exactly. You were probably having sex with that Empress right before you came over here. Alien lover!"

Kael-ven ground his mandibles together. He wasn't concerned about the hits to his ego, but if John Grimes heard this stuff it might not *only* be these idiots who felt the pain when he finished around here.

He opened his arms while looking up at the window. "I've come here to warn you. I'm not here to try to change your minds. However..." he waved at the bodies, "you have killed others. If you wish to have a fair trial rather than being killed here today, you need to lay down your arms."

Kael-ven waited. It didn't take long to get a response from those inside the building. A moment later the front door cracked open and four Yollins stepped out, looking up and down the street before moving closer to Kael-ven.

One wrinkled his nose as the smell of the dead wafted over them.

He pointed to himself. "We are the ones with the armor, we are the ones with the guns, we are the ones with the power! There is no way that we're going to go down without a fight. We have been in charge of Yoll for a long time because we are more intelligent, because we are brighter, because we are smarter, and because that is how it is to be! The religious texts tell us that *we* are the chosen ones. 'And the mighty shall vanquish the weak.'" He pointed to the street beyond Kael-ven. "And you can see the *truth* of that statement right behind you." He sneered.

Kael-ven took a moment to turn around and he looked everywhere, even up at the pock-marks on buildings where guns had gouged divots.

He understood he was being videotaped and had to play this for the news for the rest of the planet. He turned back as he waved at the revolting scene behind him.

"This is not the truth of your religious beliefs! This is the truth that you intend to stay above everybody else, regardless of whether you are *truly* better than anybody. You," he pointed at the ones confronting him and then to three open windows in the building "just wish to continue the caste system because it makes you feel superior."

Kael-ven spat on the ground in front of them.

"You're no more superior than me or anybody else. I have led teams through the stars. What have you done—sat on your asses and played games? Perhaps you had eloquent discussions at a playhouse? Our planet is going to move forward. It's going to be better, and idiots like you don't even deserve the opportunity to live on it. However, I'm here to tell you that the person that is coming down here—" he pointed to the pavement at his feet, "isn't going to offer you the opportunity to surrender once he

43

arrives. He is no Queen's Ranger worried about the law. He is a Queen's Bitch. And if you haven't gotten the message—"

A sharp *BAM* echoed from the building and Kael-ven was slammed backward to roll over and over in the street with his four legs seeking purchase before he finally stopped some thirty feet back.

Those people watching from alcoves and inside the safety of the buildings gasped in horror as they saw the result of the caste members' shooting of Kael-ven.

Everyone, even the reporter, heard the shouts of joy coming from the building the upper-caste members were holed up in.

Slowly, however, those shouts of joy faded in shock when Kael-ven just shook his head and started to stand back up.

The videographer zoomed in on the anger and disgust on Kael-ven's face as he viewed those in the building and outside it. "I came here in peace. I came here to warn you." He sneered at them. "It is time for you to pray to your gods." Kael-ven turned around and started walking slowly back to his Executive Pod, just daring those in the building to try shooting him again.

They took the bait.

Pehl-eck's videographer was able to capture the multiple muzzle flashes. Kael-ven barely noticed them as sparks flared up some feet behind him.

By the time he got to the Pod, all his security people were inside. Kael-ven looked over his shoulder at the building, flipping the shooters off with a sneer on his face. "Jean Dukes armor, bitches!" He closed his hand and entered the Pod. Snow circled him, sniffing at his feet and legs, then stopped in front of him and barked twice.

"I'm sore, but not damaged," Kael-ven reassured the pup, "and that's why you needed to stay in the Pod. Once you have your own armor, things will be different."

Snow yipped her agreement and went to lay by Kael-ven's

flight couch, picturing herself in shiny armor, tearing up people stupid enough to shoot her partner.

Pehl-eck watched as the Pod rose into the air, easily shrugging off the shots fired at it.

As it flew away, Pehl-eck felt that a hammer of doom was going to arrive.

She started scanning the sky with concern on her face.

There was movement from the building at the end of the street. Quite a few of the males were grabbing whatever they could and pulling it toward the building, placing the components in front of windows and doors to barricade the position.

The rumors of the Queen's Bitches had already made the rounds with the newscasters.

She looked at her videographer. "We should probably move back another block or two, don't you think?"

CHAPTER SIX

.

Commercial Gate 221, Yollin Space, Third Outer Ring

"Ixtali Trade Legation Representative Ixtelina, your ship has been approved to move from Commercial Gate 221 on Outer Ring Three to Outer Ring One. You will hold at that location until you have been approved to approach the QBBS *Meredith Reynolds.* Please be aware that if you attempt to approach the space station without approval, you will be fired upon. There will be no second opportunities. Do you acknowledge this information?"

Ixtelina blinked her four eyes in surprise. Her species had worked to acquire information on well over 272 different space-faring communities, and some of those had been quite militaris-tic. Usually you did not receive a warning quite so specific.

"This is Ixtali Trade Legate Ixtelina. Can you confirm that if we should pass through Outer Ring Number One without permission we will be fired upon?"

Both Ixgurl and Ixgalan turned to look at their leader, their four mandibles moving in and out of their mouths in surprise.

Ixtelina waved her right arm toward Ixgalan, who turned around and started jotting down the information. It seemed it wouldn't take too long before they would be able to report a few of the nuances of working with these humans to their corporate office.

Ring Three Traffic Control immediately answered her query. "Yes. Should you move past Outer Ring One, the humans will reduce your ship to so many pieces. This has occurred three times in the last thirteen-point..." there was a slight pause, "two-five days. We presently have a bet going as to whether anyone else will be stupid enough to make it number four. By all means, please ignore this warning, as I have over five hundred credits riding on someone ignoring this warning again, within the next forty-eight hours. Have a nice day." There was a slight pause. "Ring Three Traffic Control over."

"Understood, Ring Traffic Control. Ixtali ship recognizes the warning, and we are now named Ship Number," she leaned forward to get a view of Ixgurl's screen, "Two Zero Nine." Ixtelina motioned for Ixgurl to continue moving the Ixtali commercial ship toward the human base.

She noticed he was extremely focused on the incoming information designating where to stop the ship.

One way or another, Ixtelina was sure this was going to provide much information on the new spacefaring species. They should be able to sell this information for a large sum.

Her small spy ship was going to become very rich.

Her species had precious few things to trade. One was an incredibly rare harmonic gem they mined on their home world. It was hard to mine, and was used for a few very advanced machines that allowed space travel over large distances. Any sufficiently advanced race craved the option to trade for them.

The other was information they acquired during these trade operations.

They made an obscene amount of money trading in these rare gems.

And an even more obscene amount from the information

they sold to partners, friends, and enemies. Since they were a neutral third party, very few species tried to attack them.

During the last generation, they had been attacked twice. The mercenaries they had hired to fight on their behalf had cost them almost four years' profit.

Both the hostile species had sued for peace.

When Ixgurl was assured that his commands to the space ship's autopilot were logged appropriately and he had confirmation back from Outer Ring Number One that they were in sync with geospatial tracking, he turned to the mission's primary. "What do you think, Captain?" He pointed toward the small speck in the far distance that represented the human's space station on the forward screen. "What is your thought on their 'shoot first, ask no questions' policy?"

Ixtelina rested her elbow on her third leg, then opened her two large fingers and placed her chin in them to give Ixgurl's question some thought. "According to the information we have on Yoll, the humans are not overly antagonistic from a military perspective. Based on this plus a few other bits of information, my opinion is that they are in a highly defensive posture."

This time the question came from Ixgalan, her physical spy support specialist. "What do you think they will do if they catch us spying on them?"

Ixtelina straightened in her chair and weighed his question. "Nothing ventured, nothing gained," she finally answered. "We will probably be either very rich from this effort," she admitted, then continued her thought...

"*Or very dead.*"

QBBS *Meredith Reynolds*, Tactical Operations, Traffic Control

Bethany Anne was speaking with Lance when one of the local controllers turned around in his seat and cleared his throat.

Both Bethany Anne and Lance turned to look at the man, Bethany Anne raising an eyebrow. "Yes?"

"I'm sorry, ma'am, sir. We have a ship inbound that is on the watchlist."

Bethany Anne turned to her father, this time raising both eyebrows in surprise. "We have a watchlist?"

Lance hadn't turned back to his daughter, but rather asked the specialist a question of his own. "Are we speaking of the specific ship or the species watchlist?"

The specialist answered quickly, "Species, sir. It is an Ixtali ship."

"I understand. I will give you an answer in a moment," he turned to Bethany Anne. "The Ixtalis—" he started, but Bethany Anne put up a finger to stop him mid-sentence.

It seemed TOM was giving her an update—probably a better one than he could—so he waited. Probably wouldn't take too long.

Tell me more about these aliens, TOM.

The Ixtalis are an interesting species. During my time, and from updates I have reviewed since I have been able to acquire more recent data, they are a cross between your country's CIA and a commercial venture.

So they spy for money—is that about it?

Yes, that sums it up nicely.

Why would anyone allow them on their base?

They always market small numbers of their precious *H'Laxrick* gems. These gems provide unique properties for significant-distance space travel, similar in concept to a Kurtherian Engine to bend space and move the ship vast distances.

Bethany Anne thought about this for a moment. *So finding out how many they are willing to sell should give me an idea of what they think information about us is worth? Ok, I got this...I think.*

ADAM?

>>Yes, My Empress?<<

Bethany Anne wanted to roll her eyes. *Okay, who the hell gave you the idea you should be calling me "My Empress?"*

>>I was just trying it on for size. Since you have confirmed that I am truly sentient, I am trying to figure out where I fit in the Etherian society.<<

Bethany Anne wasn't sure if ADAM was being totally forthcoming.

You are fortunate that I can't kick your ass in martial arts practice—that's where you fit in. However, if you annoy me too much I'll figure out how I can suitably chastise you one way or another. I have been "Bethany Anne" to you from the beginning, I am "Bethany Anne" right now, and I will be "Bethany Anne" in the future. Use your incredible intellect to understand the appropriate times to call me your Empress, like in the presence of others. When it is just the three of us in the middle of my own damn head, I don't need titles. Am I clear?

>>Very clear, Bethany Anne.<<

Good. Now, how good are our defenses against Ixtali spy efforts?

>>My calculation depends on whether we allow them to dock. If we permit them to connect to the QBBS *Meredith Reynolds*, we have a fifty-fifty chance of defending ourselves. I have limited knowledge of their capabilities, and I have never tried to prevent hacking by a species that has raised that skill to an artform. Well, except humans, of course. However, if we have them come in on one of our Executive Pods, I believe our ability to protect ourselves is closer to ninety-four-point-seven percent.<<

Bethany Anne chewed on this information for a fraction of a second. *What increases the likelihood of success so much?*

>>Jean and her R&D Team. TOM and I have been working with Team BMW to create unique transfer units which allow us to attack non-organic tools and machines.<<

How can you attack non-organic machines? Couldn't they just have a shield around their bodies to protect something on them? And what about a machine inside their bodies?

We have increased the capabilities of the organic analysis probe from the Pod-doc on TOM's ship. Since it was designed to be used on multiple alien species including new ones it is incredibly accurate, but it won't be harmful to the bodies under review. Using the enhanced Pod-doc technology plus new technology integrated from Yoll in the last few weeks, we have placed sensors inside three Executive Pods. They are EI-controlled, and allow us to reliably confirm the status of any organics and non-organics we allow to transfer to the QBBS *Meredith Reynolds.*

This conversation had taken nearly half a second in real time, and Bethany Anne returned her focus to her father. "It seems we have a small ship of spies—business spies at that—seeking to come aboard. I'm told by ADAM that the teams have prepared special Executive Pods which would allow them to locate and minimize the impact of any devices they have on their bodies. What do you think about this?"

"Percentage of defense success?"

"Ninety-four-point-seven percent success expectation," she replied.

"I assume this high expectation of success has a reason?" he countered.

Bethany Anne shrugged. "This particular group, at least from what I've just been told, isn't militaristic. They wish to glean information about us and sell it on the open market. Since we are the new game in town, this information is probably going to go for a lot of money. However, they have some of the best spy technology in the business. Should we allow their ship to dock, I'm told our chances of defending ourselves drop all the way down to fifty-fifty. I don't like fifty-fifty odds."

Lance grunted. "That's a significant drop. I don't want to

throw a quarter in the air to see whether they can get into our systems and defeat us."

Meredith interrupted from a speaker near the two of them. "Me either. I can't imagine having an alien infestation in my memory banks. I've been working with ADAM on this problem for a year now to confirm I stay clean against foreign efforts. If it is all the same to you, I would prefer the possible damage be minimized."

Bethany Anne shrugged, allowing her father to take the lead.

Lance turned to the specialist. "Let them know that they are permitted to stop exactly three kilometers from the QBBS *Meredith Reynolds*. Make sure they understand what that is in their distance units. We will provide a shuttle for their crew to come on board."

Bethany Anne murmured after he was finished talking, "I guess this is as good a time as any to test the passive defenses."

Lance looked back at his daughter. "Don't you mean passive-aggressive defense?"

Bethany Anne smirked. "When have you ever known me *not* to be aggressive, Dad? I am either passive-aggressive or just aggressive-aggressive, so I am answering as if this was an algebra equation and I could leave off the extra *aggressive*. I'm either passive or aggressive."

Those around who listened anytime the Empress was close by kept their smiles to themselves.

Their Empress was *never* truly passive.

Planet Yoll, R'Chkoklet

"This is Pehl-eck, reporting from the city of R'Chkoklet. As we zoom out from our present location, you will notice that we have moved back another two blocks from the building where presently multiple upper-caste individuals are holed up. We have received word that the Etheric Empress has sent one of her team down to confront these individuals."

The reporter continued her discussion as the news organization uploaded a video over her on the newscast. "On your screens right now is video from when Empress Bethany Anne first landed and exited her ship at the arena where she challenged the king. Note those exiting her ship with her, specifically the human male on her right. This is the individual we believe is heading in our direction at this time."

"From all indications and eyewitness accounts, the human will confront at least twelve individuals inside the building. We do not expect—" Pehl-eck stopped talking for a moment and pointed toward the building. As the video zoomed in, her commentary continued. "I can see three more individuals arriving in what looks like military clothing. No, my videographer is telling me that seven military individuals are now entering the building. That is going to bring the total to nineteen individuals this one human will take on. Will this human come down with additional support, or will he or his people just blast this building into pieces from the upper atmosphere, causing those of us around the buildings to suffer with our lives? This is Pehl-eck, reporting from R'Chkoklet, and we are going to move back another couple of blocks."

QBBS _Meredith Reynolds_

>>Bethany Anne?<<

What is it, ADAM?

>> Bellatrix tells me through her partner Yelena that Dio would like to speak to you.<<

Are you shitting me? she asked her companion, _I refuse to have another puppy following me. Where is Matrix, anyway?_

TOM answered, **I had Matrix go down to the park and frolic with one of his sisters. He needed to get out and run** around, and asking you to do it at the moment didn't seem like a wise choice.

ADAM, you're not going to tell me that Dio wants to become your partner, right?

ADAM was quiet.

Bethany Anne, her mental voice upping an octave, continued her outburst, *Am I right? You have got to be kidding me! There is no fucking way I'm going to have three dogs running around with me all the damn...*

She received the mental equivalent of a snicker.

>>**Gotcha!**<<

Bethany Anne ground her teeth, trying to contain her anger. Some days it sucked having an AI in your head. *Fine, tell me where. I will go speak to him. You had just better pray to the Digital God it really isn't you.*

This time there was a pause from ADAM's side before he replied, >>**Me? Why in the world would a puppy want to connect with me? I'm not prepared to have the responsibility of a puppy.** There was another pause before ADAM continued, >>**I have just reviewed what it takes to raise a pet. I would have to**—<<

Bethany Anne interrupted his comment, *ADAM?*

>>**Yes?**<<

She snickered. *Gotcha!*

CHAPTER SEVEN

Purplish clouds swirled out of the way of the human's Black Eagle as it cut through them, the mists mixing again as the gravitic air cavitation shield kept any wind from buffeting the aircraft while it streaked across the Yollin sky.

John glanced around, enjoying the view of the colors coalescing through the atmosphere. For a moment he felt like a kid again, and wished he could stick his arm out and run his hand through the mist.

"Tell me what the nanospies have for us so far, ADAM," he requested aloud.

"We have nineteen individuals inside the building. There are seven exits. The building is five stories tall, and has multiple windows made out of a substance very similar to Earth-type glass."

"Are these windows as breakable as a standard window on Earth, or are they bulletproof- or destruction-proof-class see-through windows?"

"I do not know the answer to this question, I have now tasked multiple nanospies to gather more data."

John flipped a couple switches inside the cockpit of his Pod.

He viewed the surrounding area and zoomed in on the neighborhood blocks to see if any backup or reinforcements were making their way to the building. Satisfied he wouldn't have to face more enemies, John turned off those displays and checked the magazines on both his Jean Dukes' specials.

Fully loaded.

ADAM came back. "John, we have ascertained the breakage quality to be within the parameters of normal window glass on Earth."

"Good to know. If I throw some asshole out the window, he won't bounce right back at me. That would be fucking frustrating."

John rolled his eyes at the thought. "Can you even imagine how embarrassing that would be, ADAM? Would you be so kind as to add that to the checklist for the next time the spybots are sent down?"

"I have added the request to the list for the spybots."

John could make out the small town he was heading toward with his own eyes now.

He smiled to himself. "One riot, one Ranger." He cricked his neck back and forth to get ready for the challenge ahead.

"One planet? One Bitch!"

Planet Yoll, R'Chkoklet

Pehl-eck felt the presence rather than hearing anything arrive. She lifted her eyes and saw the small ship sliding down out of the sky.

It wasn't so much flying as floating.

As she watched the wings melted into each other, going from an "X" shape to a single line. Moments later, it hovered a mere foot off the ground and the canopy cracked open.

Pehl-eck waved to her videographer to make sure he was getting the action. A large human in blood-red armor hopped out of the ship and reached back in to grab what looked like a helmet, then additional weapons. He kept his eyes on the building at the end of the street as he holstered two pistols and put what looked like four small metal boxes across his chest.

A moment later, the canopy started closing, and the ship slowly rose into the sky.

Either he wasn't worried about getting hurt, or he was concerned with somebody trying to acquire his ship while he was busy.

Pehl-eck called to the human. Her videographer grunted behind her, and she waved her hand in a way that meant "Nothing ventured, nothing gained." Surprisingly, the human started walking in her direction even though he kept his eyes focused on the building at the end of the street.

While he was certainly encased in some sort of metal armor, it folded and molded to him as if it were fabric. Personally she preferred her males to have hard exoskeletons, not a soft skin outside, but she supposed that the armor the human wore was hard enough that it could make things interesting.

It wasn't that his looks appealed to her, it was the sheer sense of raw destruction it felt like he was about to unleash—yet she did not feel afraid for her personal safety as he strode over to her.

She put the microphone out to him when he arrived. The human nodded to her and turned so that his mouth would, in fact, speak into the microphone. Considering some of the arrogant personages she had interviewed during her career, she appreciated the courtesy.

"Hello. My name is Pehl-eck." John nodded. "I was wondering if you would mind me asking a few questions before you head down toward the end of the street?"

John smiled. "I figured you were a reporter," he nodded toward her cameraperson, "since you have the necessary staff to help you here. What would you like to ask?"

She adjusted the microphone to make sure she caught his full answer. "My first question is, how do you plan on arresting those men?"

John turned to look her straight in the eyes. "I'm sorry, you must be mistaking me for a Queen's Ranger."

She gave him a puzzled look before she caught up with his translation. "Forgive me my ignorance. I didn't even ask your name. Do you mind providing it, and would you explain to me what a Queen's Ranger is?"

Her normal ability to play the disinterested reporter was being challenged in this person's presence.

"Certainly," John answered, his eyes once again focused on the end of the street. "My name is John Grimes. You ask what a Queen's Ranger is?" She nodded her head. "The Rangers, more accurately called 'the Empress' Rangers' now, are tasked with locating and finding lawbreakers. They respond to situations according to the laws laid out by Empress Bethany Anne. While they *can* kill in the line of duty, justice, not death, is their prime directive."

A shot was fired from the end of the street, hitting the side of a building close by. John raised an eyebrow. "I guess they are ready to meet their maker." He nodded to the lady, then started walking toward the building. Pehl-eck called after him, "If you're not an Empress' Ranger, a Queen's Ranger, or whatever type of Ranger you mentioned, what are you?"

John called over his shoulder, "I'm a Queen's *Bitch*." He snagged his helmet, ready to lock it into place as he finished his statement. "We get called in when someone has taken a situation beyond the law." He jammed the helmet on his head, sealing himself into the latest Jean Dukes armor.

QBBS *Meredith Reynolds*, Transit Quarters, Fourth Group

Aerolyn had been running now for over four months through three different star systems. He had hoped that by coming into the Yollin system, he would have the opportunity to obscure his tracks due to the upheaval resulting from the aliens taking over the Yollins' system.

Unfortunately, the humans had implemented rules that had made the system more efficient.

It was just his luck to find an efficient star power. He chose to head toward the humans' space station when it became obvious he would stick out on the Yollins'. The Yollins didn't have a specific area for all the aliens to congregate. They kept them off in their ships for the most part.

At least on the humans' station, rumor had it, all sorts of aliens were congregating in an attempt to find out more about the "new kids on the block," and determine what kind of money could be made from them.

Aerolyn had two problems. The first was that he felt the king and his cronies were not ruling in the best interests of the people of his planet, and he spoke often and loudly about this in the common bars on his planet.

The second problem was his relationship with the king himself. Aerolyn called him "Dad."

When he was younger his comments were taken as humorous ignorance, but as he became an adult his father could no longer ignore his outbursts.

One evening, his older brother warned him that should he open his mouth one more time, the king—not his father—would have to act on his civil disobedience.

Unfortunately, it took all of three days for Aerolyn to forget the warning from his brother and express his opinions in a local bar.

One of his friends notified him of the Royal Decree later that night. There was a price on his head, and it took him three long agonizing hours to locate someone who would get him off the planet.

He had hoped that if he left, his stupidity would be forgiven at least. Unfortunately, he found out in the next system that the price on his head was for dead or alive, and there were no distance limitations.

He had been on the run ever since, and now he was in the Yollin system.

Where he suspected he would die when a bounty hunter found him.

Planet Yoll, Nachid

Nachid was a medium-sized city in Yoll's northern hemisphere. It had been the present size for the last four generations, never getting larger and never shrinking in population. Most Yollins ended up shipping out to the space stations, where they would then be redirected out to the commercial or military organization that needed their services.

A lottery determined who would stay behind and continue helping the city grow or ship out to the space stations.

Brylen walked the streets of his city, considering its history in light of the aliens taking over.

While everybody took standardized tests, it seemed like it didn't matter what you scored on the tests or how you answered the question "Where would you like to work?" One would be randomly assigned to whatever role they had the least ability to accomplish.

The same way it was handled in bureaucracies in whatever solar system you came from.

It was amazing that his people were able to produce the beautiful craftsmanship they did, Brylen thought.

The middle-aged Yollin walked toward the bar where he expected to meet his partner Rih-benn at a back table. He finished his musing about the government with the thought "There was no ability Yollins possess that bureaucracy can't screw up."

Stepping quickly into the bar, Brylen moved to the side. He didn't want to be outlined in the doorway any longer than he had to.

He walked the perimeter of the room and quickly located Rih-benn at the back table. Looking around surreptitiously, Brylen noticed three of Rih-benn's men sitting and talking at the bar and two more sitting in a nearby booth.

Rih-benn wasn't taking any chances. He must have heard the same rumors that Brylen had regarding this human they had chosen to meet.

"Good to see you, Brylen." Rih-benn pushed over a glass of the new beverage.

Brylen took it and sniffed. "Pepsi?" Rih-benn nodded as Brylen took a sip through the straw. "Burns."

"I actually like that feeling. Interesting that the humans introduce a gas into the drink. Similar to fermentation, but unnatural. It causes my wife to bitch at me when I expel the gas back out of my mouth. She always waves a hand at me, and tells me I am acting like a kid again."

"Oh, well in that case," Brylen raised the drink to his mouth again and took in a large amount through the straw before setting the drink back down on the table, "I'm not happy with Chr-len right now. She wants to say I'm childish? Bring it on!"

Rih-benn chuckled. "Living dangerously?"

Brylen looked around the bar before turning back to Rih-benn and tilting his head toward the bar. "No different than you, apparently. Why the large number of head-breakers?"

Rih-benn looked at his guys. "Options," he answered and took a drink of the Yollin version of beer, which was made from a local plant which fermented quickly. "I have the option of taking the information I want on pain of death, or making sure if our contact does something stupid he doesn't touch me."

"Still sensitive to pain?"

"Always. Aren't you?"

61

"I live with pain every day," Brylen answered.

Rih-benn smiled. "Yes, but your wife doesn't count."

Brylen grimaced. "Oh, well if that is the case, then no. I'm good not feeling too much pain."

The two males picked up their drinks and clinked them together.

"What's with the pack on the table," Brylen asked, nodding to the bostok pack. Bostok was a semi-legal way to drug oneself. It was mostly frowned upon in public, but allowed many Yollins to relax at the end of a hard day.

"Options," Rih-benn replied cryptically.

The silence went on for a few moments before Brylen spoke again. "Ok, I'll bite."

Rih-benn took the pack of bostok and flipped it end over end on the table. "If I leave this on the table, my men are going to take this jackhole out when he leaves. We will stick him in the ship and take him out to the back canyons. A few choice whacks and he gives us what we need to know."

"What about Krylen?" Brylen asked. "Won't it force him to tell the truth?"

"Don't know yet if it works on humans. I'd hate to have our human be the first to die when we want him to answer more questions."

Brylen thought about Rih-benn's answer for a moment while Rih-benn turned the bostok box over and over. "What about when you are done asking questions?"

Rih-benn stopped turning the box. "Well, you know, there isn't a good reason not to use it then." He shrugged. "We would find out something useful if we shoot him with the stuff. Why waste the opportunity if he isn't going live anyway?"

CHAPTER EIGHT

Nathan walked the last mile into a medium-sized town on planet Yoll. He found the bar, fronted by a nondescript door in a nondescript wall connected to a nondescript building in a warehouse district on the west side of town.

Basically it was symmetrical, and he would have to admit that in its bleakness it had a form of beauty. However, it was bland as shit in its perfection.

He reached into his pockets and pulled out a small box. It was black and made of metal, and he flipped the lock and opened it. His sensitive eyes could see a few sparkles of light reflecting off the little metal pieces that left the box. Seconds later he received a little beep from his implant that produced vibrations that his ears translated as sound.

He closed the box again and put it back into his pocket. Moments later he was informed there were no obvious traps inside the building, so he moved forward. "This," he muttered, "should be fun."

Nathan opened the door and allowed it to close behind him after he entered. Unlike others, his eyes could adjust to the darkness quite easily. He received a minute head nod from a pair of

Yollins off to the left toward the back, so he made his way between a couple of tables heading in their direction. The few extra Yollins in the bar looked at the human.

One grimaced. However, three of the four looked around, then decided to pay their bar tabs and leave early. There were better drinking partners just two warehouses down.

Nathan grabbed a chair from a nearby table and pulled it up to the booth to sit down without asking permission. "Gentlemen."

Both the Yollins looked at each other in confusion and Nathan grimaced. "I apologize. There is no translation for gentlemen in your language, but in our language it is a respectful salutation."

Brylen shrugged. "I don't know if there's a reason to be respectful, but I'll admit it's nice to hear once in a while."

Rih-benn just chuckled.

After the first couple of minutes of discussion, the bootlegger on Nathan's right took out a small box and his Wechselbalg nose wanted to twist in annoyance. Whatever root this product was made from, it smelled to high heaven.

Rih-benn took a small pinch of the product and put it in his mouth before closing the box and setting it on the table.

Rih-benn looked up at the human and tapped two of his mandibles together. "I'm sorry," he reached down and grabbed the box, "did you want some?"

Nathan shook his head. "On our planet that would be considered a chew, and I'm not really fond of them. Plus, I'm not really sure what effect that plant would have on my physiology. Not a good idea. I hope you understand?"

The alien made a twist of his hands that Nathan had learned a while back was the equivalent of a human shrug. It had been easier with Kael-ven and the other Yollins he knew because they had picked up human mannerisms.

Nathan wondered how long it would be before those on this

planet, which had such a large population, started adopting human mannerisms as well. He supposed it had as much to do with familiarity with humans as anything else.

Now that ADAM was streaming some of the videos to the Yollins he had…borrowed from the Internet on Earth, it would be interesting to find out what happened with Yollin society. Right now Nathan could imagine dozens—no, hundreds—of research scientists having heart attacks about humans infesting the universe with their pop culture.

Nathan had to smile at that thought.

There was some commotion from behind him, and Nathan turned to look over his shoulder as Ecaterina, with Christina in wolf form, walked into the bar. Most of the eyes were on the two new humans, but Christina got a fair amount of attention as well.

When Nathan turned back around to the table, Brylen had grabbed the box of root off the table and stuck it into his pocket.

Nathan raised an eyebrow.

Christina followed her mother until she sat on a bar stool and got comfortable. The small wolf made a face at the dirt on the floor, then laid beside the stool and started watching the room.

She knew what her responsibilities were: keep an eye on anything her mom couldn't see right away. If she saw a problem? Well, then she would yip or growl to get Mom's attention.

Ecaterina lifted her hand and pointed to the place on the bar in front of herself. "I want a Kleric, and not the cheap stuff they gave me at the last bar."

While looking at the bartender, Ecaterina was listening to those around her.

"Did you see that? Brylen took the box off the table." One upset Yollin turned in his seat to grab his drink. "The boss doesn't want us to take this guy out when he leaves."

"Well, there goes the bonus we would've gotten this afternoon. This job is a bust." The first guy slapped the second and nodded in Ecaterina's direction. The second Yollin opened and closed his mandibles a couple times when he noticed the human's eyes glowing yellow.

And looking straight at them both.

Ecaterina kept her voice low. "Nathan, there is talk over here at the bar about a plan to hurt you as you leave your meeting. Tactics?"

Nathan received the communication from his mate and nodded.

He stood up from the table and rapped on it twice with his knuckles to get the attention of both Brylen and Rih-benn. "You guys," he pointed at each of them, "have just lost your opportunity to acquire the spice for the Pepsi drink. I don't appreciate you thinking you might do me harm when I left this conversation. Because of your bullshit, one of you is going to die."

Rih-benn grunted at him, not concerned about the alien's threat. "What's to stop us from killing you right now?"

Nathan allowed his eyes to go yellow and lifted one of his hands as it gained claws. His voice was guttural as he responded, "Go ahead. That just means both of you will die. If you do not attack me right now, at least one of you has a chance."

The Yollins at the bar turned to watch him leave and noticed the other human had a pistol out and pointing in their direction. She waved her fingers and called, "Toodles."

Her eyes were glowing yellow as well.

After the two humans had left the bar, Rih-benn slammed his hand on the table. "Why did you take the bostok off the table?"

Brylen pulled it out of his pocket and set it back on the table. "Have you not been listening to the rumors?" He pointed to the bar. "That small animal was the one that got a ship's security guard ripped apart. That wasn't someone to try to kill—and do you think he brought his mate in here if she wouldn't provide more protection?" He grunted and pushed himself back in the seat before standing up. "She had a pistol ready. I doubt your people," nodding toward the bar, "would've appreciated being shot in the back."

"Where are you going?" Rih-benn spat at him.

Brylen answered, frustration evident in his voice, "To the restroom." To himself, he added, *Then out the back door, dickhead.*

QBBS *Meredith Reynolds*

The atmosphere in the Ixtali ship was thick with impatience. Ixgurl looked over his shoulder, and the *click-click, click-click* of taloned fingers on plastic suddenly stopped. He returned his gaze to his instruments with surprise on his face. Normally, the lead on any Ixtali mission would be calm.

Ixtelina's mandibles twitched in annoyance. "That is the fifth commercial craft I have now seen permitted to dock with the human station. Don't they know how important we are, and what an opportunity our ship brings them?"

"They are new to the system. Perhaps these humans are seeking information about us?"

Ixgurl lifted his hands in the air and replied with a hint of frustration evident in his voice, "So far I am unable to piggyback on any communications between commercial ships and the human station. They are either using a frequency I'm unaware of, which is unlikely since they communicate with other ships, or they have such tight communication beams we are unable to capture leakage.

"What about our microspies?" Ixtelina asked.

"We lose them as soon as they go approximately two ship lengths in any direction. I've also tried sending them away from us to circle back. It seems the humans want to keep this area of space clean of microdebris."

"Interesting," Ixgalan murmured.

Ixtelina leaned forward in her chair to review the screens in front of both Ixgurl and Ixgalan. "So far the humans are ahead of us on knowledge of who is trying to get information from whom. I would expect—"

Her comment was cut off when a voice on the radio interrupted her. "Special trade legation, this is the QBBS *Meredith Reynolds*. Please be prepared to receive an executive shuttle to transport two contacts to the station, per your earlier request."

Ixtelina leaned back in her chair, her eyes closing slightly. "Executive shuttle?" She let the question hang there for a moment, teasing it as her brain worked on what it could mean. "Perhaps this trade mission is going to be a little more difficult than we had assumed. The challenge might be enough to warrant us getting a difficulty bonus, which would be very nice."

Ixtelina pushed herself up from the chair and headed to her suite to put on a fresh robe. Whether she wanted to or not, she could not leave this mission in a huff. Once the humans understood the value of the information products and the gems they could provide, they would understand their mistake of treating her legation so poorly.

She looked forward to watching the face of their human negotiator when she pulled half their product away from them.

Ixgalan unclipped from the seat next to Ixgurl and leaned over. "Why do you think they are doing it this way?"

Ixgurl shrugged. "I think Ixtelina is right. They know more about us than we know about them."

Ixgalan stood up and started toward the back to change into his own robe. "That's what I'm afraid of. However, since we know nothing about them it wouldn't take much to know more about us."

A short time later, the two Ixtali waited patiently as a docking connection was made with their ship. A slight noise could be heard as the locks connected.

Once Ixgurl confirmed they had a tight seal, Ixgalan reached forward and pressed the button to open their side of the connection.

He and Ixtelina glanced at each other before stepping into the Executive Pod. Ixtelina made an appreciative sound. "Well, if they plan on killing us at least we are going to go out in style." She ran her hand across the seats. "I believe this is genuine leather, from down on the planet or maybe from theirs. These are not synthetics."

Ixgalan, a couple seats away, had bent down and was tapping on the frames of the seats. "Yes, and these are organic, taken from a plant."

A voice spoke to them in Yollin from the ship's speaker system. "Please take a seat. This ship will not commence moving until all individuals are properly seated and buckled in. This is for your protection."

Ixtelina turned to Ixgalan and nodded, and the two of them sat down and adjusted their robes before looking at the buckling device and easily manipulating it to lock themselves in. Once that had been accomplished, the doors to their ship closed. Moments later there was a click so faint it was felt more than heard, and the two vehicles separated.

Ixgalan leaned forward in his seat and looked toward the front of the ship, but he saw no person up there. He looked at Ixtelina as he leaned back and asked, "I wonder who is piloting?"

The voice came from the speakers again, "No biologics are piloting this Pod. Presently this ship is being piloted by an Entity Intelligence. Welcome to the *Meredith Reynolds*."

Ixtelina sat for a moment, digesting what she just heard., "This ship is being piloted by what type of intelligence?"

"Entity."

"What type of entity?"

"Now that, Special Trade Legate Ixtelina, is a very good question. Unfortunately, I am not sure I have the ability to explain it in this language. What other languages are you fluent in? Perhaps I can offer a broader context for cybernetic beings?"

"I am sorry, what does 'cybernetic' mean?"

"That is a human word for which the Yollin language does not have a direct translation. Are there other languages you understand? Perhaps I can speak in one of those?"

Damn, the humans were going to make her give up the first bit of information.

A formidable adversary, truly.

QBBS *Meredith Reynolds*, Space Traffic Control, Special Unit

"The first scan of the aliens is coming back at this time."

Outside of testing the Executive Pods, Specialist Marilyn had yet to have the opportunity of using her systems to check out a potential alien liaison. This was going to be the highlight of her day.

The gruff voice of General Reynolds came over the speaker. "I am patched into what you are finding, along with EI Reynolds. What can you tell us?"

Marilyn *wanted* to tell the General, "Probably nothing that Reynolds hasn't already," but she was there as additional eyes and ears. As smart as the EIs had been in the past, they had been unable to make the leaps of understanding that most humans called "gut checks" or intuition.

Presently Marilyn was feeling nothing in her gut, and certainly nothing was coming up in her brain. "At this time, sir, everything looks to be appropriate. I am not registering anything that causes me to second-guess the detailed information."

There was a pause before the General came back over the line. "Understood, Marilyn. Please interrupt what I am doing if you sense something out of the ordinary. I won't jiggle your shoulder while you do this. Reynolds out."

CHAPTER NINE

R'Chkoklet, Planet Yoll

As John walked down the street, he waited for the first shots to ring out.

So far, his stroll toward the building had been eerily quiet.

As the Queen's representative and one of her bodyguards, he needed to project quiet calm as he headed toward their building. That part wasn't so hard. After fighting as a normal human against Nosferatu, this was a walk in the park.

Against aliens.

John chuckled. At least he would make the Armed Forces proud. *See the galaxy, meet interesting new aliens, and kill them.*

Were these guys really going to let him walk right into the building? What were they expecting, that he would stop and chat?

"I'm telling you, he will stop to talk with us!" Tol-bek hissed to his brother Gry-bek.

Gry-bek stared at him while pointing out the door toward the human. "Does he *look* like he is stopping?"

"Not at the moment, but you have to be seen as trying to communicate. We will wait until he starts his speech, then we will shoot him dead," Tol-bek ground out. "We will be remembered for our bravery as the revolution goes forward, fertilized by the ashes of our bodies!"

Gry-bek replied, his voice quiet, "So you are suggesting our lives are worth shit?"

John looked at the HUD in his helmet and turned on the advanced tactical EI.

John? his tactical EI spoke up in his ear.

Yes?

There are presently four Yollins on the other side of the front door arguing about when it is best to attack you, now or when you stop to talk to them.

Do you have that on tape?

Tape? his EI asked.

John rolled his eyes. *Recorded?*

Yes.

Good, because it is going to suck to be them.

"And I am *telling* you—" Tol-bek was starting to get wound up, but his next words were cut off when his head shattered. Shrapnel from the door and the walls exploded around the four in the entry.

Gry-bek barely had time to register his brother's death before his body was peppered with more than twenty slivers coming from a high-velocity Jean Dukes pistol. His expression, if someone could have taken a picture in the microsecond before his skull exploded, would have been one of surprise.

He really hadn't expected the human to walk right in.

One of the other two Yollins died in the first attack by John Grimes, the personal protector of the Empress of the Etheric Empire.

The last, his leg mangled and chest his bleeding from multiple holes, laid on the floor in the back of the entry. He had dragged himself away from the front door, which was now a shattered piece of glass and metal that barely hung on one hinge.

Yollin doors, designed to be used by upper and lower-caste Yollins, were easily large enough for the red-suited human to step through. His boots crunched on the broken glass.

Are there any more combatants on this level?

Negative.

John walked over to the last Yollin and stared down at him.

"Mercy?" the male grunted, blood leaking from his mouth and over his mandibles.

"You get mercy when you give mercy." John lifted his pistol and shot him in the head. "When you plan to kill me? Don't expect mercy from an Empress' Bitch," John told the dead alien. He looked around the entry, the white marble rock was pockmarked from his high-velocity rounds

John stepped toward the stairway leading to the second floor.

"This is Pehl-eck, still reporting from R'Chkoklet. We are zooming in on the massive amount of destruction the Etheric Empire's representative has caused, and you can see he didn't come here to negotiate. Apparently shooting at the Yollin leader, who came here earlier to negotiate, was the fatal flaw in their plans."

Glass shattered loudly as the cameraperson focused on the

front door, and he zoomed out enough to see a Yollin rolling around on the street in front of the building, obviously in pain. Almost immediately thereafter the red-armored human leaned out of the second story window, his arm and pistol in view, and casually shot the Yollin.

The Yollin's exploding head was now a matter of public record.

The human disappeared back into the building.

It was a moment or two before the reporter could compose herself.

"Oh, my ancestors," she whispered. "What have those idiots unleashed?"

John brought his head back into the building.

Update?

Two more on this floor, both armed with hand weapons.

Pistols?

No, an ax and some type of sword.

John holstered his pistol and walked toward the two, who were lying in wait, ready to ambush him as he turned a corner.

The first swung his ax too fast, and his partner's attempt to stab John at the same time was also a failure—not that John cared. He freely allowed both attacks to come at him.

Record the trauma from both attacks, and any damage they cause to the suit.

Understood, his EI responded.

The Yollins stared at the alien in front of them in disbelief when both attacks failed. Hitting him was similar to trying to cut a rock wall, and resulted in about the same amount of damage.

The one with the ax recovered first and pulled his weapon back for a second try.

"Oh no you don't, motherfucker," John growled. "It's my turn."

His punch caved in the Yollin's chest, crushing his skeleton and sending a piece into his heart. The second never saw the backhand that caved in his face, cracking one of his mandibles and killing him instantly.

Both bodies dropped to the floor.

Pehl-eck's reporting on the latest update from the building was interrupted by more glass breaking. This time the videographer barely recorded the body flying from the fourth-floor window. The human looked out the window and down before pulling back into the building.

Pehl-eck's comment, which later became the video news snippet shared in five solar systems, was, "I guess if you throw your enemy from the fourth floor of a building, you don't need to waste ammunition on a confirmation shot to the head."

"Well," John commented as he pulled his head back in the building, "that was effective."

Any more combatants on this level? John subvocalized.

No.

"Ok, that makes twelve down. Seven more assholes behind Floor Number Five."

Pehl-eck provided more color commentary after she had made the decision to move closer to the building. The videographer jerked his camera to the side, and she turned around. "It looks like," she told those watching her feed, "those inside have a few reinforcements coming in." Moments later an armored Yollin walked casually into the building.

Like the human had.

Pehl-eck turned back to the camera. "Including armored support."

John.

John pulled his clips and replaced them. They were still two-thirds full, but no reason not to be prepared.

We have five additional combatants coming up from below, one in Yollin armor.

"Oh?" John looked at the feed from the cameras he had been leaving behind him. "Huh. Old armor, maybe two generations older than the stuff Kiel had. Decent, but the mobility on that shit must suck."

John jumped down the stairs to get to the floor below. No time like the present to test out Jean's group's new armor.

God, he wished he had a metal bat right now.

Drk-vaen reveled in the power he felt in the armor he had taken from his parents' home. It was invigorating. There was nothing that could stop him; certainly not this human. He towered over his four friends, who had watched with joy as the lower-caste Yollins had been shot for daring to think they could step up. Their revolution was dying in front of them.

Then the human had arrived. When he shot the counter-revolutionary in the head, Drk-vaen and his friends had howled in anger.

It wasn't fair!

They all decided to head to the building and offer their

support. Then Rhu'glik asked Drk-vaen if his parents still had the armor from when his dad was in the military.

Oh, yeah! It hadn't taken Drk-vaen any time to run over to their compound. His family was gone, either to work or out of town on business, which allowed him easy access to the powered armor. It turned on and went through the activation sequences smoothly.

Then the five were on their way.

Drk-vaen walked past his comrades, taking the lead as he moved up the stairs. He flinched when he placed a metal foot down too hard on a stair and cracked the marble. He sure hoped his parents didn't have to pay for that.

As he moved through the second floor he turned in the armor a little too sharply and hit a wall, halfway embedding himself before extracting himself and proceeding to the stairs that led to level three. His four friends cautiously followed. They had seen the two deaths out in the street, and their idea of a fun time was rapidly being challenged by the harsh reality of the dead.

"Are you fucking kidding me?" John asked no one in particular. He was viewing the video feed from the floors beneath and watched as the person in the armor ran into the wall.

"This is a kid," he muttered. The cameras showed the four other Yollin youths slowly following their compatriot.

Drk-vaen turned the corner on the third floor and scanned the hall. A sudden loud *ping* startled him and he jerked around.

The human was waiting for him.

He spoke to Drk-vaen through speakers from his helmet. "You

know, you have two options here. Well, three, but I don't really expect you to turn around."

Drk-vaen sincerely wished that *was* an option at the moment. The human had obviously seen his armored suit, and wasn't running in fear. That was what he would have done if he were in the same place as the human.

"Either you can die, or you are going to suffer severe pain. You are sticking your nose in the Empress' business. Your actions won't go without a lesson, trust me."

"The Empress is false!" Drk-vaen blustered, his bravado lost on the human since the Yollin hadn't turned on his suit's speakers.

Dammit.

Once the speakers were on, he tried again. "The Empress is false!" he croaked.

"No," the human told him, "the Empress is real enough. The falsehoods are the religious beliefs about superiority and your caste system." The alien moved to Drk-vaen's left. "I'm here to bring the Queen's Justice. Well, shit. I guess I mean the Empress' Justice. Old names die hard."

"I'll not stand here and accept you berating our world's system of—" Drk-vaen ranted.

The alien interrupted, "Oh, you are right." He ran forward and grabbed Drk-vaen, who wasn't able to track the fast alien under his armored arms. "You won't be standing here," John told him as he used his strength and that provided by the armor to heave the Yollin toward the windows.

This time Pehl-eck wasn't talking, just watching the building when the armored Yollin shattered two windows exiting from the third floor. The crunch as the armored figure landed on the street reverberated off the buildings, and sand and dust billowed up from the landing spot.

This time the human walked to the now-open window and stopped a moment, then hopped to the street below.

From a three-story window.

She wasn't sure, but she would have sworn the human floated the last few feet to the ground.

She would have to go back and look at the video.

John walked over to the young idiot who was writhing, probably trying to figure out how to get all his limbs working inside the suit.

"Lesson number one..." John began. "You have to practice in suits of armor. It isn't like putting on a new pair of pants and a shirt. You knew enough to walk around, but you didn't have a damned clue how to fight in this stuff."

Drk-vaen's compatriots rushed out of the building and skidded to a stop when they realized the alien was talking to their friend.

"Second lesson," John continued, aware of the Yollin's friends behind him. "Never let your friends tell you what to do. In this case they might literally get you killed. The armor doesn't make you impervious to stupidity."

John leaned over as Drk-vaen turned his helmet in his direction. "Third and final lesson." John grabbed a small unit at the junction of Drk-vaen's neck and shoulder and ripped it off. Metal screeched in anguish and sparks flew.

John stood up and tossed the small metal box onto Drk-vaen's chest. "These old units have a design flaw, so they are easy to overcome. Always know the limitations of your armor." As he turned and walked back into the building, Drk-vaen's friends all gave him a wide berth.

Drk-vaen just laid there, horrified as all his systems locked up and his suit powered down.

Twenty years later on another planet, Drk-vaen would use that bit of wisdom to overcome a Kurtherian adversary for his people, and ultimately for the Etheric Empress.

Unfortunately for his future adversary, he couldn't provide a second chance in the heat of battle.

Executive Pod, Outside *Meredith Reynolds*

The EI told the Ixtalis, "You have multiple electronic devices stored about your bodies. There is a lock box in the front of the Pod, which you may take with you out of the Pod. Keep it with you at all times. There is a shield to confirm your valuables are inside."

Ixtelina asked the question on Ixgalan's mind. "Why?"

"These electronics are not known to the Etheric Empire, so they may not be used in our presence without a review of their capabilities. I'm sure you Ixtalis, with your core commercial interest in data acquisition, will understand our caution?"

Well, that blew it. These humans certainly knew more about her people than she did about them at this time.

"And if we do not wish to give them up?" Ixtelina inquired.

"That is certainly an option," the EI responded. "We will return you to your ship and allow you to leave."

"What about our offer to trade?" Ixtelina asked.

"Are we speaking about information or the H'Laxrick gems?"

Ixtelina pressed her teeth together. "I would say 'something other,' but would you believe it?"

"I'm informed by the Empress that it wouldn't matter. Those electronic devices are not coming onto the *Meredith Reynolds* outside the holding box without an explanation about what they do and how to confirm they are not working. She is responsible for too many people to throw the dice trusting a mercenary group."

"We are *not* mercenaries!" Ixgalan shot back. "We don't get involved in wars."

"Excuse my specialist's outburst," Ixtelina requested. They were back to speaking in Yollin. "But he is correct. Why do you call us mercenaries?"

The EI responded, "To the highest bidder—and sometimes multiple bidders—goes the information. Whether the information will be used for good or ill is not relevant to the Ixtalis."

Ixtelina wanted to spit. Of all the alien species the Ixtali worked with, the ones with morals were the most difficult. They often judged the Ixtalis and their neutrality.

A new voice came through the speaker system, interrupting her thoughts. "Do not believe that we do not understand the dance on the edge of the knife when someone is outgunned, outmanned, and often outmaneuvered. Ixtalis are working to keep themselves relevant and protected in the only way they know how, but if you think I give a shit you are vastly mistaken. I will judge Ixtalis by their actions, not the whys behind them."

"Hmm." Ixgalan paused a moment. "That was a new voice."

Ixtelina parsed the comment. "Who is this?"

"This is the EI," the previous voice answered.

"Ok, who just spoke?"

"That...was the Empress."

CHAPTER TEN

Ixtelina was bothered as she and Ixgalan left the transfer Pod. A Customs Agent documented their arrival and which ship they belonged to, provided them papers containing the information, and, interestingly enough, took their pictures.

"Aren't those two-dimensional images rather useless?" Ixtelina asked. The images had been printed in the small book she had been provided and asked to keep.

The human waited for the translation before responding, "We are used to looking at them, but there is more information encoded in your records which allow positive identification. While we do not expect to need it, should something happen we will have the data. The book—we call it a 'passport'—is your promise to be honest with us."

Ixtelina looked down at the passport she had been handed. "How is this a promise?"

The human smiled. "We promise that if you don't have it, we will make it very unpleasant for you."

Ixtelina looked back down at her document. "What if it gets stolen?"

The human made a facial gesture that Ixtelina hadn't categorized yet. "Oh, we promise to space the person who took it."

Ixtelina stared at the man for a moment before his words clicked. "Wait, do you mean you'll throw the thief out into space?"

"Why, yes! How else would we encourage individuals not to steal someone's passport?"

There went one of their preferred methods of walking around space stations. Most advanced societies understood mistakes and provided second chances.

Yes, this operation would be rated highly enough to include both a difficulty bonus and a danger bonus.

She put the passport into her robe and zipped up the pocket. "Our instruments." She nodded to Ixgalan, who lifted the box they had retrieved from the Pod. "How do we get them reviewed?"

"Go by Station Location ARD001. They will ask you to explain their purpose and how to lock them down. Be aware that if your stated purpose is ever determined to be false, you—and perhaps your organization—will be forever banned from the Etheric Empire. Your superiors will be able to argue the charge, of course, but the person who falsely explained the purpose will not be allowed back into our space."

Ixtelina smiled, but the reaction of the human let her know he didn't understand. He nodded to her as she went through the last short hall to the inside of the humans' Outer Docks.

She stood just inside the hatch and took in the massive room, the almost eye-searing amount of light, and the smells that were foreign to her.

She was on the bottom floor of a large shopping and food area.

It went up five levels. The floor she was standing on had seating areas interspersed with large plant and liquid arrangements. Each higher level had its own walkways, and seating by the edge that allowed those above to look down on the lower levels and the final floor at the bottom.

Almost like this was a large amphitheater. A place to shop, eat, and see and be seen by whoever and whatever happened to be visiting the station.

At the far end was a two-story-tall sign—a picture of weapons, humans, and something else she didn't recognize, which was ferocious and furry. She pulled out the tablet the human had provided and clicked the instructions to translate the language to one she understood.

The name translated to "All Guns Blazing."

It was a bar, a place to drink and eat. The hall indicated by the sign had traffic going in and out of it.

Quite a bit of the traffic was human, some Yollin, and there were others as well. She recognized an Akkafuln and several other species. It was hard to miss those very tall, very skinny, hairless aliens.

Ixtelina thought of them as all legs and no personality.

Ixgalan came up beside her. "You decided not to have the items reviewed?"

Ixtelina made a sound of distaste. "The humans are a little too straightforward for me to answer their questions without advice from our leaders." She looked at Ixgalan, who was scanning the large cavern with its noises and lights shining everywhere.

After a moment he whispered, "This place is huge." Then he looked at the very top of the cavern.

Ixtelina followed his eyes as he wondered, "How do they power a little sun in here?"

QBBS *Meredith Reynolds*, Space Traffic Control, Special Unit

Marilyn reviewed the full body scans from both the Executive Pod and the Customs area.

There was a potential problem.

She talked to Meredith, then Reynolds before contacting the General.

"Reynolds here." His gruff voice was consistent, at least.

"Marilyn from SU. We have...anomalies...on the two Ixtalis, and I've reviewed them with both Meredith and Reynolds. Both aliens have unique devices planted near what looks to be their brain stems."

"One moment," he replied. Marilyn waited, wondering if the General would arrive at the same conclusion she had.

He came back on almost a minute later. "Confirmed by TOM. Most likely those are suicide devices. TOM and ADAM are now talking with Bethany Anne, but both believe the devices have been in place for a long time. These agents may not even know about them."

"Well, that just sucks," Marilyn murmured.

"Agreed," the General answered. Marilyn's face went red; she hadn't expected the General to hear her observation. Then she heard some murmuring from his side of the line. "Marilyn, Dan Bosse is heading your way. Sit tight. He is going to take the lead on this case."

"Understood, sir."

"Reynolds out."

Her line went dead.

Oh hell, she thought. *Now the Empress' inner circle was getting involved.*

Planet Yoll, R'Chkoklet

John passed the bodies from earlier and went back up the stairs after confirming with the tactical EI that no enemy combatants had created new ambush locations.

He arrived on the fifth floor after a large number of steps and turns and paused for a moment to look around, then shrugged.

There was only one way to go from here, and it was down the

hall to a pair of very fancy doors. Fine. If the hall went to the executives' offices, then to the executives' offices he would go. Nothing these Yollins had was giving him or the new armor a serious workout.

That was when the alarms sounded and a rocket burst through the doors, heading in his direction.

One more time window glass was shattered, but this time it was half the windows on the top floor. Fire exploded out of several sections, their pieces cascading down to shatter on the ground below.

Somewhere a female Yollin screamed in pain.

One body encased in red armor was violently ejected from the building. It headed toward Pehl-eck, looking like it might slam into the street just feet from her.

"Oh my—" She cut off her comment when the figure stopped in the air a block away and hovered some two stories above the ground.

She continued reporting. "Stars! There was a large explosion from the fifth floor of the building. The human was ejected forcefully, perhaps by a rocket or a trap that triggered the explosion. The human stopped two stories from the ground in mid-air, as if he has the same technology in his armor that his ship uses, and is now starting to move back toward the building. It looks like he is flying as he heads back up to the fifth floor."

"YEAH!" Silus yelled as the executive offices' doors were ripped off. Once the shoulder-mounted missile was fired at the representative from the Etheric Empress, he and his team had dropped behind overturned furniture to protect themselves from the blowback.

Which had been a good idea. The doors had exploded back into their room, one slamming into the table they were hiding behind, another partially exiting through the window behind them. It hadn't shattered the glass, but the glass looked like it was about to go.

His ears were ringing.

The smell of paper on fire was intense. The guys grabbed their packs.

"Don't want to burn!" Soc'vele yelled, pushing Kr'chen next to him to "move his soft ass."

They stopped when they heard footsteps coming toward them.

Crunch, crunch, crunch...click.

A figure strode through the smoke and fire and entered the chamber. None of the Yollins said anything, since the shock of seeing the alien still alive kept them quiet momentarily.

Silus ground out, "We will die before we accept the new regime."

The human's movements were too fast for any of the Yollins to see, but as seven bodies collapsed to the floor the human holstered his pistol and headed back toward the broken windows.

"Telling me that was redundant, asshole," John told the dead.

QBBS *Meredith Reynolds*

Ixtelina and Ixgalan made their way around the outside of the lower level's central congregation area. It was set up to facilitate food purchase and consumption, and meetings in the same area. She noted at least five alien species she hadn't expected to see here.

Ixtelina and Ixgalan wandered around for a while, walking

into different shops, and found one small store had handmade kv-chet. It was a Yollin specialty that Ixtalis considered a sweet.

Most considered it sour.

After some negotiation the proprietor handed them two long cylinders, and the Ixtalis found themselves a table and began to suck on the viscous substance. Ixgalan laid down the box with their electronics and grabbed a chair. Both of them were slightly on the small side of standard-sized human, so the seats fit them just fine.

Ixtelina used the device the store owner provided to suck the Yollin treat into her mouth. "That...is good," she admitted.

Ixgalan only nodded as he continued to ingest the kv-chet.

"Did you notice," Ixtelina asked, as much to herself as to Ixgalan, "that the exchange for our gold was as fair as they could provide?"

Ixgalan stopped for a moment and looked at his food. "What did the person call this?" Ixgalan shook the cylinder.

"A straw."

"We should purchase more of these. I can't believe we haven't considered stocking these as standard supplies whenever we go into new locations."

Ixtelina looked down at her straw and back at the store. "Do you think they will sell us these straws?"

Ixgalan rose and headed toward the store, but stopped three paces away and turned around. Grabbing his kv-chet, he chortled and started back to the store.

Ixtelina guessed he didn't trust her. She sucked down more of her kv-chet.

Good call.

She let her thoughts wander as she took in the five levels. Apparently these humans had built with the idea that other species would use this...bazaar?

No, it didn't have the feel of a bazaar.

At least half the stores on the third level and almost all on Levels Four and Five were shuttered.

Not ready for business.

It either spoke to massive plans to grow, or a lack of ability to open enough stores of their own.

Ixgalan came back and placed a box on the table.

"Five hundred straws," he declared proudly. "Apparently they have manufacturing facilities inside this station that make the products they use, including these wondrous straws."

"It doesn't take much to satisfy you, does it?" Ixtelina asked.

"No. Do you know how many times I have had to look like a baby on stations that were not set up to serve our kind?"

"More than once?"

"And it was too many, even then," Ixgalan admitted.

"Why did you become a physical specialist if you hate eating in strange places?"

"I like seeing them, so you take the good with the bad."

"And now?"

"I know of a product that will liquefy almost anything." He pointed up. "My future is now as bright as their fake sun up there."

"That light *is* a marvel," Ixtelina admitted. The salesperson had shown Ixtelina how to use the camera capabilities on the tablet the Customs agent had allowed them to use and then informed her they could purchase the units if they desired.

Ixtelina had quickly agreed to purchase the tablet and tried to negotiate down the price.

The salesperson wouldn't budge. Apparently the humans didn't believe in negotiations. The salesperson did say that the larger the purchase was the more likely humans were to negotiate, but not for common items.

Ixtelina had also found out what the bumps on the salesperson's chest were after pointedly asking. The human laughed, changed colors slightly, and explained they were for providing nourishment for their young.

"What is over there?" Ixgalan pointed to the other side of the floor. Some humans exited the hall and others went in. Ixtelina picked up her tablet and figured out the function that provided a map of the local area.

She looked up. "It is a hallway to take you to the tram that goes inside the space station."

Ixgalan started slurping the last of his drink. "Finished." He stood up, adding, "I'll be back."

Ixtelina watched as he went to the other side, threw his cup away, and disappeared into the hall.

He came back out a little while later, returned to their table, and sat down. "Etheric Empire citizens or invited guests only."

Ixtelina nodded. "That isn't entirely unexpected. What has you dejected?"

Ixgalan turned to look at her. "There will be no unexpected options to get inside. There are only two trams and trust me, those are some vicious-looking aliens you would have to get by to get on the trams. I'm sure they have security protocols in place to shut down the tram if they have undesirables in one of the cars." He glanced around the area and leaned toward Ixtelina, switching to their language. "Plus, the cars just fit inside the tunnel. I would not be surprised if they use a form of suction to move them."

"That would require quite a bit of engineering and power," Ixtelina murmured.

Ixgalan pointed up again. "Like that fake sun doesn't?"

"Well, no time like the present. Let's figure out a way to release the macros, and we will walk around this area. I'll need to reach out to those in charge of trade and let them know I would like to meet. I would like a little more information on this species before I do that, though."

Ixgalan nodded his understanding, and stood up and left once more.

Ixtelina looked at the different shops, wondering which ones might provide more information, and decided the one which suggested it was a type of monetary institution looked promising.

She was halfway around the concourse when she saw Ixgalan coming in her direction, his face calm. His eyes, however, were annoyed.

She was waiting, her hands in the sleeves of her opposing arms when he walked up. "The macros are dead," he told her.

Ixtelina let out her breath in a long, controlled exhalation as she looked around. "Humans?"

Ixgalan nodded. "Humans."

Ixtelina considered the next step before she took her hand out and pointed toward the monetary location. "The game is afoot, Ixgalan, the game is afoot."

CHAPTER ELEVEN

Rih-benn nodded to his last two guards, releasing them as he strode into his home. Three full-time guards roamed the place, and he had high levels of security as well. He would admit, if only to himself, that the human they had met to exchange money for the spice had scared him, if only a little.

It would be Brylen who died tonight, not him.

After walking through the front entry, he headed down the hall and took a right to stop in front of a door. He entered the security code and let himself into his home office. Locking the door behind him, he tossed the box of bostok onto his desk and turned to the small group of plants he had cultivated as a side project.

One of the four rectangular plots was empty. He had been planning on growing his first successful batch of the spice needed for the soda project right here in his office.

Then he would have the stranglehold on the market, since Yollins would prefer to know the source wasn't the aliens.

Well, ok...most Yollins. There were a few who would go straight to the source for the thrill or the promise it was truly the right spice.

He, however, would have all the rest.

He picked a berry from the leftmost planter and popped it in his mouth. It had taken him over three years and multiple operations to acquire the precious seedling that was now a plant. "Keep growing like the little rebel you are," Rih-benn told it, "because I'm going to make you a star."

The shock of the berry hit his system, energizing the ends of his pleasure nodes for almost half a minute. He closed his eyes and accepted the joy of success and the pleasure the chemicals brought him.

Opening his eyes, he smiled. "I'm so sorry. You were my greatest achievement, but now you are yesterday's news." He patted the empty planter that now had only sand and some chemicals. He would have to figure out the right chemicals to grow the plant, the right solar mixture, and the liquid quantities. It was a puzzle he would enjoy solving.

Rih-benn grimaced and turned to his desk and sat down in his chair. He rubbed his mandibles together.

"How the hell," he asked himself aloud, "am I going to get another shot at those seeds?"

Over a hundred miles away in their ship, Nathan and Ecaterina watched the feedback from the nanobots that had infected the Yollin drug and crime boss.

"That was an interesting peek into his physiology," Nathan murmured. He was tapping into the information coming from the host's system as the Yollin ate the berry.

Ecaterina walked to the front of the ship. For this trip, Nathan had used a baby *G'laxix Sphaea*-class vessel that had been cut down in size to half the original. With a full EI component and a direct link to ADAM, Nathan and Ecaterina just had to do whatever the ship told them needed to be done by someone with two arms and two legs.

Everything else was run by the onboard EI.

"Christina is asleep," she told her mate. Sliding a hand up his shoulder, she looked at what he was doing. "Is this the guy who was going to set you up?"

Nathan nodded. "Yes."

He didn't see Ecaterina's eyes flash yellow. "Those are his physiological and biometric readouts?"

"Yes," Nathan agreed, still paying attention to the feedback coming back from the crook.

"So when the nanocytes finally kill him we will receive the medical information?" she continued.

This time Nathan nodded.

"Good." Ecaterina patted her mate on his shoulder as she dropped into the chair next to him. "No reason to waste this opportunity to understand Yollin physiology."

Nathan finally caught on that his mate was not pleased and looked over his shoulder at her. His eyes widened as Ecaterina's eyes flared yellow and her mouth opened in a snarl as she thought about the crime boss trying to kill her mate.

She looked back at him. "This asshole was going to die one way or another."

Planet Yoll, Yollin Capital

Kiel, dressed in the normal clothes of a Mont-level project planner, entered the fifth bar he had worked so far this week.

In his frequent updates to Dan Bosse, he mentioned drinking so much due to the job that it was beginning to cause him problems during workouts to get rid of the excess weight.

Dan informed him he was aware how little the Yollin alcohol truly affected a Yollin's weight, and that he appreciated the hellacious amount of sacrifice that going out drinking was causing the Yollin mercenary.

Kiel smiled, shrugged, and just muttered, "I tried..." But now, after a month of working the bars, it was indeed becoming a sacrifice.

It was just so damned *boring.*

He was nursing his second beer when his implanted audio activated. "That's what I'm telling you," a Yollin speaking with an upper-caste accent hissed, his voice low compared to the ambient sound. "Some of us in the Straiphus system need a few good contacts. Further..."

Kiel lost the connection; too much noise was interfering. He put the mug up to his mouth to cover it. "ADAM?"

"Yes, Kiel?"

"Can you clean up the audio that is piping in? This is legit."

"When we have the necessary ships we will make our run and force this alien to surrender, then hang her head in the king's palace as the first of a new monarchy."

Kiel grimaced. "ADAM, clean up, translate, and route to Dan. Where is this coming from?"

"A drinking establishment named 'Mont's the Best,' two streets over and one toward the stadium, on Chk'klock."

Kiel tossed two coins on his table and stood up, then stopped and braced himself for a moment before looking the wrong way for the door, but finally located the exit and nodded to himself. He put his head down and walked like a Yollin with a mission, making sure he could finish the job of getting out of the bar without falling down.

Once outside, he turned left and kept up his act. After crossing the street, he changed his stride from half-falling forward to a determined gait as soon as he was outside the range of the bar's video cameras.

"We have a strategy to move the aliens where we want them so they fight us on our terms."

Kiel turned the corner.

"Wrong direction," ADAM told him.

Kiel turned around. "Sorry, thinking about how to yank this asshole's spine out of his mouth."

"Dan says not to detain him. We have a photo, we just need you to release your tags. Kiel, he is heading out the other side of the building."

Kiel cursed in Yollin and reached into his pocket to pull out a cylinder, then moved closer to a building and cracked it open. From inside four small spheres, each the size of a small rock, floated out and zoomed over his shoulder.

He faked drinking from the cylinder and then put it back together, then stood up and looked around. "What do we know?"

"One moment," ADAM answered.

Kiel started walking slowly down the sidewalk. It was a few moments before he received an answer.

"We know he got away," ADAM finally replied.

Kiel looked both ways down the street and turned to his left. After a few paces, he was able to duck into a small alley and wait for the tags to come back. The four black orbs returned, and Kiel grabbed them and stuck them in the cylinder. "Shame these are too expensive to leave around."

ADAM replied, "Sorry, but it isn't just their cost. It might become a PR problem if they are found, according to Cheryl Lynn."

Kiel opened a messaging app on his tablet and requested to see Kael-ven as soon as possible.

Seconds later he was pinged with a time and place.

QBBS *Meredith Reynolds*

Hirotoshi, Ryu, Katsu, and Shin followed the female in front of them. She had her hair tied back in a ponytail, and her long black synthetic leather coat flowed behind her.

Typically the Tontos would be in some form of casual dress, but now they were on a mission.

The five of them walked down the hall behind All Guns Blazing, and when they reached it Tabitha knocked on the nondescript door.

The lock clicked for her, and she pushed it open.

Tabitha raised an eyebrow and bowed as she and her team flowed into the room. "My Empress."

Barnabas snorted. He was sitting next to Bethany Anne and she punched him as she told Tabitha, "Oh, for fuck's sake straighten up, you twerp." The Empress grinned as Ranger Two walked the length of the table to hug her friend. Bethany Anne rolled her eyes and called, "You Tontos as well."

The four Japanese vampires stopped bowing, but Bethany Anne took care to look them all in the eye and nod. They owed their lives to her people, and they took their vows very seriously.

While Tabitha was only partially respectful, there was nothing but respect coming from her team.

Protect your lead, she sent them.

Hirotoshi and Ryu subtly nodded. They got the message.

"How are they hanging, Number One?" Tabitha cracked a smile as Barnabas frowned. He caught the play on words.

"I see that young Anne hasn't taught you anything yet," he chastised her.

Tabitha's face gave her away before she could lie.

She chose to drop the discussion rather than answer his question. "What are we doing?" She looked at Barnabas, then Bethany Anne, then back at her boss.

"We have data that says the Eubos system is barely above anarchy," Barnabas started the information dump. "Well, that's not true. They have plenty of structure. What they lack is an implementation of law."

"They didn't get the memo?" Tabitha asked.

"What memo would that be?" the Empress asked.

Tabitha turned to Katsu. "Didn't you send an all-Yollin dispatch that shared the new rules from Empress Bethany Anne?"

"God, let me go back to just being Queen," Bethany Anne grumped.

Tabitha winked at Bethany Anne as Katsu answered, "Yes, I sent the memo as directed. We have confirmation receipts from over a month ago."

Tabitha turned back to her bosses. "See, we sent the memo."

Bethany Anne turned her head to look at Barnabas, who was staring at his number two Ranger. "Oh, do tell, Barnabas."

Barnabas turned to Bethany Anne. "As much as it pains me to say this, she implemented a tactically sound plan."

Tabitha shrugged. "Hey, ignorance of the law doesn't excuse you. Plus, we warned them someday we would come calling, and God help them if they hadn't read the memo."

Bethany Anne wanted to either smile or put her head in her hands. She wondered what her Ranger had just done. "Oh shit," she muttered. "I bet you just started a meme in this solar system."

"Didn't you get the Empress' memo?" Barnabas asked.

"That is what I plan to ask right before I plant my size-eight boots up their asses." Tabitha agreed.

Bethany Anne nodded. "Ok, Ranger Tabitha. You are commissioned to go to the Eubos system and seek out the slave trade," Bethany Anne got serious, "and stop it with all speed." She pointed at the table and stabbed it with her finger. "I will not have slaves in my Empire. Slavers get one chance to listen. Second time they can explain their reasoning to their personal gods." Her eyes started glowing. "Those who have used their slaves sexually or victimized them? They don't even get one chance."

Tabitha swallowed and nodded her understanding. This was the Queen Bitch speaking.

She was going to need a lot of ammo.

Bethany Anne stood up. "Barnabas has the files for you and

your team, but I wanted to present you and your team with something."

Bethany Anne walked around the table, heading out the door Tabitha and her team had just come in. This time, when the door opened Darryl was standing there.

Where the hell was he when she'd shown up?

As Tabitha walked past her guys she whispered, "We are going to need a lot of ammo."

Ryu nodded in understanding.

Tabitha walked out the door and followed Bethany Anne and Darryl. She turned back in time to see Barnabas talking with Hirotoshi for a moment before he went the other direction and Hirotoshi started following them. Moments later, Darryl was in the lead, Bethany Anne and Tabitha were next, and the four Tontos brought up the rear.

As they headed down the hall, a sliding door opened, and the seven of them swept through before the wall slid closed behind them. Seconds later, they left the hall that headed back toward All Guns Blazing and Darryl led them across the bottom of the large shopping and eating area.

Bethany Anne seemed to ignore the looks and whispers and pointing fingers as she and the group walked across the floor.

"*Hai!*" Ryu hissed behind her.

Tabitha looked at the two aliens ahead, who were Ixtalis, based on the images Tabitha had studied. She thought they looked like standing spiders. The couple were a male and a female. They headed in their direction, perhaps thinking they would be able to intercept Bethany Anne.

That was when the fear hit.

Darryl had a hand out in the direction of the two Ixtali and spoke in their language. "Not now. Thank you for your interest." He kept to his fast pace as Bethany Anne nodded to them, and the team reached the entrance to the special docks beyond.

Tabitha noticed the look of shock on more than one alien—at least if she was reading their body language correctly.

And perhaps a new level of respect for their Empress from a few of her fellow humans who hadn't been around Bethany Anne for a while.

Darryl stepped aside as Bethany Anne caught up and then passed him in the hall once they got through the commercial areas. She nodded to the guards at each checkpoint.

Bethany Anne had told Meredith she was tired of going through security stations and the EI needed to warn each that she was on her way.

Apparently age hadn't provided any extra doses of patience to Bethany Anne—at least not yet.

At the last station, however, she slowed down. She had personally told these guards that everyone—including her—was to be checked before entering this work area.

"Gentlemen." She nodded to both black-clad guards, although she couldn't see their faces since their helmets were in place. They should be confirming with both Meredith and Reynolds who the people in front of them were. If there was any doubt, they had additional tools as well as protocols to follow.

While Earth had thousands of stories of body snatchers, TOM had said it was unlikely anything would truly be able to fake being human.

Bethany Anne had breathed a sigh of relief.

They would be unable to fake being a human any time *soon,* TOM had finished.

She sucked back in the air she had just exhaled. *You are lucky I can't strangle your scrawny neck,* she told him.

She could feel his amusement. She still didn't know if he had been joking that it could happen, or was just pleased that his timing on delivering the warning had been so effective.

If she hadn't planned before to find out how to provide TOM with his own body again, she was now—just so she could beat the shit out of him just once for old times' sake.

The guards had finally confirmed everyone's identity, and the doors unlocked. Darryl moved in first to verify it was safe for Bethany Anne. "Clear."

"One of these times," Bethany Anne grumped, "I'm going to have a practical joke waiting on the other side of these doors." She walked into the hanger and turned to watch Ranger Tabitha and her team come in.

Tabitha walked through the door, and her mouth dropped open. "Oh, my," she whispered as she walked past Bethany Anne.

Bethany Anne continued to watch her reactions.

Tabitha completely ignored her.

Bethany Anne looked at Darryl, who was grinning. "I won't give you the pleasure."

Darryl chuckled at Bethany Anne's words as he walked toward the other side of the ship.

Hirotoshi stopped next to Bethany Anne. "That is a Ranger's ship?"

"Well," Bethany Anne told him, turning to take in the beautiful ship, "it is *this* Ranger's ship. Specially made to handle her and her team of six Tontos, plus three passengers. Six, if those passengers are really close," she admitted. The black human version of the *G'laxix Sphaea*-class ship gleamed under the bright lights of the hangar.

Tabitha called over her shoulder as she ran a hand along the side of the ship, "What's its name?"

"What would you expect?" a somewhat electronic voice snarked from underneath the ship.

Tabitha pulled her hand down as if stung. "Oh, God!"

Bethany Anne and Hirotoshi walked over to the Ranger. "Welcome to the *Achronyx*, Tabitha."

Tabitha lowered her head into her right hand, her middle finger somehow the only one running up the side of her face and aimed in Bethany Anne's direction. "*OWWW!*" Tabitha screamed as she yanked her hand down, shaking it to deal with the pain. When she looked at it, a thin line of blood showed where something sharp had cut it.

She looked at Bethany Anne, who raised her eyebrows.

"I deserved that," Tabitha admitted. "I've been around a teenager too much."

There was a commotion from the doors through which they had entered, and Barnabas walked in with the other two Tontos following him. They carried additional boxes labeled "Ammunition."

Barnabas walked up to Bethany Anne and pursed his lips, staring at Tabitha's hand.

"What happened?" he asked. Bethany Anne looked at Tabitha.

"Well, since there aren't any buildings to fall out of, this time I decided to let my hand do something stupid, and it got reprimanded," Tabitha replied.

Hirotoshi nodded to his Ranger. "I will see to the new supplies and make sure the ship is ready, Kemosabe."

Tabitha nodded to Hirotoshi and turned to Bethany Anne. "Are you sure Achronyx is up to handling this ship?"

Barnabas chuckled.

"Keep it up, boss." She looked at him. "I swear he is the most obstinate EI anyone has ever heard about. He forces me to rephrase shit just because he knows it annoys the fuck out of me."

Bethany Anne folded her arms and raised an eyebrow. "Tabitha, are we going to have the same discussion about the inability of an EI to actively choose to be obstinate like that? As a programmer yourself—"

"I was a hacker. There is a difference," Tabitha interrupted.

"Programmers worked in corporations playing with their databases."

"And what were you doing?" Bethany Anne asked, one eyebrow raised.

"I was on the outside, busting in and retrieving the data they were putting into the databases." The ex-hacker Ranger thought about it for half a second. "They were filling the data vault while I was making withdrawals."

Bethany Ann tapped her lips before asking, "So, a common thief?"

There was a snort from the other side of the ship.

"My Empress," Tabitha answered, a gleam in her eye as she waved a hand up and down her body, "there was never anything common about this."

Bethany Anne smiled. "Good, we have the old Tabitha back."

Tabitha's smile turned melancholy as she considered the past couple of months. "Yeah, I'm sorry about that. Leaving Earth, and no boyfriend—it kinda walloped me."

Bethany Anne's voice was soft. "You aren't the only one to suffer from leaving Earth behind," she told her Ranger, "but you came out of it. It only took a spunky teenager to help you."

This time Tabitha made a face not unlike one Barnabas might have made when thinking about Tabitha. "Not the method I would have suggested, but you're right, she helped," she admitted.

"Well, we finally recognized the problem with Anne's mom when she was taking it out on Anne. Then Jinx chose the girl, and we had the Pod-doc episode. You helped her through it and did very well, but it is time to get back on the horse."

Tabitha smiled, a glint in her eye. "I think it is, at that." Tabitha looked down, stomped her right foot once and grimaced, then stomped it a second time.

Chink.

Then she did her left.

Chink.

Tabitha lifted her head and smiled. "Round them up, Tontos!" she called as she walked toward the entrance ramp on the side of the ship, "We have a party to crash!"

There was a slight *chink, chink, chink* as Tabitha walked away.

Barnabas stared down at her boots in horror. "Is she wearing *spurs?*"

Bethany Anne just shook her head and patted Barnabas on the shoulder. "I'm sure it was a gag gift from her team."

Barnabas watched his Ranger walk up the ramp and disappear into the spaceship before saying to Bethany Anne over his shoulder as he pointed to where Tabitha had just disappeared, "You realize that young Hispanic Ranger could be the first representative of *your* Empire. She is wearing a black leather coat, leads four Japanese vampires who all respond to 'Tonto,' and her boots have *spurs.*"

Bethany Anne started walking toward the exit, so Barnabas followed. "There isn't a cow for a hundred light-years around here, Bethany Anne."

Darryl was waiting at the door to lead the Empress out.

Barnabas kept talking. "And I don't think there's a horse on this whole space station!" he complained.

The two remaining Tontos followed Barnabas through the doors.

The guards chuckled as the team went down the hall and around the corner. Barnabas' voice floated back to them, "Oh, for God's sake! She had better not come back saying 'y'all' in her Latina accent!"

CHAPTER TWELVE

QBBS _Meredith Reynolds_, Open Court, Outer Docks

Aerolyn was struggling to figure out what options—if any—he had to hide here on the Etheric Empire's space station when the buzz of conversation on the floor increased.

There was a group of humans threading through the center of the large area.

"No, that's her!" he heard someone whispering in Yollin. He wanted to turn around and see who was talking, but kept his focus on the procession. Out of the corner of his eye, he noticed a couple figures heading toward the parade.

They were Ixtalis.

Aerolyn grimaced. Those aliens would screw you over and make you smile while they did it. Every chance the Ixtalis got, they hooked you on either their rare gems or the information they traded.

Usually both.

The big dark man in front of the Empress put his arm out, and then a sense of fear hit. It wasn't only him—most of the people on the floor felt something. Those nearest the male seemed to be affected the worst. One of the humans off to the side turned away and threw up.

The Ixtalis backed off, and the Empress and her people disappeared in the direction of the ship berths.

"What was that?" Aerolyn looked around in shock. Most of the humans seemed to know what was going on, and a few were casting irritated glances at the two Ixtalis. They had sat down, obviously shaken.

Aerolyn got up and left his table. If this Empress was willing to upset an Ixtali, maybe he had a chance. He needed to find out who he could talk to about his problem—and if the Etheric Empire was willing to help him.

Ixtelina found the nearest table and sat down.

Ixgalan dropped into a chair beside her. "What just happened?"

Ixtelina looked at him. "Do you have a guess? Because I do, and I do not like the idea much."

Ixgalan reached up and scratched his face. "We were hit by some kind of emotional weapon?"

"Did you see a weapon pointed at us?"

"Sure. His hand."

Ixtelina was quiet for a moment. "Do you believe there was a weapon in his hand?"

It was Ixgalan's turn to pause. "My mind says he had to have a weapon." He made a gesture with his arm to show he didn't believe it.

"That is my point, Ixgalan," Ixtelina admitted. "If he could push out a wave that messed with our emotions at such a basic level, and it isn't a technical ability but rather an organic one..." She left the statement open.

"How would they know how to affect our physiology?"

"I'm trying to work on that right now," Ixtelina admitted. "It's scary as well as interesting."

Ixgalan leaned toward his lead and put a hand on her arm. "Are you ok?"

Ixtelina looked around, leaving Ixgalan's hand where it was for the moment. "No." She turned to her team member. "I'll be straightforward. The implications of this are far-reaching. We can sit and ponder it all we want, but there are very few species that can do what they just did. We are the first Ixtalis on their space station, but perhaps they recorded our genetics when they took our pictures earlier. If they did, what is their technology? We were only in front of the camera for seconds."

"Maybe while on the transfer ship?"

"That Executive Pod?" Ixtelina thought about that a moment. "If so, that was the most luxurious medical scanner I've ever been on."

"Yeah, I didn't think so either, but I had to ask," Ixgalan lamented. "Then again, why aren't my tiny spies working?" Ixtelina shook her head, and Ixgalan grimaced. "Sorry, that was inappropriate."

"We are both out of sorts at the moment. If we had been able to connect the ship to the station, we would have been able to employ a significant amount of attacks."

"Which," Ixgalan finished, "was why they didn't allow us to dock."

"Exactly." Ixtelina leaned forward and rested her elbows on the table. "They know who we are, and they know what we sell."

Ixgalan thought about it for a moment. "And they don't care."

"Ignorance, lack of need, or pride?" Ixtelina whispered.

"Well, we could just ask them," Ixgalan suggested.

Ixtelina looked at him to register her opinion of that idea. He was looking at the entrances to the ship's berths, where the Empress was coming back through. This time, however, she had a new male beside her and was obviously in a heated (and one-sided) conversation. The two males that followed them looked similar to the ones who had guarded her going the other direction, but she was sure they were different.

Ixtelina pushed herself up from the chair. While she didn't relish the thought of feeling the fear again, she had a job to do.

Darryl turned his head just a small amount. "Incoming at two o'clock."

Bethany Anne's eyes flitted that way as Darryl called, "Those are Ixtalis, right?"

>>**Affirmative.**<<

"Ok, we will see what she has to say this time. This could be fun." Bethany Anne slowed as Darryl halted their procession.

Darryl went forward to meet the two aliens and Barnabas took his place, calmly waiting and looking around. He made it obvious that he was keeping others from the Empress. Jun and Kouki spread out behind Bethany Anne, scanning as well.

It wasn't lost on Ixtelina how quickly the team around the Empress spread out to protect her as she approached the Ixtalis. The lead security person was headed in her direction, and she worked not to shake in fear—even a little—as he approached.

"Hello, Special Trade Legate Ixtelina. What do you wish to speak with Empress Bethany Anne about?"

Not surprised he knew who she was, Ixtelina forged ahead. "There seems to be strife concerning my mission here to set up trade between our people and yours. I would like to see what could be done to reduce the friction."

Darryl caught Bethany Anne's barely whispered, "Let her pass" and waved the Trade Legate through. "Just you."

She nodded her understanding.

―――――――

Bethany Anne listened to the burst of information about the Ixtalis ADAM sent.

I got all that information the first time, ADAM.

>> **Right, but your father requested I remind you. Dan is looking into a situation with the two Ixtalis. They might have suicide implants, or their people have set them up to be killed if they are in harm's way.** <<

Understood.

Bethany Anne nodded slightly to the alien. "How can I help your faction, Trade Legate?"

Ixtelina looked around. "You wish to discuss this..."

Bethany Anne smirked. "I didn't approach you, Trade Legate, but rather the opposite. I will make a few assumptions and cut this short. I think I have the basics of how the Ixtalis work, and I'm willing to share them with you right here and now. I imagine nothing I'm going to say isn't already thought by beings all through this section of the galaxy, so I doubt it will affect the Ixtalis' reputation."

Ixtelina placed her hands inside her robes and considered her options. She was quickly coming to grips with the blunt attitude of the Etheric Empire, and apparently it started at the top. It was too early to decide if it were true, or only a front and a negotiating ploy.

It wouldn't be the first time.

The Empress looked at her guard. "Darryl?"

"Yes ma'am?" he replied, but didn't look at his Empress.

"There is an ice cream shop on the second level. What flavor?"

Ixtelina, trying to follow along, wasn't sure what to think. However, the Empress' security guard merely replied, "Mint."

"Good choice," she told him. "One scoop or two?"

"Better get it packed, unless you are going to change roles with me?" he asked, and she chuckled.

"I'm not sure you want the role."

"There isn't any doubt; I don't want your part." Her guard turned to look at her and flashed the human smile. "I'm happy right where I am."

"I'll eat it for him," the other male offered.

Ixtelina was still trying to figure out what ice cream was.

"Ok, Barnabas, but you will owe Darryl a scoop of mint when this is all over."

"Deal." He smiled. "It will help me deal with my errant Ranger."

"She's not errant," the Empress argued. "She is doing what we told her to do."

"You will have to excuse me." Barnabas grinned. "I'm not using the archaic version. I mean she is straying from the proper standards."

"That's so much bullshit and you know it, Number One. Now hold my place." She reached out and touched her guard, who had backed up a couple of steps to be near her.

Ixtelina's mind blanked in shock as the Etheric Empress took a small step to her left and she and her guard disappeared. The crowd on the floor became so quiet, she wondered if everyone was holding their breath.

A moment later the Empress called from the second floor, "Barnabas!"

Everyone on the floor looked up at the Empress on the second level. "They are out of mint, but they have chocolate."

"Sure!"

Ixtelina looked around and noticed that Ixgalan was using his tablet to record his observations. Her mind was working feverishly. The Empress was doing this for a reason, and that she *could* do it was known, because the people on the floor had resumed their conversations.

But logic dictated it was a rare demonstration.

"So you see…" The Empress popped back in with her guard next to her and handed the human Barnabas some of the 'ice cream.' Ixtelina stared at the Empress, who was using a utensil to move something light-colored from a cup into her mouth. "It isn't like we really need your gems."

Ixtelina didn't say anything, but she got the message.

"So why would I want to work with a data acquisition group who brings me nothing in return?" She used her utensil to point around her. "My goal here—my responsibility—is to make sure they have as long a life as possible." She pointed the utensil at Ixtelina. "Ixtalis, as near as I can tell, offer negative benefits as trading partners."

"You have the option of re-trading the gems," Ixtelina told her. Although that was a common negotiation, she hadn't realized there was a chance it would ever be true.

"I don't think we care enough to do that." Bethany Anne took another bite of her ice cream.

"Then you may be right. We may *not* have a basis for trade."

"Yes, that is true, so you have two options. You may stay here," she pointed to the location they were standing in, "and ponder your course of action, or you may go back to your ship. You will not be allowed outside this area."

"Why do you treat us so harshly?" Ixtelina asked.

"That is an easy question to answer. You are users. In the end, it is all about the Ixtalis at the expense of everyone else in the universe. Until you pick a side you are against everyone, and therefore you are my foe. I'll not have an opponent roaming free in the Etheric Empire. You either convince me Ixtalis aren't my enemies, or you leave now and don't return. Be aware that actively working to attack, subvert our information, or reduce our ability to work with other species will be considered a declaration of war."

This trade mission was rapidly going down in flames. Ixtelina wasn't sure how it went so wrong, so quickly.

The Empress pointed the spoon at her again. "You have a few decisions to make, Trade Legate Ixtelina. The first is whether you care to attack our Empire by trying to acquire information for your trade. Using your eyes and ears is permitted." She pointed to the box sitting next to Ixgalan. "However, if you continue to try to use your technology, and we confirm you are doing so?" Ixtelina took an involuntary step backward when a new expression appeared on the Empress' face and changed her demeanor. "Then you will return to your planet with the news that the Ixtalis are now at war, and you and your team are at fault. Am I making myself clear?"

"That is preposterous," Ixtelina, her mind in total shock, argued. "No one goes to war over information!"

"Apparently you didn't have information on our species in your database, did you?"

"Well, of course not. We have—" Ixtelina stopped talking. *Dammit,* this Empress just confirmed another bit of information from her.

"Don't worry about it." the Empress waved her utensil. "I know you have no information about us."

"Why do you say that?" Ixtelina asked.

"Because you still wonder if you can hire someone to attack us."

Ixtelina squeezed her hands in frustration inside of her sleeves. *What was this Empress doing, reading her mind?*

"Just think about this," Bethany Anne told Ixtelina. "Do you think a group that is trying to find Kurtherians and kick their asses will give a fuck about whoever you can hire to attack us?" The Empress turned to her guard. "We can go, Darryl."

She turned back to Ixtelina as they started walking away. "Bring your mercs on. We could use the target practice."

Ixtelina watched the group walk toward the hall that led to All Guns Blazing.

She just stood there as Ixgalan walked up to her side. "We need to go back to headquarters. This is way above us."

Ixtelina nodded. "They need to know what we know and provide guidance."

The two Ixtalis never noticed the grins of the humans who had heard the conversation, or that the humans made fists and bumped them with each other as the two aliens left.

Matthew, one of the Mining and Ores crew, watched the two aliens depart and shook his head. He turned to his friends, who were enjoying a lunch break. "One of these days, this part of the galaxy is going to figure out that you don't try to put one over on the Empress."

Alicia, who worked the same working shift and was sitting next to him, snorted her agreement.

CHAPTER THIRTEEN

QBS _Achronyx_, En Route to Eubos system

Tabitha had stored her stuff in the Ranger's Cabin. She had easily been able to tell it was her cabin because Bethany Anne had stuck those damned yellow sticky notes, complete with arrows, to the walls to point her down the hall to her door.

She had taken down every one of the yellow stickies on her way down the corridor.

The envelope affixed to her door had the Empress' handwriting. "Yes, this is your room, Tabitha."

She pushed open the door and took in her room. The bed wouldn't allow for two very easily. "Achronyx?"

"Yes, Ranger Tabitha?"

"Are there any beds that can handle two people on this ship?"

"Every bed will handle two people," the EI replied.

"Mmmm." She moved over to the bed and examined it. Sure enough, she didn't have one six-inch mattress but two three-inch mattresses. She found a lock, and when she flipped it she was able to pull the under-mattress out to make the bed a double.

Apparently companionship was permitted—or at least there was an understanding that it could happen.

She bumped against the other wall.

"Ok, close quarters when it's open." She shoved the second half of the bed back under and locked it in place.

She tossed her go-bag on the bed and looked around. Sitting down, she opened her envelope.

Tabitha,

Those in Eubos did not get the request to refrain from slavery, although slavery will not be permitted. I suspect it will take a while for the understanding that "No slavery" means "No slavery!" I would provide stories on how bad it is, but then you might be as pissed off as I am about it and I don't want to be the one to color your response.

Make it stop.

Bethany Anne.

She stood up. "Achronyx, call the team to the meeting room."

"Confirmed, Ranger Tabitha. All team members have been notified to assemble in the main meeting room."

Tabitha walked to her door and opened it. She took a step out, paused, then turned back and stuck her head into her cabin.

"Achronyx," she whispered, "how the fuck do I get to the team's main meeting room?"

Tabitha walked down the hall to the room the team would use to meet, and interestingly enough it was also where they would eat. She waved to her Tontos as she went to the coffee maker and punched in her order.

Moments later, her hot chocolate was ready. God, she would have killed earlier in her life for a body that could eat as much chocolate as she could now and not show it.

Well, she supposed she *had* killed once she had gotten it. Did that count?

The table the Tontos were sitting at had lifted out of the floor and locked into place. The right side of the rectangular room was empty, but she could see the outline of another table in the floor.

This table held ten easily, so there was no reason to pull up another table.

She set her hot chocolate down. "Here is the very short version," she started. "There have been sightings of slavers in the Eubos system even after our Empress sent an edict forbidding the practice. Our responsibility is to go to Eubos, make friends, and slap some heads if need be. They are now under the aegis of the Etheric Empire, and apparently we need to give them another memo. We will be armored at all times, everybody will go with their partner, and we'll kick ass and decide if we take names or leave corpses."

She took a sip of her drink. "Questions?"

Katsu asked, "Data acquisition?"

Tabitha smiled. "You have to ask?"

"Ranger Tabitha," Achronyx interrupted, "we are twelve minutes from Gate transfer. Do you have any commands for the ship?"

Hirotoshi advised, "Go in hot."

She smirked. "We'll always go in hot."

"Understood. *Achronyx* will always go through transfer Gates armed."

Tabitha looked at the nearest speaker. "No, that wasn't what I was suggesting."

"You do not wish to go in with weapons activated?" Achronyx asked.

"Well, yes," Tabitha replied, but then looked at Hirotoshi. She pointed to the speaker and mouthed, "See?"

Hirotoshi shook his head.

Tabitha rolled her eyes. "Achronyx, we will go in hot until I say otherwise. Do we need to be seated anywhere specific?"

"The bridge has the best defensive shields, and the best seats in case we need to maneuver."

Tabitha stood up, walked her mug over to the sink, and set it in the cleanser.

"Let's do this."

She waited for the guys to go first—to confirm which way she needed to go to get to the bridge.

Planet Yoll, Capital City

Kiel made his way across town and quietly entered a building that held a total of four different restaurants, three at street level and one on the top floor. The building next door had a landing pad on the roof.

Not that Kael-ven needed one, but he preferred not to show off his Pod's capabilities if he could help it. Kiel, on the other hand, would have shown off if he were allowed.

Nothing was terribly sexy about Kiel's walking abilities, however.

Kiel was playing with his dinnerware in the small private dining room when there was a sharp knock. He had barely stood up when a Yollin head appeared, looked around, and ducked back out. The door opened wider, and Kael-ven walked in. Kael-ven's annoyance was obvious when the door shut behind him.

"Captain." Kiel reached out to shake Kael-ven's hand before the four-legged Yollin reclined on a couch made for his body type. Kiel turned back to his side of the table and reclined in his chair.

"As the humans would say," Kael-ven muttered, "'God, it's good to be captain again.'"

"What, being 'Plenipotentiary Leader Kael-ven' isn't to your liking?" Kiel asked.

"No, but 'King Kael-ven' and 'Traitor Kael-ven' are the ones I hate to hear most because I expect one of the Empress' Bitches to show up when they say something bad about Bethany Anne."

Kiel shrugged. "They can't be everywhere."

"Well, they are certainly watching me closely enough," Kael-ven countered.

"Trust issues?" Kiel asked.

"What? No." He waved the thought away. "They are concerned my," Kael-ven pointed to the door, "security isn't up to standard."

Kiel looked toward the door. "They seemed fine." He scratched a mandible. "Although perhaps it would have been better if they had come in here and checked under the table."

Kael-ven reached for the drink that was waiting for him. "Trust me, he wanted to, but I told him not to disrespect the Yollin Mercenary Leader that way."

Kiel shrugged, then grabbed his own drink and took a sip. "It wouldn't have bothered me, as many times as John, Eric, Darryl, or Scott practically picked me up and looked under my feet before Bethany Anne came in." He chuckled. "Like I could have hurt her either."

"You could have had a bomb," Kael-ven pointed out.

"Uh…" Kiel stopped for a moment. "Yes, I guess you are right. I hadn't considered that."

"No matter. Eric came down yesterday and tore my people new assholes about their sorry abilities, then he showed them their mistakes. One person chose to be offended by Eric." Kael-ven paused. "He's not with me anymore."

"What, Eric killed him?" Kiel asked, not surprised.

Kael-ven chuckled. "No, but he is in the hospital recuperating. He is allowed to return to the team if he wants to come back, but no one will give any of the Empress' people lip anymore. By the time Eric was done, the guard was apologizing and saying over and over he was happy he was learning the lesson from Eric rather than John."

Kiel laughed. "Eric does like to make it seem like the beatdown he is delivering is, 'only half the shit John would do to you, so you better thank me for not letting John teach you this stuff.'"

Kael-ven nodded. "Said that right after he broke my guard's leg. That human is amazing."

"No," Kiel corrected. "He just makes John seem that much worse."

Kael-ven lifted his drink in Kiel's direction. "Good point."

A minute later, one of the security guards knocked and stuck his head in to announce the waiter was here. Within moments the two Yollins had ordered, and the door was shut once more.

Kael-ven reached into a leather bag and pulled out a small tablet, then logged in and chose an app that would block all known bugs. He looked up at Kiel. "Physical?"

"Checked the place out, and it's clean."

"Ok." The captain accepted his assurance. "What do we have?"

Kiel brought out his own tablet. "ADAM?"

The AI responded, "Yes, Kiel?"

"I'm in a secure room with Kael-ven. Would you transfer the recordings from today into his implant?"

"Certainly," ADAM confirmed. A moment later, Kael-ven's eyes became a touch distant as he focused on the conversations coming through the implants he had received from Bethany Anne. His mandibles started grinding together.

"Idiots!" he finally growled.

"Finished?" Kiel asked, and Kael-ven nodded.

"Ok, thoughts, boss?"

Kael-ven tapped his fingers on the table. "Oh, it doesn't surprise me. They are going to waste a lot of good Yollin blood trying to bring back the aristocracy. I've seen the latest reports, and spoken with the lead scientist on the Yollin population challenges here on our planet."

"What did he say?" Kiel asked. It was no surprise that the biggest issue facing Kael-ven was how to deal with the burgeoning population. That was the reason Yollins had gone to space for decades and become the aggressive species they were.

"He said we *have* no damned population problem!" Kael-ven

spat. "It seems King Yoll made it all up. We could bring all the Yollins in the galaxy back home and still have centuries more growth. Hell," he waved toward the ceiling, "those on the space stations could come back down too, and not be so damned crowded."

"So…"

Kael-ven continued his tirade. "Furthermore, that sphincter plug of a king created useless engineering requirements that hampered our ability to construct bigger buildings, which when you see some of the structures we have created makes no sense. The only times we built to our capabilities, the engineering went through the king's group. In those instances amazing feats of intellect occurred, and no one cared to question the king about why only a few buildings could be so tall."

"And…" Kiel tried to interrupt once more—unsuccessfully— as Kael-ven continued.

"May that rat-faced finger-fucked shit-goblin forever be tormented in the acid belly of a Deer'ghlock!" he hissed as he slapped the table.

Kiel waited for a moment to see if Kael-ven was finished.

"What?" Kael-ven asked, rubbing his hand.

"Ok, just wondering about that tirade. I seem to have noticed a little Bethany Anne-inspired motivational conversation there at the end."

"Oh, yes." Kael-ven tapped the side of his head. "I memorized some of the colorful language she used on multiple occasions."

"Do you have any idea what it means?"

"Not a damned clue. For instance, what's a rat?" Kael-ven started chuckling. "I have no idea."

"Something ugly, I'm sure. I imagine that in the future whole university classes will be based around her colorful language and tear it apart to find the nuggets of wisdom each contains, no doubt making up complete stories about the true meaning when really she just meant they were fucktards."

"Another one of my personal favorites," Kael-ven admitted.

Kiel got back to the problem at hand. "Ok, Straiphus?"

"Talk with the Empress, find out what they know and how we might help if she needs us."

"That simple?" Kiel asked.

"I would think you need to worry more than I do," Kael-ven pointed out. "You are the mercenary in her employ. My job is to help run Yoll. She is responsible for the rest of Yoll's territories in her Empire."

ADAM interrupted, "Do you want me to patch Bethany Anne in? She has just left a meeting and has a few minutes."

"Yes," Kael-ven answered.

Both Yollins had waited a moment before ADAM came back on. "Bethany Anne, Kiel, and Kael-ven are on the other side of the line. They are discussing the situation with Straiphus, and want to make you aware of what they know."

"Hi, guys." Bethany Anne's voice popped in. "Sorry, no video."

"That's a shame," Kiel told her. "My muscles have muscles now."

"How the hell can a human tell?" she asked. "You guys have that chitinous armor, so aren't your muscles hidden?"

"That is why he is saying he has more muscles," Kael-ven answered. "It is a favorite strategy of militarily-focused Yollins."

"Which strategy?" she asked.

"The time-honored strategy called 'lying through our mandibles to get a female to touch us in appreciation,'" Kiel answered.

"Same shit, different species," she muttered, but there was amusement coloring her voice.

"Yes," Kael-ven answered. "I don't want to continue taking up your time with Kiel's attempts at humor."

"No, it's ok. I find him funny," she replied.

"Ok, may I admit I didn't want Kiel taking up more of *my* time with his attempts at humor?" Kael-ven ignored Kiel's smile at her catching his lie.

"Mmmhmmm," she told him across the tablet. "Now *that* I believe."

"I didn't think you could read minds at this distance," Kael-ven stated.

"Same shit, different species," she repeated.

"That wasn't a full answer," Kiel pointed out.

There was silence.

Kael-ven got the message. "All right, we asked you to join this call to discuss new information Kiel has found related to an effort by Yollins in the Straiphus system to attack here in the home system. They are both formulating a plan externally in the Straiphus system and seeking support here."

"I understand," she replied. "We were made aware of some questionable maneuvers in their system by a few spy ships we have over there, but we haven't pushed into the system because we needed to get the damaged ships from the first fight fixed. Also, I'd like to have additional weapons capabilities tested and online."

"They have three capital ships over there, right?" Kael-ven asked.

"Yes, but that isn't our biggest concern, Kael-ven," she replied. "We can only find two."

"How the hell do you hide a capital ship?" Kiel interrupted. "It's not like you can park the sonofa*Gro'lick* in a barn somewhere."

"Well, on the other side of a moon works," Kael-ven started before Bethany Anne interrupted.

"We looked everywhere we could think of, and while it should be around, it isn't." There was a pause before she added, "Suggestions, guys?"

Kael-ven tapped the table, then answered, "Why don't we talk with the defense minister?"

. . .

Planet Yoll, Executive Prison

E'Kolorn had been considering the implications since his wife had left his cell with the promise that she would be back in a week's time. That she had spoken of what amounted to better conditions under the aliens, not worse, had been very surprising.

No one had come to get him and no one had changed the routine, but something had changed inside him.

He had hope.

Hope that he hadn't made the wrong decision to stop King Yoll, to force him to fight the alien Empress. He hadn't expected the king to fail—and his people to fall into the hands of the aliens.

No different, he supposed, than the Yollins forcing other people to be under Yollins.

Except that the Etheric Empire was making the Yollin world better, at least according to his wife.

He was pondering these things when continued knocking on his door finally grabbed his attention. "Yes?"

"You are requested to clean up and meet with the Etheric Empire's agent. Do you consent to this meeting?"

"I have a choice?" he asked.

"Yes, I'm told you do," admitted his guard from the other side of the door. "But I can tell you that if I were you, I'd go."

E'Kolorn stood up from his bed, walked to the door, and spoke through the slot. "Why is that?" he replied, his voice normal since he wasn't yelling from across the room.

The slot opened and his jailor stared at him. "Because the alien is offering you a choice. I confirmed that you saying 'no' is just that...no. They want you to come because they have questions you can answer. I'm told if your heart isn't in it, to have you stay."

"What is 'it?'"

"Above my responsibility," the guard replied.

E'Kolorn softly tapped his mandibles together in thought for a moment before he answered, "I'll go."

It had taken only a short while to shower, fix his face, and put on the clean badge of office which had been brought to him.

When he walked out of the shower room, the guard was waiting. "No locking devices?" E'Kolorn asked, expecting to be cuffed before they left the prison.

The guard shook his head. "No." The guard looked around and then stepped closer to the ex-defense minister. "But if you want some unasked-for advice?"

E'Kolorn nodded. "Sure, I'll listen."

"The person here to escort you is one of those aliens who stays around the alien Empress. Those guys don't play around. They are professional, and they take care of business. I watched one go into a building this week and wipe out everyone in there who was trying to kill him. He was blown out of the damned building from the fifth floor, and he never hit the ground—just flew back to it and finished his job. Not one of those who had killed other Yollins made it out alive."

"He just killed everyone?" E'Kolorn asked.

"No, he spared some stupid youth who thought he knew how to operate powered armor."

E'Kolorn grimaced. "How badly did the fight go between the two?"

The guard looked at him. "You really have been out of touch. What fight? He knocked the kid out of the window, then dropped down from the third floor, yanked something from the back of the kid's armor, and walked back into the building." He shrugged. "He just ignored all the idiots thinking they were joining a grand riot."

E'Kolorn shook his head. "How badly are we overmatched?"

"What overmatched?" the guard asked. "The aliens are bringing good changes to our planet. Sure, there are some hotheads, but so far I'm thinking the leader is doing a better job than the king ever did."

"Their Empress?" E'Kolorn asked, surprised.

"No, Leader Kael-ven, the Yollin captain who had been sent by King Yoll to spy on their system."

Now E'Kolorn realized he hadn't asked his wife enough questions, but he was willing to forgive himself. He had needed the companionship, as well as the knowledge and reassurance his family were safe.

He had needed her time, her affection, her respect, and her love, and she had provided all of that and more.

He nodded to the guard and the two of them started heading out of the prison—to what future, he wasn't sure.

CHAPTER FOURTEEN

Skaine Slaver Ship _Kalifo_, Eubos System (Etheric Empire, Yollin Territory)

"What do you mean, 'we need to keep our heads down?'" The five-foot-tall blue skinned large-headed, bulbous-blue-eyed and thin-bodied Skaine yelled at the communications device.

The space station manager's voice was annoyed. "Keep yelling at me, Gyrm, and I'll forget to warn your ass and you can suffer your ignorance."

Gyrm looked down and made a note, taking ten points off Space Station Two-Seven's manager's score. The station manager had been in the good zone, but two more drops like this and Gyrm would need to make a permanent example of the Yollin.

No one talked to the Skaines like this, no matter how powerful they were.

"I find your communications disrespectful, Ghy'luck," Gyrm answered. "Why would you think there is anything in this pitiful excuse for a system that would make me worry?"

"Don't you know shit about what has happened, Gyrm?" the frustrated Yollin's voice came back. "Damn, didn't you get the memo?"

"I would have to know what a memo is to know if I got one, ass," Gyrm replied. "I've got over one hundred and thirty prime candidates for the outer marker mining efforts. No tags, no tracebacks, and all clean."

"That is the shit I'm trying to warn you about, Gyrm." On the other side of the conversation, Ghy'luck wiped his mandibles. "Hold on... Go to active frequency 222.72."

"Frequency 222.72," Gyrm confirmed and set the new frequency on his communicator. This time the connection had video, not just audio. The station manager wasn't on the screen yet, but Gyrm could hear movement off-screen. A door shut, and then he came into view and sat down.

"Video, Gyrm?"

"Right." Gyrm set the communication to two-way video. "There."

"Better." The Yollin stared at the screen a moment. "Weren't you in green robes last time?"

"Yes, you are perceptive. The blue you see me wearing is due to a rise in rank. I'm now in charge of our group."

The Yollin glanced off-screen. "I see only one ship, Gyrm."

"There are three of us here. The other two are lying silently in the asteroids."

The Yollin nodded his understanding before facing the screen. "Ok, I'm going to assume you have been out in the scavenger worlds." He put up a hand to forestall any comment from Gyrm. "Don't deny it, I don't care." He dropped his hand. "Yoll has been conquered by an alien group."

Gyrm barked out sibilant laughter. "Isn't that some shit?" The Yollin looked uncomfortable. "Wait, did you guys try to take over someone who fought back and kicked your ass?"

Gyrm slapped his chair and hooted. "That's it! Oh, that is just too rich for words." The Skaine continued to laugh.

"Keep it up, you pirate prick," Ghy'luck ground out, "and I'll let you learn at the end of one of their lasers."

Gyrm's eyes narrowed, but his laughter continued. "I'm in the slaving group, not the pirate group, as you should well know. Those 'pirate pricks,' as you call them, couldn't navigate their way out of a tub you wash in if you drained it of liquid. Idiots, by and large."

Ghy'luck interrupted, "Weren't you in the pirate group at one point?"

"That's why I know how bad they are. Notice how quickly I moved to slaving."

"I've no idea. You never told me," Ghy'luck admitted.

"It was quick, trust me." Gyrm finally settled down. "So, who are these alien overlords now?"

"They call themselves 'the Etheric Empire,' with a human Empress as their lead. A while back we received a torp with a lot of video related to the battle, and frankly they kicked our Home Fleet's ass. There isn't much there except them now. I'm not sure what the other two systems are going to do, but Eubos couldn't stage a counterattack for shit even if we wanted to. This system is only good for raw materials. The local planet's people are useless as slave labor."

"Wasn't that what you just told me...no slaves?" Gyrm asked.

"Yes, they sent something they call a 'memo,' which said slaving was to stop immediately. So you need to stop it." The Yollin smiled into the screen. "Make sure you have no slaves on your ships, and whatever you do, don't even consider trying to do a system-wide notice like you would have done before. We don't know if they have spy ships here."

"What ships *do* they have there?" Gyrm asked, leaning forward in his chair.

"Well," Ghy'luck waved his hand, "that's unknown at this time. We don't have any on our scopes, but the information in the torp suggested they have cloaking technology."

The Skaine slaver's commander thought about the information Ghy'luck was entrusting to him, then glanced down and erased the deduction in his points. He wouldn't provide Ghy'luck any extra benefit for the warning, but his disrespect had been warranted since his stress level must be high right now.

No one could say that the Skaines couldn't understand and adjust to the particulars of their contacts.

Gyrm finally looked up. "So, I'm completely good delivering those who wish employment in the far outer asteroid fields for room and board, which is a much better solution than the life they had on their decrepit planets before?"

Not much of a life, Gyrm thought, but completely within the limits of the memo (whatever the hell that was) Ghy'luck was sharing with him right now.

"That sounds agreeable, Captain of the *Kalifo*. It is my judgment as an Etheric Empire representative in the Yollin-controlled Eubos system that providing transportation for a fee to those who seek employment in other systems is a beneficial occupation."

Gyrm smiled. The Yollin was speaking bureaucratic like he had sucked on the tit of a politician.

His kind of contact.

The Skaine reached down and added twenty points for the lesson Ghy'luck had just delivered to him. Now, how to pay Ghy'luck his fee...

Gyrm rushed to get ahead of Ghy'luck's effort to stop him from talking. "Am I to pay the usual charge for recharging our systems from the local sun?"

Ghy'luck shut his mandibles. He had been concerned that the Skaine was going to be stupid. There had never been a fee for solar recharging levied by any system government, except for those whose governments were completely inefficient. They were worse than bandits.

"Yes," Ghy'luck replied. "I will give you the account number for transferring your fees once you confirm total usage." He

MICHAEL ANDERLE

looked around on his desk. "What did we charge you last time for solar charging?"

"I'll have my second send you the previous bill so you can confirm with your accounting. I wouldn't want any paperwork to be misplaced," Gyrm answered.

"That works for me. Good luck with your transportation efforts. May you provide homes for all of those seeking a better life."

"Agreed, Station Manager. Captain of the *Kalifo* out." The Skaine shut down the connection and leaned back in his chair, staring up at the ceiling.

There was more than one way to accomplish one's goals. You didn't have to use the same playbook as those in the pirate group would most every time.

Bunch of non-creative hacks.

He leaned forward and touched two buttons on his console. "This is Gyrm to ships' captains. You need to bring your weapons up and place them on standby. This system may be hot."

Once the two captains of his support vessels confirmed their orders, Gyrm leaned back in his chair once again.

Now, how to sell his slaves legally...

QBS *Achronyx*

"Achronyx, can we go through the Annex Gate cloaked?" Tabitha asked as she and the four Tontos sat in their chairs on the ship's bridge.

"Technically, yes, but the chance for problems during the Gate transfer increase. It is possible the system could jettison the ship on a different trajectory or at a different speed, or even drop it into the system in another location outside normal operation parameters."

"So you're telling me it can be done, but it is a bad idea?"

"I don't have parameters to quantify good or bad, Captain Tabitha. I am simply explaining the risks."

Tabitha pressed her lips together. She didn't want to be called "Captain" by Achronyx, but any time she asked something related to the navigation or fighting of the ship he switched to calling her "Captain" instead of "Ranger."

Typical EI behavior.

Right?

She couldn't tell. It was like all her hacking into computers and making them her bitch had created a karmic imbalance, and the universe was delivering the bill—and Achronyx was its name.

Fucking shit. She grimaced.

"What is the chance of us having a reduction of abilities and/or dying on the other side of the Annex Gate if we do this?"

"First pass at calculating chances is, three-point-two percent chance of a reduction in capabilities including cloaking and damage to the ship's body."

Tabitha blinked a moment. "Achronyx, what is the reduction?"

"It fluctuates, but the average is two-point-two percent."

"What is it on the high side?" Tabitha asked. Something was working here in their communication.

"Unity," Achronyx answered.

Tabitha sighed. That wasn't the best answer to her question. "Chance of that happening?"

"One in three-point-four million."

Hirotoshi looked at his leader. "Why do you wish to go in cloaked, Kemosabe?"

It was a testament to Tabitha's acceptance of her guys' ribbing that she didn't even question the title anymore. "What if they are just waiting on the other side of the Annex Gate to blow away the Etheric Empire's lawful representatives?"

"Can we not cloak immediately upon exit, when the Annex Gate flare occurs?" Katsu asked.

"Achronyx, please answer that question."

"Yes, Katsu, we can cloak immediately upon exit."

You jackass! Tabitha thought. "Not that question, the one about doing the cloaking during the exit flare when we arrive?"

"There is a high probability that we can successfully cloak in time if you permit me to deal with the timing."

Like I'm thinking I'm going to push a button? Maybe Bethany Anne was right. Maybe she was too sensitive.

"Because the chance of success if a human were to push the button is reduced by seventy-two-point-three percent."

You fucking electronic pain-in-my-ass, she fumed, and bit off her retort. "Yes, I am assuming my EI would cloak since the EI is also taking care of the chauffeuring of the ship."

"Piloting," the EI corrected.

"Same thing," Tabitha replied, then added, "Make it so, Achronyx."

Tabitha snickered to herself.

The QBS *Achronyx* sat in space a half-hour from the Annex Gate. The 3D map was displaying the system star while Achronyx provided an update about Eubos.

The EI explained, "There are a hundred and twelve different space stations, bases on planets, and major areas. Two of the planetoids have archaeological digs that existed before the Yollins took over this system. There are both Yollins and other aliens in this area of the system. King Yoll didn't mind the illegalities, so long as the mining throughput was sufficient—apparently the bible according to King Yoll didn't apply here. There is a small planet of marsupials which have been forced into slave labor upon occasion, but they really aren't equipped to be in outer space. The local Yollins don't have a reason to help stop slave trading because they need bodies."

"It seems we have several issues to handle. First, the present methods of production using slaves. Second, the future changeover to a slave-less production, and lastly, dealing with those providing the slaves."

"And, who are slaves?" Ryu added.

"Come again?" Tabitha asked.

"Who do we classify as slaves?" Ryu asked. "What about individuals who are working something off? What about prisoners stuck out here? There are three separate issues which might include debtors, prisoners, and legal guard of prisoners (if any) to deal with—all examples of people who would like to be released because they are slaves, and would probably lie through their teeth so we would force the issue and potentially release criminals back into society."

"Well, fuck," Tabitha murmured.

Sometimes, she thought, having centuries-old history books walking around with you could be *such* a *molesta y fastidio*.

Planet Yoll, Executive Prison

Scott waited patiently for the former Yollin defense minister. He had reviewed all the notes that ADAM provided, and had asked Kael-ven his opinion on this individual.

E'Kolorn had just been a person doing his job to the best of his ability, who had used his only remaining option to protect his people as best he could. He had no way of knowing Bethany Anne had been bluffing about slamming rocks into the space stations.

Nor would she have dropped the space stations out of orbit. She would have, however, dropped a puck on the king's palace grounds. That place would have been a large hole in the ground if she had been forced to continue the fight.

Cheating aside, the result Bethany Anne accomplished had been the best they could hope for from the challenge.

Scott heard footsteps coming down the hall and stood up.

Two Yollins came into the room. One was a guard, and the other had a badge of office attached at his breast.

Dressing a Yollin would have been about as beneficial as dressing a Wookie—or maybe a horse, considering Kael-ven. Scott smiled, wondering how a Yollin with four legs would put on pants.

The defense minister, who himself had four legs, walked over to Scott and nodded.

"I am formally taking responsibility for this prisoner, Guard K'lrek," Scott told the guard, who looked at him in surprise. "What? You thought I wouldn't?" Scott asked.

"No," the guard answered, "but I didn't think it would be formal."

Scott lifted his arm and pointed to a device strapped to his forearm. "This records everything I do. The Empress is very persnickety about how her personal guards act. Should I have failed to act accordingly, my next sparring session with her would have been much more painful."

"Excuse me," E'Kolorn interjected, and both men turned to him. "What do you mean, 'would have been much more painful?'"

"It means my healing time for fucking up would have been increased due to me getting my ass kicked. Bethany Anne is a high-contact boss. As in, the bigger the fuck-up, the higher the amount of contact. While we get our own licks in from time to time, a fight with her can sometimes be one-sided."

"You hit your Empress?" the ex-defense minister asked.

"How else would you spar?" Scott asked. "Just stand there and take it? That wouldn't do Bethany Anne any good. Trust me, we know she can take most anything we can throw at her, so if we get a chance we make sure to teach her a lesson."

The human scratched his face. "Unfortunately she doesn't usually fall for the same trick twice, so we have to figure out new ways to get through her defenses." He stuck out his hand. "I'm Scott. I'll be your partner for today. Keep all hands to yourself, and everything will go just fine. If you mouth off to the Empress, which I don't suggest, you will earn pain, although perhaps not in front of her. However," Scott pointed to E'Kolorn, "she is offering you dignity and an opportunity to act civil. I don't care how mad you might be...she cares, and doesn't deserve to hear about anything you don't like, am I clear?"

The previous defense minister thought about it for a moment. "If I am disrespectful you will hurt me later."

Scott considered his answer. "A little blunt, but that is the basic message. So don't fuck up."

The two left the prison and boarded a ship that was floating above the ground. It had a Yollin symbol next to one he guessed was an alien skull with pointed teeth.

E'Kolorn looked over the city at the stadium in the distance that had been the end of King Yoll.

And the Kurtherian who was using the Yollin body like a puppet.

"Where are we going?" he asked.

"The new government leadership's building. We will land on the top, and go down from there. You will be seen on news video, so you decide if you want to walk like a hero or a prisoner."

"No beating me to make sure I walk a certain way?" E'Kolorn asked.

"That's up to you, but we have a saying on our planet: 'Act like you want to be treated.' So, if you want to be treated like a prisoner, feel free to act like it. I imagine I can facilitate your act. I have already reviewed your records. You are treated well, and not abused. It isn't a hotel, but killing many of our people when we asked for safe passage doesn't rate you a king-sized bed, either."

E'Kolorn didn't argue that he had been under orders. The aliens knew it.

Moments later, the Pod landed on the new government building and the two got out. They went past the guards stationed at the top. E'Kolorn looked up to see the massive ship the Empress used hovering not that far above them in the sky.

A warning that idiots flying around wouldn't be permitted to live, he imagined. He wondered for a moment about their method of propulsion. What he wouldn't give to know if the Ixtalis had gotten their hooks in them already! Or had the Ixtalis gotten their hooks into the aliens *before* they had shown up in his planet's backyard?

The two of them went down five floors and passed more guards as they left the elevator.

When they finally arrived at the last set of doors, there were two more aliens in red armor like Scott's. One had skin somewhat darker than Scott's, and the other was significantly darker than Scott.

Neither carried the wounds that being blown out a fifth story window would cause.

The two entered the meeting room and walked up to Kaelven and Bethany Anne. "My Empress, I would like to introduce you to former defense minister, E'Kolorn."

Bethany Anne stood up and reached toward him, holding out her hand as his guard had done. He took it, and she shook his hand before releasing it. "How was the meeting with your wife?"

"That was you?" he asked. He had wondered if she had been the person who had made the meeting happen.

A Yollin who was standing next to the Empress held out his hand in the same fashion the Empress had. "No, that was me. My name is Kael-ven."

Perhaps it was true that she had a docile Yollin standing in for her?

Kael-ven continued, "I could not confirm for a while why you obeyed King Yoll's orders but then capitulated, or encouraged him to fight Bethany Anne when you did."

"That was an easy decision. She," and E'Kolorn tilted his head to Bethany Anne, "could have easily killed those on the space stations or pummeled the planet with kinetic weapons. As defense minister, my job was to defend the people. It seemed an easy decision once she requested to fight for the role of king."

The Empress pursed her lips, which was odd to see in someone with no mandibles. "What if we had started with attacks like that?"

E'Kolorn shrugged. "Well, then I would have fought you tooth and nail."

The Empress seemed to withdraw into herself for a few moments, and E'Kolorn wondered if he had just messed up.

"I think you will work well, E'Kolorn. I think you will work well indeed," she told him.

Work well on what? he wondered.

CHAPTER FIFTEEN

<u>Eubos System, Station One-Eight-Two</u>

Yollin Station Manager Denigh closed his eyes, then tapped his mandibles twice, before turning in his chair and stabbing the call button. "Yes, Comms?"

"Station Manager, we are being hailed by aliens, sir."

"Coc'li," Denigh answered slowly, "we know about hundreds of species, ourselves. Do you know which particular alien race, or are you going to make me play 'five questions before I put my clawed foot up your ass?'"

There was a moment as Coc'li seemed to parse his comments. "The humans, sir."

"You imbecile!" Denigh stood up. "I'm coming to Communications. You should have said that first!"

Denigh slammed the button again and grabbed his tablet.

It seemed his boring time was officially over.

So was his curiosity about whether the humans would show up in this backward area of Yollin space.

—

Tabitha watched the seconds tick up on the clock. "Well, the

138

bet is now between Ryu and Hirotoshi as to who wins. We still haven't heard from the station manager."

"That was a sucker bet." Ryu commented. "The manager over there is going to want to be in the communications room. It was unlikely he was sitting in there, and now he is trying to figure out where we are."

Tabitha smirked. There were twenty seconds to go before Hirotoshi lost and Ryu won.

"Well, let's test that theory, shall we?"

"Wait, Kemosabe," Ryu interjected. "That wasn't instruction to suggest—"

"Achronyx," Tabitha requested, "please cancel the cloaking, provided we are in no danger."

"There is always danger," the EI replied.

"Danger of more than one percent," she clarified.

"Uncloaking," Achronyx confirmed.

"This is Station One-Eight-Two," came a voice over the comm.

Ryu groaned behind Tabitha as she, Katsu, and Shin chuckled. She could hear the small gold coins that were legal tender in the Etheric Empire jingle as they were taken off the table by Hirotoshi.

"This is the Etheric Empire's QBS *Achronyx*," Tabitha replied. "Ranger Tabitha speaking. We would like instructions on how to dock, information on the internal atmosphere, and an opportunity to speak with the station manager."

"We do not recognize the ship design," the voice came back. "It seems to be based on a Yollin scout vessel, but it is not the same size."

"True," Tabitha replied. "But the connections are standard, I assure you."

"Well," the Yollin voice came back, "I would like to confirm..."

This time Tabitha overrode the person speaking. "Look, here is how it will go. This is Her Majesty's Ranger Tabitha. You will provide docking instructions, or I'll shoot a hole in the nearest surface in order to dock. Keep dicking with me, and when I get on the space station I'll make sure to look three times as hard for infractions. When I find those infractions, I will immediately implement Justice. Since I don't have any detention facilities, I'll just throw whoever fucked up off the station without a suit. Have I made myself clear?"

There was a pause.

"Please use docking location B-14. It seems we have a few ships leaving quickly."

"I'll just bet you do," Tabitha murmured to herself. "Achronyx, are there any issues locating B-14?"

"No."

"Then take us there, but maintain active defenses."

"Understood," he supplied.

"Well." The station manager thought about the discussion after the call disconnected. "I guess that answers the question about whether they are friendly, unfriendly, or willing to put a clawed foot up my ass."

"We have four different ships requesting immediate depar-ture," Comms spoke to the station manager. "We will need to unlock those ships at the right time for balance issues."

"I guess the R'cklickn are leaving before the light gets shined on them." He rubbed his mandible.

"Sir, did you see the image of their ship?"

"Just a glance, why?"

Coc'li pulled the station's video up and dialed in the magni-fication.

"That's…" the station manager paused a moment, "a lot of guns."

"That is not a normal scouting vessel," Coc'li agreed.

The station manager pointed to the screen. "Dial up the magnification on the ship emblem."

Coc'li leaned forward. "Are those pointed teeth?"

Denigh stood up. "They aren't herbivores, not with pointed teeth."

The station manager started walking out of the Comms room to head toward berth B-14 and called over his shoulder, "Next time aliens that conquer our home world show up, how about you start off the conversation with that information?"

Tabitha checked her guns, made sure her equipment was in each pocket, and confirmed she had plenty of ammo.

She dialed the gun down to three. She didn't want to blow any unnecessary holes in the space station's walls if she could help it —for now.

She grabbed her soft helmet and stuffed it into one of her pockets. It would help if she was in a bad place and needed air.

She considered kicking out her spurs, but decided not to. Those should come out, she decided, at an opportune time.

"Achronyx," she called, "are we good with gravity and air?"

"Yes. Gravity is three percent above the norm, air is acceptable. The additional trace gasses are not detrimental to your physiology."

Tabitha reached up to pat between her breasts, just confirming her Ranger's medallion was lodged there. She had other identification, but it had been decided that the medallion was one form every Ranger would carry. It had chips embedded in the casting that would confirm its validity, as well as tell if the wearer was the correct Ranger—and whether that Ranger was alive.

If not, it would send information through the Etheric to the *Meredith Reynolds*. That information would be used to locate the

Empress' Rangers who died, and facilitate finding the ones who killed them.

Tabitha left her cabin and walked to the bridge. "Katsu, when we dock, make sure you work on their computer systems with Achronyx. I want to have everything sucked out of their system and any other ships you can get by the time we leave."

"Isn't that illegal?" he asked as he started bringing up the necessary screens to work on her request.

Tabitha tapped herself on the chest and smiled. "Interestingly enough, we are still under Etheric Martial Law in these areas, so the answer is no."

"And when we revert back to normal Etheric Law?"

"Then the choice is left up to the Ranger when said Ranger is on an operation. So, since I am the Ranger in question..."

"The answer will still be 'suck it all dry,'" her Tonto responded. "Yes, Kemosabe."

Tabitha left the bridge and worked her way to the docking area. The connection between the ship and the station had been established, and Hirotoshi was waiting for her. Ryu and a Yollin were standing on the deck of the space station.

"Shall we, Number One?" she asked.

Hirotoshi harrumphed, and Tabitha walked out of the ship with him following. The ship's door irised closed behind them.

"Welcome to Station One-Eight-Two," the Yollin greeted. "My name is Denigh. How can I help you?"

Tabitha held out her hand, and the Yollin looked down at it, then up to her face. "Do I take your hand?"

Tabitha nodded before remembering he wouldn't understand human mannerisms. "Yes, in our world it is a customary greeting. The practice goes back in time, where it showed we didn't have a weapon to stick into the person we were meeting."

Denigh reached out and grabbed the smaller alien's hand. "I assume, since your hand is so soft, that squeezing hard would harm you."

Tabitha raised an eyebrow. "How about we give it a try? The first one who says 'Uncle' has to buy the other a drink."

Tabitha grinned and the Yollin didn't answer, just started squeezing. Tabitha continued smiling as his mandibles started making an almost imperceptible noise like two horns rubbing against each other. Denigh looked at her as she calmly accepted his effort.

"Now, Station Manager Denigh, it is my turn," she told him and started to squeeze.

The larger Yollin, whose hands had minor levels of chitinous armor protecting his fingers, looked down in surprise as the smaller hand began to cause him substantial pain. "I'm not sure if you need your hands, Station Manager, but I guarantee I will continue squeezing until you say 'Uncle' or I break through your hand's tough outer shell to get to the squishy insides."

Denigh's mandibles started tapping together quicker and quicker as he put everything he had into smashing the alien's hand. "*YIELD!*" he screamed.

But she didn't let up.

"Benkle!" he yelled as he went to his knees, the cracking of his hand's armor loud in his ears. "No, *UNCLE!*" he cried, and the pressure was released.

"I hope you have some good drinks," Tabitha told him. "You owe me. What say we go get some now?"

Denigh was rubbing his hand. "Sure. It will probably help me with this pain."

Moments later, Ryu walked ahead of the group and Hirotoshi brought up the rear as Denigh and Tabitha walked through the space station, the manager explaining what they were seeing as he rubbed his hand.

"Down this hall," he pointed left, "are the quarters for most who live and work here. We are a smaller station, with docks for twenty ships. If a ship is too large, we have two shuttlecraft that can each hold twenty Yollins. We use them to ferry crew and passengers back and forth."

"How many work on this station?" Tabitha asked. "From the outside, it looked like this station was at least a hundred stories tall."

"What are these 'tales' you talk about?" Denigh asked. "and how do you use 'tales' to figure out size?"

Tabitha thought about her comment for a moment. "Sorry, stories in our world also speak to levels of a building. I'm suggesting it's a thousand feet tall."

The Yollin worked the height difference out in his head. "We are actually about twenty percent taller than what you suggest if my translation is correct about your feet to Yollin units."

Tabitha whistled. "It should be, and damn, that is huge."

The Yollin puffed out his chest. "We aren't the largest station in the Eubos system. We are sixth, and those that are larger than us exceed our size by a large margin."

"Why so many?" Tabitha asked.

"Well…" Denigh started warming up to the conversation, but then pointed to his right, "oh, and down that way is my office, if you should need me." Finally he continued the explanation. "This solar system doesn't have a decent world to inhabit. It's smaller—considerably smaller than Yoll—and has had a significant amount of meteorite impacts that have taken out a large part of the population, so the local species never got off planet. However, for those of us who can mine in space, it is like going around and picking up precious metals off the ground."

He looked at the alien. "It isn't *quite* so easy as that, but it is significantly easier than trying to dig far into a planet."

Tabitha nodded. "I understand."

Two turns later the four reached the area on the station which had a few places to eat, and as many places to drink. When they entered the double doors of one of the drinking establishments, Tabitha did a double-take.

There were humans here?

"Who is that?" Chrillen pointed to the four who had just walked into the bar. He and the other two Skaines had dropped into Station One-Eight-Two just hours before. They had spent the last three days in the back of nowhere, having finally sold their last two slaves to a small mining outfit.

"Probably someone working on this damned station," Mrik told him, raising his drink to his mouth. "But it is my first time here, so it's a guess."

Chrillen turned to look back at his business partner. "Most Yollins you see work for the station, idiot." He rolled his eyes. "I'm talking about the new aliens next to him. The two in the corner look like Torcellans, but their skin is darker, their hair is not white, and I don't think they have purple eyes." He looked again. "Too dark in here to see that much detail."

Avar leaned forward in the booth to look at the new people. "Torcellans make excellent slaves. Very practical with their hands, and damned easy to train." He leaned back. "Shame the two here are protected."

"What about the Yollin?" Mrik asked, his curiosity peaked. Three Torcellans would be worth as much as a dozen of the slaves they just sold.

Plus, they had buyers already lined up.

"Try to pay him off?" Chrillen asked.

"Aww, damn," Denigh complained aloud.

"What?" Tabitha asked.

"There is a table of Skaines in the back. I suppose they just landed recently, or I'd have heard complaints already. As a race,

MICHAEL ANDERLE

I've never found one who isn't into some business that is usually forbidden or frowned upon."

"Murder?" Tabitha asked.

"For profit?" Denigh considered. "Actually, not normally. They rob, steal, cheat, slave, pimp, cheat... Wait, did I say cheat already?"

"Yes, and I'm confirming you said 'slave,' right?" Tabitha asked.

"Yes, certainly. In fact, they are wearing the colors of a slaving ship."

"Oh, perfect," Tabitha answered. "They seem to be getting up."

"Probably thinking you are a type of Torcellan or," he looked at the top of Tabitha's head, "no, not even a Skaine would think you are an Aen."

"Why not?" she asked.

"You have hair on the top of your head," he answered.

"You think they are coming over here?" Tabitha asked.

"Oh, definitely. I'll get rid of them. They will talk to me first, to make sure they can buy me off before they try to take you."

"Oh, get your cut, Denigh," she told the surprised station manager. "Just make sure you get it up front, because anything that is on their bodies after we get done with them is ours."

Denigh looked sideways at the alien. "You aren't trying to catch me doing something wrong?"

"Actually, I consider it wages for acting," Tabitha told him. "Make it look good, so they won't realize it isn't for real."

Worked for him.

The three Skaines walked up, and the whole bar turned to watch the groups face off.

"Achronyx?" she subvocalized. "Anything about Skaines that can cause us problems in a bar brawl?"

"They cheat," he responded through their implant, "and they are pirates and slavers. Assume that if you lose you will be enslaved."

Nothing like a little encouragement. "Pass that on to Tontos

One and Two." Both vampires turned to look at their boss, and Ryu rolled his eyes when the EI passed on the warning.

The first Skaine, his outfit dark blue with gold edges, looked the three up and down. "Torcellans?"

Tabitha raised an eyebrow as she slowly looked at the three aliens, their big heads hooded, and replied, "Assholes?"

Ryu snorted before he could stop himself, and Tabitha chuckled. One of these days she would catch Hirotoshi off-guard, and then her life would be complete.

Apparently, the translation programs worked just fine. All three aliens became agitated.

Next to her, the Yollin started speaking in a language she didn't have loaded. "What the hell, Achronyx?" she subvocalized again. "Why can't we understand anything they are saying?"

"Working on it, Ranger Tabitha."

Damn, her EI got all proper when it was his underwear down at *his* ankles, didn't he? She would have to see if the EI's ego was deflated by comments about previous mistakes, just like a guy's. If so, then her communications with the EI were going to be so much easier.

"They are using a rare dialect. A trading language. Updating your implants...now."

"And that is why they are worth the money, Chrillen. They are twice as useful as a Torcellan." He pointed to Tabitha. "She might be puny-looking, but she is stronger than she looks. Perhaps they are from a high-gravity world...I don't know."

"One-sixty is the highest I'll go for the men. I'll give you two hundred for the female. I can always say she is a good incubator," the alien told Denigh.

Tabitha carefully kept a comment safely tucked behind her teeth, although she planned on knocking this asshat's teeth right out.

"Ok, but I want payment up front. If they understood what we are saying, my future will be shit."

147

The middle alien paused, then nodded. The one to his right reached in his clothing and pulled out a purse. He dumped the contents into his hand, then grimaced. "It's four-eighty...just a little short."

Tabitha noticed he had pocketed four coins at the last moment.

Denigh hmmphed, but held out his hand. The Skaine slipped the coins back into the purse and tightened the top, then tossed it to the Yollin, who turned to walk away. "Good luck."

Tabitha watched him leave. Who the hell was he wishing good luck to?

CHAPTER SIXTEEN

So, you didn't get the memo?" Tabitha asked the middle Skaine, who was wearing blue robes. The two on each side of him were dressed in gray. "Don't suppose the clothes colors tell me anything about you guys?"

"If you aren't an ignorant Torcellan, what are you?" Chrillen asked. "I'd like to know so I can sell you appropriately."

Tabitha, keeping an eye on the three but turned her head slightly to Ryu, asked, "You got that, right?"

"*Hai.*"

"Ok, just making sure." She turned back to the three Skaines. "One second, you jackasses are my first bag in Eubos, so please be patient," she put up a finger, "for one fucking second while I find out if my recalcitrant pain-in-the-ass EI has your ship locked down."

"I did not," Achronyx replied in her ear, "but I should have. Ok, they are locked from leaving. I have taken over the Yollin station's systems, but it will take me time to confirm their ship is under control. I don't have any Skaine protocols."

"Well, get them," Tabitha told him. "Don't make me show you how to do it."

Back in the ship, the EI calculated whether the Ranger could accomplish her threat. He calculated a twenty-three-point-seven percent chance of success on her first try. After two days, she had an eight-eight-point-one percent chance of success.

The EI finally replied, "Working on it."

"Ok, so here is what the memo said." Tabitha spoke loudly so as many people in the bar as possible would hear her. "Yollins, and the systems claimed by the Yollins, are now part of the Etheric Empire. That places the Eubos system under Empress Bethany Anne, and she has issued an edict that slavery is to stop. Those who are slaves will need to be moved to non-slave status. For those who continue working the slave trade inside the Etheric Empire—you will be summarily executed if you choose not to comply immediately."

"Uh huh," Chrillen commented. "For a slave-to-be you have a big mouth, I'll give you that." The Skaine leader commented. "Any particular reason you think you won't be a slave in a few moments?"

"You know, you should probably never ask a Ranger shit like —" Tabitha, Hirotoshi, and Ryu *moved*.

The Skaines on either side of Chrillen were turning something in their pockets, and little bumps became visible. The two Skaines were definitely pointing something through their robes.

Tabitha jumped into the air, and Hirotoshi and Ryu went out to the sides.

There was a high-pitched *thrumm*, and she heard Ryu bitching. Hirotoshi grabbed a chair made out of some sort of plastic and used it like a fly-swatter, hitting his target upside his head.

Ryu pivoted on his right leg and swung a fist behind him as he moved forward. Ryu's eyes were red. The surprised Skaine caught a backhanded fist in his face, and his eyes blanked before the sheer power of the punch threw him backward.

The lead Skaine's eyes registered surprise, then narrowed in annoyance. He tried to keep her in sight, looking up and over his shoulder to find her behind him, and he had only managed to turn halfway around when her kick caught him under the arm.

———

Two Yollins were arguing. "We can't drop the gravitics energy twenty percent and still have the food grow properly. They need to strive against gravity to strengthen the fibers in their stalks…" The first Yollin reached for the door to the bar, yanking it open as he continued his argument, "in order to…"

A body in a dark blue robe flew out of the now-open door and slammed against the wall to their left.

Both Yollins froze, surprised at the unexpected violence, as the *clang* of the body hitting the wall reverberated. A few individuals came out of their doors to look up and down the hall to see what was going on.

"That's a Skaine," the second Yollin told his friend.

The Yollins stood transfixed as another person walked out of the bar.

She was dressed in black and was wearing a bulky coat, and she looked pissed. "Come back here, you lazy-assed cheating nut-knocker! I'm not done with you yet." She grabbed the obviously unconscious Skaine's foot and turned around, dragging him back into the bar. "Try to start the fight before we say 'Go?' Fuck you and the ship you rode in on. I'm going to shove my size-eight boots up your alien ass, you fucktardian asshatus maximus. *Gott Verdammt*, trying to shoot my guys like that." She looked at the two surprised Yollins.

"Thank you for holding the door. That was very gentlemanly of you," she told the first Yollin, who was still holding the door open. "I'll be done in a moment," she called back as she walked back into the establishment. Unfortunately, the Skaine's head caught on the frame. They heard her say from inside the place, "Oh, give me a break!"

They watched as the Skaine's head bounced twice against the door *hard* before it moved enough that the lady inside could pull the body back into the bar.

Crack!

Chrillen felt the pain blast through his senses. "Wakey-wakey, asshat!"

He opened his groggy eyes to find himself staring into the eyes of the alien. He was still in the bar, but his arms were bound behind him.

Chrillen heard Mrik next to him. "I'm telling you…" he started, but the female looked to her left.

"Didn't I already tell you to shut the hell up?" Chrillen heard a tearing sound, and one of her associates placed a strip of something gray into her hand. She leaned toward Mrik and placed it over his lips. "Now maybe you will give me a little damned peace and quiet. Who knew you dipshits were so talkative when your little cheats don't work?"

"I think you broke my ribs." Chrillen coughed.

She looked back at him. "I fucking hope so. I was going for maximum power, and my teacher would be pretty disappointed with his student if I weren't good enough to break a few ribs."

Chrillen could taste the blood in his mouth. "What will it cost to release us?" It pained him to admit he needed to buy their freedom. This was going to get him busted in rank, but he could argue that no one had fought these non-Torcellans and therefore they should be given a pass.

"Your lives, of course," she told him. "I'm working with my trusted advisor—"

Ryu cut in from behind her, "I thought you called him your recalcitrant pain-in-the-ass EI?"

She looked over her shoulder at her man. "That was before he got into their ship's computers and located another slaver group operating near one of the commercial Gates, trying to deliver slaves under the auspices of paying off transfer fees."

They had gotten into his ship's computers?

She turned back to Chrillen. "Don't worry, we already found the destruct codes and changed them. We aren't sure how you got the message to it, so we changed the passcode too."

Chrillen's lips pressed together. That explained why he hadn't felt the explosion rock the space station. "Just kill me now, because if you don't, other Skaines certainly will."

"Oh, don't worry." Tabitha smiled. "You will be punished, trust me. I'm not big on slaps on the hand," she looked at the Skaine, "but I'm the law, so Justice will be part of the program."

Tabitha stood up and looked at the three Skaines sitting on the floor with their backs against the bar. She raised her voice. "I really appreciate all the information you guys have provided. Your lives will be spared."

"Grab one each, guys. I'll take this one." Tabitha reached behind Chrillen and grabbed a fistful of his clothing. She pulled him up with one arm and turned him around, so everyone in the bar could see his face. Most of them were smiling, and a few of them looked like they were thinking about how to use the information they now had.

For one, they now knew that the aliens could pick up a Skaine without straining. They watched the little procession leave the bar. Tabitha stopped and looked to her right. "Denigh?"

"Coming, Ranger." The station manager joined the alien, who was easily holding the Skaine leader behind her back. She didn't seem to be bothered by his weight.

"Please show me to the detention area. I don't want to litter your space around here with new items that your customers would have to dodge."

"Of course." Denigh nodded (useful gesture) as he stepped through the door and held it for the three aliens. "Please head in

153

that direction." He nodded to the left. "I will follow as soon as everyone is out."

A Skaine was complaining loudly ahead of Denigh, and when he came around the corner, he found that the female had stopped. The reverberations from Chrillen hitting the wall twice and his quick assurance that he would shut up echoed down the hall.

The rest of the walk to the jail area was pleasant. Many at the station had heard the rumors, and they'd stick their heads out of their businesses or come out to see the three aliens carrying the Skaines like sacks of food as the procession walked past.

It was almost like a parade.

Denigh punched the button on his phone. "Comms?"

"Sir?"

"Please confirm the QBS *Achronyx* has provided final call?"

"Yes, Station Manager. I confirmed with Station Control the QBS *Achronyx* is outbound and they have the Skaine ship slaved —er, poor choice of words, Station Manager—they have the Skaine ship *following* them."

"I don't think they are worried about inanimate objects, Comms. So, the humans are gone, and the Skaines and the Skaines' ship with them?"

"That is correct."

"Thank you," Denigh replied and lifted his finger, leaning back in his chair.

On his desk were three small columns of coins, two worth one hundred and forty credits, and one, the middle stack, worth two hundred credits.

He kept looking at the money sitting there, wondering what to do. For whatever reason, he felt it was special and needed to be saved. He reached for his tablet and punched the video button, routing a connection to a friend.

"Hello, Tro'lick speaking," responded a female's voice.

"Hit your video," Denigh told her.

Tro'lick's face came up, and she smiled. "Denigh! Haven't seen you in a while. Did you hear about the fight in the bar?"

How had the fact that he *was* part of the story gotten dropped? "Yes, Tro'lick, I've heard. I had a good seat for it, as a matter of fact."

"Oh?"

"Yes." Denigh punched a button to turn on a camera on the back. "Do you see these three piles of coins?"

Her face got closer to the camera. "Yes?"

"Did your story include the Skaines paying off someone?"

Her mandibles opened for a moment. "That was you?"

"The very same," he replied. "I was wondering... I would like to encase these three piles of coins to commemorate them."

"Why?" she asked, her mandibles askew in confusion.

"I just think these are going to be special in the future. They will be the coins that started the Skaines' downfall. Certainly in the Eubos system, but maybe in this corner of the galaxy."

His friend looked at the screen, not saying anything for a moment. "You think this money is that special?" He nodded to her. "Ok, then you stay put. Keep the video on those piles, and while you're at it, have Security pull all the video from the bar to you walking down the hall and into your office."

Now Denigh's mandibles to proclaimed confusion. "Why?"

"Because," she told him, "if they are that important, we will need to prove those are the coins. And if we can?" She smiled. "They might be worth a thousand times more than their value, Denigh!"

She laughed at the look of astonishment on her friend's face.

. . .

QBBS *Meredith Reynolds*

How bizarre, Shi-tan thought as he looked around the multi-story shopping and eating area. It was just off the exit from the Customs area of the huge space station, which had been formed out of an asteroid, and so far he was impressed.

He hadn't been allowed to fly all the way around the exterior of the asteroid. He would have enjoyed a chance to see if there were soft points and a closer look at the large dish on one side of the station, but ships were prohibited from getting too close to that side

"Raaak'd," a voice called from behind him. Shi-tan continued moving forward, then stepped to the side to get out of the way of someone trying to get around him. He had followed the damned son of the king for his bounty, and now he was here in this completely new alien station, having tracked him to this...place. He looked around.

These aliens looked like a multi-color variant of Torcellans.

Except, *feisty*.

Feisty Torcellans. Shi-tan liked that thought. Feisty was good. He looked around to find a bar, and he noticed a store selling the tablets the agent who checked him in had spoken about so he headed in that direction.

A few minutes later, he had a tablet and understood how to use the programmed translation capability. He changed the tablet to use a language he could readily read and raised it. Sure enough, the signs all over the place changed into a language he could understand. He swept it across the different levels, then he pointed it at the end of the cavern.

There was a huge sign for a bar.

Shi-tan smiled and pulled the tablet down.

All Guns Blazing was a name he understood. Certainly a bar after his own heart.

CHAPTER SEVENTEEN

Charrlock Mining, Asteroid 9881, Eubos System

It had taken the Yollins in the small mining company operations group about thirty seconds to realize their internal communications had been subverted. The aliens' system had turned off the link between the operations office and those who were a few hundred steps across the surface of the asteroid in the main mine.

The Yollin in charge of the mining operations might have sent one of his subordinates to see to the problem, but the very imposing alien spaceship was hovering right outside with its guns pointing at his office.

They were relatively safe where they were, but getting information to the mine itself—and the company owner, who had been in the mine checking on things for the last couple hours—was impossible.

"Attention, Charrlock Comms." Br'ockchrellick's communications worked again! He grabbed the microphone, switched the comm over to the correct frequency, and hit the button.

"Hey Boss, we got a problem out here," he started.

"No," an alien voice came back. The aliens were speaking

Yollin, but they certainly *weren't* Yollin. "What you have is an annoyed Ranger who is tired of your lack of communication. So, are you going to talk to us, or shall I just start blasting?"

Brock, short for Br'ockchrellick, looked down at his communication systems. Everything was set correctly, but he wasn't speaking with the mine. He slowly clicked the button to talk. "This is Charrlock Comms, Second Lead Brock speaking. Who is this?"

"This would be Empress' Ranger Tabitha speaking. We have some horse-trading to do with your mine manager, so would you be so kind as to—"

The halt in communication surprised Brock, and he was looking to see what had changed when the voice of the alien came back online. "Never mind, I see that we have a group coming out of the mine right now."

Chan'on, the mine and the company's owner, was pissed. He had lost contact with the main office, and those guys had not sent anyone to check on those in the mine. This was against safety regulations.

Safety regulations he had written himself.

He was walking back to the operations center to tear a strip off Brock's back. "He's getting too complacent," he grumbled to himself.

"Sir?" one of his two assistants asked.

"Nothing," he called back over their intercom, then made sure he was on mute this time.

"Brock, come in, you poor excuse for a...for a..." Chan'on stopped at the mine's opening when he saw the craft hovering right above the asteroid. The ship moved with the slight gyrations of the asteroid.

For a ship that size to get this close to the asteroid was beyond insane.

Someone *really* good was piloting that ship. His thoughts were interrupted when he noticed activities at the stern. Two turrets that looked like they were big enough for him to crawl into turned around and pointed right at him and his two assistants.

Tabitha watched the three Yollins stop at the mine entrance. They had on suits that were more rigid than shipsuits, but didn't give the same level of protection the armor Kiel used offered. Still, she didn't want to get into a fight and be punched by one if she could skip that part.

"Achronyx, patch me into the helmets of those new Yollins behind us."

Company owner Chan'on wasn't too surprised when his comm crackled to life, but he *was* surprised to hear the alien's speech pattern. It was Yollin, but...different.

"Attention, individuals coming out of the mine," the voice announced. "I am Ranger Tabitha of the Etheric Empire. I have been sent to stop the use of slaves here in the Eubos system."

"Fat chance of that," Chan'on grumped into his helmet. "Those damn Skaines—"

"Are sitting in a ship above me right now, and there are more I'm sure I'll speak with soon," she interrupted him.

Alarmed, Chan'on looked at his display on the inside of his suit's helmet, realizing his microphone was on. He sent the command to turn off his mic, but it remained open.

He clicked his mandibles twice in agitation, then Chan'on

took two more steps out of the mine and looked up. Sure enough, above the larger ship was one of the smaller Skaine slavers. "Hey!" Chan'on looked at the ship nearest him. "I run a tight company here. We don't have any slaves."

"I am aware of that," she told him. "I'm here to ask you if you need workers, because these Skaines are going to die if you don't."

Chan'on thought about it a moment, then started walking toward the entrance to his operations offices. "I suppose the least I can do is talk," he agreed, then glanced up at the alien ship hanging above him as he walked underneath it. It was large enough he felt he could reach up and touch it, but not so large it seemed bulky.

It was, he conceded, a very svelte ship.

"Your ship or my offices?" he asked, not even bothering to see if his mic was on. His communications were obviously in their control.

"Your offices are suitable, Company Manager Chan'on. Ranger Tabitha out."

The frantic voice of his second-in-command came over his comm immediately when the alien dropped off. "Chan'on! Chan'on! We have company! Oh..." Brock stopped yelling when his boss walked out of the shadows cast by the ship.

"I'll be there in a moment. Set up the meeting room for visitors," Chan'on told his second.

Anything else he needed to say, he would say after he got this damned suit off.

The QBS *Achronyx* slowly pulled away from Asteroid 9881.

From inside the mining company's operations and communications room, Chan'on and Brock watched the human ship turn gracefully. The Skaine ship turned to follow, and both ships left.

"That," Chan'on stated as the ships rapidly disappeared on the video monitor, "was the strangest experience I've had in my life." He stopped looking at the screen.

Brock turned to his boss after glancing at the monitor one last time. "You think these Skaines will work well for us?"

"They have seven years, then they can go free. If they don't comply, their own technology will punish them." Chan'on shrugged. "They made the choice to accept her punishment for slavery."

Brock chuckled. "Boss, I'm not sure ejection without a suit into space is a choice."

Chan'on shrugged. "That head guy, Chrillen, straight up told her no. Said some things I didn't even realize you could translate into Yollin, and looked straight into the video camera and bragged how she was too nice to kill them."

Brock shivered. *Do not ever mistake compassion for inability to implement Justice, Skaine.* the Ranger had told Chrillen. Damn, it was like she had shut off all emotions. The next thing those watching knew, she had grabbed the Skaine and told a video bot to follow them. Dragging him as he screamed, she took him into the airlock. By then the Skaine had started pleading, because he finally understood there was no bluff in her. The Yollin watched the video as she tossed the Skaine out the airlock, her suit providing a helmet that no one realized had been folded into her collar.

"It was a good message," Chan'on admitted as he stepped out of Comms. "I've got to make sure our two new recruits are situated with their equipment."

"What was the message?" Brock asked, thinking back to the video of her flinging the body into space.

"When she says the punishment for slavery is death," Chan'on called as he turned the corner to walk down the hall, "she means it."

· · ·

QBS _Meredith Reynolds_

The bounty hunter Shi-tan downed his fourth glass of Coke. He had tried three different drinks these humans called "beer," but the alcohol was playing with his perception. He couldn't allow that.

If a fight occurred, he wanted to be able to remember it. Although, looking around at those in the bar, it seemed a sedate group.

Shi-tan smiled when the next glass of the brew was dropped off at his table. The alien was male, but Shi-tan didn't care. He was strong and graceful, and therefore, enjoyable to watch as he took care of his group of tables.

There was something...not right here. Shi-tan could feel the emotions of those around him leaking danger, and he could feel the desire from most here in the bar area to fight.

But no fight was happening.

He had asked a few people about the alien he was trying to find, but had received no information.

He turned the tablet back on and paged around using the interface, then hit one button and jerked his hand back.

The tablet had created a 3D effect.

Slowly, he moved his hand into the picture, and found he could manipulate the different screens easily. He put the tablet on the table and left it there, then stood up from his barstool and moved to his right, looking at the tablet.

He couldn't see anything. Shi-tan moved to the other side of the table.

Nothing again. Finally the bounty hunter walked around the table, and it wasn't until he was back in front of the tablet that the screen could be seen again. Well, that wasn't totally true—there were about ten degrees on either side when he leaned over.

Nice technology, and it wasn't super-expensive. Shi-tan wasn't sure what the catch was, but he was sure there was one.

After going through the different levels of applications, he found one that searched for people.

He raised an eyebrow. "Why not?" he grumped, and plugged in Aerolyn's name. One hit came up, with a note that the photo was being withheld.

He clicked the detail, and found out that the person (or alien) in question was on a thirty-day visa for possible political asylum.

Shi-tan started laughing, and his grin was infectious. When he looked up two of the humans had lifted their glasses in his direction, so he grabbed his Coke and returned their salute.

He upended his glass, and finished the contents in one long drink. His eyes got big when his stomach tried to expel the gas in the drink, and he finally belched loudly. There was one female to his right who did something with her hand under her nose, but to his left, three of the darker Torcellan-looking aliens started clapping their hands and smiling at him.

He lifted his now-empty glass in their direction and they returned the favor, everyone smiling.

He wasn't expecting to be able to get Aerolyn back from these humans, but the bounty had a conditional clause. He would receive half the bounty, in exchange for providing the location of where the little runt had run off to.

With this new alien group's own technology, he could prove to the king where his little bastard had run to and receive half the award. Which, considering it was only a two-Gate jump back to his home planet, would mean a seventy-percent gain on this trip.

"Are you done, sir?" the human interrupted. Shi-tan turned to his waiter and asked in halting Yollin, "Do you have a barrel of this Coke I can take with me?"

"Yes. Do you want it here, or shall we deliver it to your ship, sir?"

Shi-tan thought about it. "What is the charge?"

"No charge if you buy a barrel, sir. We just need two hours to deliver."

Shi-tan grimaced. "How about a charge to make the delivery quicker?"

"That is ten percent of the barrel charge," the waiter replied.

"Yes, let us do that." Shi-tan grabbed his tablet. He was going to use the alien's own technology against them. "I need to close out my tab."

"Then we can run this against your ship, sir." The waiter pulled up a smaller tablet and hit two buttons. "There. Please confirm the bill. I appreciate you joining us here at All Guns Blazing."

Shi-tan looked at his tablet and confirmed the charge, then headed out and walked through the bazaar area again. It was very impressive.

Too bad it would probably be destroyed when Aerolyn's dad came over here to retrieve his son. He hadn't started a bar fight this time, but he had to admit...

Starting an intergalactic war sounded damned impressive.

CHAPTER EIGHTEEN

QBBS *Meredith Reynolds*, Special Operations Room

E'Kolorn looked around the large operations room in shock.

While the experience of having an alien and another Yollin search his mind was horrifying, it was something he could compartmentalize as being "alien."

The moment he had stepped into the transportation room had been disturbing.

The Empress walking with him through the Etheric had been exhilarating.

The sophistication and sheer abilities of this group to make war, however, were *frightening*.

"Those screens," E'Kolorn pointed to three displays in the lower left-hand corner of a complete wall of monitors, "are slaves to our defense systems." He turned to look at the Empress' General. "Right?"

"That is correct," Lance agreed. "There is no reason for us to route that through the planet and then up here, so we pull it directly from your satellites."

"How? Did you have the ability before you came into our system?" He turned back to the displays. "It would be nice to know if you saw everything we did, and yet I would have a feeling of betrayal as well."

"No." The Empress walked up beside the two men. She had changed clothes again, E'Kolorn noticed. These humans changed their outer garments more often than the weather changed down on the planet. Which was to say, multiple times in a day.

There were seven displays across the top, and five going down. Bethany Anne pointed to the upper two displays. "Red line numbers one and two, those two starting on the left, are the sensors we used coming out of the Gate. They were some of the first passive sensors we brought online in this system. We didn't have access to the Yollin internal network until our efforts to take over Yollin Twenty-One succeeded." She turned to look at the defense minister. "That was our identifier for your main command ship, which came to attack us from behind."

He nodded his understanding.

She continued, "When we got on that ship we were able to plant our connections into your ship link, then your communications link. We had studied everything we could on the *G'laxix Sphaea*. This was without Kael-ven's help, just so you know."

It took a moment longer for the previous defense minister to register what she was explaining. He pointed to the input displays and turned to face Admiral Thomas and General Reynolds. "Why show me all of this?"

"Because," the General admitted, "we want to know if you would once more accept the responsibility to keep your planet safe."

This time it was E'Kolorn who blinked and wished desperately to have the ability to read the aliens' minds.

Bethany Anne looked at the taller Yollin. "E'Kolorn, you did your job, and you protected your people. What you did wasn't appropriate to our way of thinking based on what we wanted to accomplish, but who were you to know this? You had been led by a modified Yollin with a Kurtherian master, and under those circumstances you did your job appropriately. Your intent—your *role*—was to protect the planet."

"If I—" E'Kolorn stopped for a moment, but then nodded and continued, "If I should take on this role, the act will provide legitimacy to your present leader."

Bethany Anne stayed silent for a moment, but the pause allowed Admiral Thomas to ask, "So what?"

E'Kolorn turned to the human advisor. "Is that your reason for offering me this position?"

Admiral Thomas looked at Bethany Anne. "Is it?"

"Not really," she admitted. "Oh, we know it would be a byproduct of the move, but frankly I don't care about that. Long term, the benefit of having E'Kolorn in the role supports Kaelven about two percent on the positive side while benefiting us twelve percent on the military side."

The Yollin military advisor turned to the Empress, confused. "Only twelve percent?"

Instead of answering him, Bethany Anne looked up and spoke louder. "Meredith?"

"Yes, ma'am?" A voice floated to E'Kolorn's ears, and he looked up and around for the speaker.

"Please put your face on the middle screens," Bethany Anne commanded the EI.

E'Kolorn stopped looking around when a human face— someone who looked like the Empress, perhaps older but with red hair—was displayed on the middle fifteen monitors. "Yes, ma'am?"

Bethany Anne waved to the screens. "E'Kolorn, please meet Meredith, a very advanced Entity Intelligence which runs the major portion of our non-defensive operations. Presently she is also managing the three main space stations around the planet, as well as other projects down on the planet." Bethany Anne turned to the screen. "Thank you, Meredith."

"You are welcome, Empress."

E'Kolorn missed Bethany Anne's annoyed glance at the screens when the EI blanked out.

General Reynolds stifled a snort.

Bethany Anne turned back to E'Kolorn. "I introduced you to Meredith first so you understand we have a massive EI helping us run this space station, but..."

"She isn't your military?" he guessed.

"Correct," she agreed. "Meredith isn't our military EI" She turned back to the video screen. "Reynolds? Please present yourself on the screen."

Bethany Anne laughed as the General grunted. "Well, shit."

Bethany Anne asked the face that was now on the video screen, "I guess we haven't ever asked you to show your face, Reynolds." She jerked a thumb toward her dad. "What made you decide to look like him, but older?"

"Because," the General's older, gruff voice came out of the speakers, "it seemed appropriate that if the female EI in residence chose a modified Empress look based on her mother, as the male of the duo and a Reynolds I would select the General."

"Please, Reynolds," Admiral Thomas asked, "would you change your voice back to the previous one? If I have to listen to both Lance," he pointed to the General next to him, "and you using that same voice, I'm going to start drinking."

"You already drink," Lance retorted.

"I'll drink *more*," Admiral Thomas shot back, and there were a few snickers from those sitting at their desks in the large operations room who were listening in on the conversation.

"You are more...open...with each other," the Yollin haltingly commented to the three humans.

"We do what we have to do for the operation," Bethany Anne answered. "These two men are responsible for our space navy, and our overall military operations." She looked around and smiled at everyone in the room; they weren't even pretending to try to work while she was present. "These people, who should probably be looking at screens or something, are responsible for making sure information is collected and reviewed. Those who are in the field have their communications streamed back into the nexus here."

The Yollin opened and closed his mandibles a few times, and Bethany Anne waited for him to speak. "I understand the purpose of the effort," he explained finally. "What I don't understand is the humor you offer each other. It borders on disrespect."

"Ma'am?" One of the specialists seated a couple chairs down from where the four were talking interrupted with a barely audible whisper. Bethany Anne turned and leaned back to view the person. Both men turned as well, and the Yollin followed their eyes.

"Yes, Franklin?" she replied.

"May I answer the question?"

Bethany Anne nodded, and the two leaders stepped back to allow the Yollin a clear view of the speaker.

A younger-looking human with blond hair smiled at the Yollin visitor. "Humans, sir, are capable of much. However, you will find that when we follow willingly, there is little that can stop us. There are a lot of stories in our history where a small number of humans beat a larger group because they trusted their friends and compatriots, and believed in what they were doing. We joke, but that doesn't mean that any person in this room right now wouldn't charge into a barrage of weapons fire to protect our Empress, the Admiral or the General," he nodded to Admiral Thomas and General Reynolds, "without hesitation. In fact, you can say it is *because* we have this relationship with them that we would do it. Humans, as a rule, don't like to be told what to do, but we will fight like hell for those we follow."

E'Kolorn thought back to his discussions with King Yoll, and his attitude and method of rule. He turned to Bethany Anne. "Why did you introduce me to the Entity Intelligences?"

"Because either of those two could do your job better than you can," she told him.

His mandibles opened and stayed that way for a moment, then closed. "Then why have me here?"

"Remember that comment about supporting Kael-ven and the military?"

He nodded.

"Having either of the EIs or another human in the position would be a negative to supporting Kael-ven, but a net twenty-five percent boost to the military. However, if you understand that we wish to support the planet Yoll, not be a detriment, then the numbers slide to net eight percent boost to Kael-ven and a thirty-four percent boost to the military."

"Why not thirty-seven percent if I am twelve percent and the EI is twenty-five percent?"

The General spoke. "Not all the benefits are cumulative. Further, it isn't even the same thirty-four percent. Some factors change, and will cause you more trouble."

E'Kolorn nodded his understanding, then the four were interrupted. "My Empress, may I continue with the presentation?"

Bethany Anne turned to view the screen. "Yes, Reynolds. Please show E'Kolorn the present disposition of the ships in the Straiphus system."

Reynolds' visage was replaced by a stellar map of the Straiphus system. E'Kolorn moved forward, his four claws making little noise on the floor as he got closer to the screen.

Bethany Anne told the EI, "Reynolds, take over all screens and display the map."

All screens changed to show the expanded map. The labels pointing to certain ships grew, and E'Kolorn's eyes opened wide. He turned to the men. "Where is the Yollin superdreadnought *Empires Broken?*"

"That," Admiral Thomas answered, "is what we want to know."

Straiphus System, Yollin Capital Ship *Bridged-ael*

Those in the room quieted down as the recently elevated Admiral of the Straiphus Fleet arrived and walked to the head of the long table, his protection detail taking up positions behind him. When he took over the fleet in the Straiphus system, those who supported the existing caste system quickly located and executed the higher-ranking officers who were part of the lower caste or were known to harbor sympathy for those in the lower castes.

They would not be trusted to run the future of the Yollin systems.

Their bodies now floated in space. Some of the ships used the bodies as targets for firing practice.

They needed to clean the area of potentially harmful objects, right? Couldn't have bodies slamming into unsuspecting ships and causing damage.

"We are now," Admiral Thlock-nod started his speech, "only waiting on the last few ships to move into positions naturally. We are assuming the aliens have spies in this system. Unfortunately for them, they cannot find what isn't here." He looked around the room and included the cameras pointed at him, which were streaming his speech to the other ships in the fleet.

"I have waited," he continued, "to unveil the truth: that the superdreadnought *Empires Broken* did not run out on us, but rather was sent on purpose out of the system immediately upon receipt of the information sent to us by Defense Minister E'Kolorn!"

There was a loud banging of feet on the ground in support of the brave defense minister. "The aliens have sent their memos and their demands, but they dare not send in their ships. Do you know *why* they dare not?"

Admiral Thlock-nod smiled, his mandibles wide open. *"Because they fear the Straiphus fleet!"*

The admiral paused to allow the roar of approval from those

in the room to wash over him and then subside before he continued.

"We will force their Empress to surrender under the might of the Straiphus Fleet. We have spies even now in their system, acquiring support on the ground, in the space stations, and on the two moons." He slammed his hand on the table in front of him. "We will take these aliens apart piece by piece, ship by ship, and decimate their space station."

"We have time for this last war council now, to confirm we all know our parts in this attack. The humans think themselves smart, but let's teach them how nasty Yollins can be!"

QBBS *Meredith Reynolds*, Special Operations Room

Help, or go back to his prison cell?

The humans had allowed E'Kolorn to retire to a room off the massive operations complex after answering all his questions, and some he didn't think to ask.

The real question, and the one only he had to personally answer was, *did he trust them?*

Further, did he believe the Yollins would be better as a member of the Etheric Empire—the only member so far. Well, that wasn't true. The Empress deemed the three other systems that had been part of the Yollin Empire now independent members of the Etheric Empire.

Not that Eubos would be considered anything but the unruliest member of an unruly bunch. The Empress didn't say much, except that she had sent an emissary to start "whacking that bunch of children into shape."

Whatever *whacking* meant. He assumed it meant something violent, but not deadly. He hadn't received the impression that these aliens used punishments that would kill their children to correct them.

As he reclined on the Yollin couch in the meeting room, he

found himself studying the seat and thinking.

This was where Kael-ven had sat. This was, for better or worse, a bench that had seen the overthrow of his king and those who supported the previous system. It was that support which was causing the most trouble down on the planet, and to some degree on the space stations.

Those who had held power in the previous system did not wish to surrender that power and influence willingly. No one wanted to be told they weren't special, it seemed. E'Kolorn thought about his four legs, which had been instrumental in his own rise in the military. Four legs, the mark of the upper caste.

The mark that proved he was special, that his body and mind were unique. The physical proof that was on display for all to see.

Nothing but a manipulation, falsehoods on the part of a Kurtherian to keep the race subjugated through lies.

He breathed hard, squeezing his hands tight and releasing them. To make this decision, he first needed to decide whether this couch, this physical seat really was indicative of whether he was special.

He placed his elbows on the table and then put his chin in his hands.

And thought.

The aliens had provided him a tablet that allowed him to call for refreshments should he want any.

He didn't use it.

He allowed his mind to wander, to consider those he had known through the many stages of his life. He thought of all of those he knew with only two legs and considered each one he knew well enough to judge. Were they any less capable than him?

E'Kolorn's voice broke the silence in the meeting room. "They were *not*."

. . .

Skaine Slaver Ship _Kalifo_, Eubos System (Etheric Empire, Yollin Territory)

Gyrm continued searching the notes, but the information he was seeking wasn't in the log. "Tell me again, where did Chrillen go?"

"Station One-Eight-Two, Captain," was the quick response from his intelligence officer.

"Something is wrong." Gyrm tapped his lip in thought.

Off to his right, his Comms Specialist called over his shoulder, "Sir, we have a coded message arriving through the channels."

Gyrm pulled his message screen around and called it up. It was the station manager of Two-Seven. He ignored the inconsequential information and implemented the function to decode the message. Inside was a small video, which he played. His eyes narrowed as it continued, and those on the bridge jumped when he slammed his fist down hard in anger.

"Never mind looking for Chrillen's group," he softly told everyone who had turned to stare at him.

"He died a true Skaine and will be avenged."

Well, he thought mentally, _he was a true Skaine until the end. Then he died like a whimpering youngling._

She looked like a Torcella, except she didn't mind killing.

That wasn't very Torcellan.

CHAPTER NINETEEN

Personal Ship *Powerdrive*, Leaving through Commercial Gate Five, Yollin System Ring Three

Shi-Tan accepted his slot in the queue to transfer out through the commercial Gate. After setting up the alarm should anything go wrong, he got up from his pilot's chair and walked to the back, where he entered his little lab area. He pulled up the analysis screen for the alien tablet to see what energy it emitted once he turned off the connectivity.

Nothing.

Shi-tan tapped the tablet in front of him, thinking. Either these new aliens weren't very devious—something he wasn't willing to believe given what he'd learned about them so far—or this tablet wasn't trying to connect to anything and send out information.

Yet.

That, he could believe. He reset the systems to check on the output of the tablet, and left it inside the box. He wouldn't need it until he got back to the bounty's home system, and he imagined if it were going to call home, it would have done that by then.

Shi-tan left his lab and made his way back up to the pilot's chair. If he hadn't needed to go back to earn his bounty, he would have liked to try fighting a few of those bigger humans.

If they had the willingness to get hurt, that was. It was too bad this little peon of a son was going to mess up a perfectly good opportunity for a grand barfight.

The *Powerdrive* went through another commercial Gate before arriving back in the king's system, where it took Shi-tan fourteen long hours to approach the final space station and gain approval to dock.

Once docked, it took only a minor amount of time before his buzzer sounded. Each time you docked, part of the connection was the outside buzzer that rang inside your ship, letting you know someone wanted to see you.

Shi-tan made sure to have a few obvious weapons, a few less obvious ones, and at least two well hidden.

He made his way to the airlock and viewed the outdoor monitor. He hadn't had time to set up his own cameras to confirm if this was a double cross, but he doubted it. He was a bounty hunter, not a mercenary.

He punched the button to open the airlock. On the other side were a king's representative and two guards.

"May I enter, Honored Shi-tan?" the larger alien, bald head and all, asked.

"Of course, Representative…"

The older being, his gray skin sagging, smiled. "You may call me 'Surce,' but it is only a temporary name."

"I understand, Representative Surce." Shi-tan stepped aside. "You and who?"

"Oh, they will stay outside, Shi-tan," the representative informed him as he stepped aboard the smaller ship. "They are only there in case I don't come back. I know of your pride, Shrillexian," he nodded to the taller being, "and I trust we have business. I'm not here to screw you over, therefore I don't fear for my life. In fact," the representative asked as Shi-tan punched the code to close the airlock, "now that I'm on your ship with your permission, aren't you honor-bound to protect me?"

Shi-tan smiled. "Yes, but since the only one who would harm you is you, I'm not too worried. I'm not here to stop you from killing yourself."

"It would be a bit of a problem if I committed suicide, wouldn't it?" Surce asked.

Shi-tan started down the short hall to his lab, commenting over his shoulder, "We are under full-time surveillance, with authenticity code. If you kill yourself, I have to trust I am in a legitimate polity. If I am not, then it wouldn't matter what I wanted. The court would punish me regardless of the truth."

"You are most cynical," Surce replied as he followed the Shrillexian, looking around the ship as he walked behind the tall alien. "I admire that in a contact."

"Truly?" Shi-tan turned to look at Surce. "I find that interesting."

The aging alien shrugged. "It is true. It means a contact has a good head on their shoulders, a thinking head." Surce looked past Shi-tan into the small room and recognized the lab equipment. "You said you have a solution for us?"

"Yes," Shi-tan agreed, "but before I pull it out, I want you to see what I've done, in case these new aliens are tricky."

Over the next half-hour, the bounty hunter explained all his tests to the representative and what the results had been.

All tests had come back negative.

"And what is on this tablet that makes it so important?" Surce finally asked.

"The king's son is now under the protection of these new aliens, and that tablet has the information you need to move forward with his apprehension. The bounty lists half-payment plus bonuses for information. I have spent a long time tracking him down. It is my belief he will be there for an additional twenty-two turns."

"Is that so?" Surce murmured. "You provide us not only the location of the boy, but also a legitimate reason to attack those providing him refuge."

Shi-tan kept quiet.

Surce smiled. "Yes, bounty hunter, you have done well. You have done very well indeed."

Surce's eyes lit up as he considered the opportunities this might provide, and how his king could use the excuse of grabbing his son in the Yollin system to acquire the needed permissions to send his warships across the territories of others. "Twenty-two turns?" Surce finally asked.

Shi-tan nodded his agreement.

"That is just enough time." He waved toward the box holding the device. "Give me the tablet. I will confirm you have fulfilled the bounty, and give you enough bonuses to make it the full value without providing the boy, provided the tablet confirms your information."

"Your technical people?"

"Bah, we need to move on this." Surce frowned. "They will hold the tablet, like you, for another fifteen turns and then require us to sign that they did everything correctly. Show me how to operate this tablet, and the payment will be in your account before we finish."

"Of course, honored Representative," was what Shi-tan answered.

What he thought was, *you fool!*

QBS *Achronyx*, Meeting Room, Eubos System

"So, three of them, one of us," Tabitha stated. She and her four Tontos were looking at the map. There were three designations for Skaine ships. Thanks to the information pulled from Chrillen's ship, they had a good idea what type of ships they would be fighting.

"It isn't the ships, Kemosabe," Hirotoshi admitted. "It is those on them who are innocent that we need to think about."

"Well, fuck," she answered, leaning back in her chair. "How the hell do we get on a ship only slightly larger than our own?" She pointed to the main ship's icon on the screen. "It's not like we can offer them a bottle of wine so they will invite us to come aboard!"

"Why not make sure they have slaves on their ship?" Ryu asked. "We are only assuming they still have innocents there."

"You cannot assume they don't," Hirotoshi replied.

"Both of you are right," Tabitha agreed. "We need to make sure, but if they don't have passengers, do we agree that blowing them out of the sky is the right decision?"

"Yes," Hirotoshi advised. "We have proof they have carried slaves in the past. This is a designated slaver ship, with two support vessels."

"Which are also armed," Ryu butted in.

"Troy," Katsu offered.

"What?" Tabitha asked.

"Why not use the Trojan Horse technique, like was done in the battle for Troy?"

"Perhaps because large wooden horses don't fly too well in space?" Tabitha answered.

"No, they don't," Hirotoshi agreed, "but we happen to have a Skaine ship. What if we can convince them to come get it and connect it to their vessel?"

"I have to imagine they can scan the vessel somehow, and anyone inside will be seen," Tabitha argued. "Then they just fill it full of holes."

"How are they going to find bodies?"

"Hell, easily," Tabitha pointed to the five of them. "Heartbeats, ambient temperature differences, uh…" She shrugged. "That's enough right there."

Shin nudged Katsu and winked. "Easy-peasy." Katsu smiled and nodded back.

Pretty soon all four vampires were smiling at their boss, who was confused. "Why do I think I missed the class on whatever-the-hell-it-is that has all four of you smirking at me?"

"Because," Ryu answered, "we are vampires. We can stop our heartbeats and reduce our ambient temperature to match that of our surroundings."

"Well, I can't!" Tabitha argued. "So…"

"You, Kemosabe," Hirotoshi told her, "will not be on the ship, so your inability to accomplish this is irrelevant."

"No no no *no!*" Tabitha argued. "The hell I'm going to allow you twat-waffles to have all the fun and leave me out of it!"

Hirotoshi shrugged. "I don't think you have a choice. We all have to do what is needed to accomplish the mission, Ranger Tabitha—or have you forgotten the command of the Empress?"

Tabitha's lips pressed together. "No, I haven't forgotten."

She looked at her men. "But if any of you get killed, I'm going to figure out a way to haunt your ass."

Skaine Slaver Ship *Kalifo*

"Captain, we have communications coming in from those who claim they are part of the Etheric Empire. They are hailing us."

"Put it on the loudspeakers. This should prove interesting," Gyrm replied to his Comms Specialist.

It was but a second before the alien's voice could be heard through the speakers, "Attention, Skaine Slaver Ship *Kalifo*. Ranger Tabitha of the Etheric Empire commands you to shut down your engines and prepare to be boarded, or we will blow your ship out of space."

Gyrm turned in his seat to ask, "Is that a proper translation?"

"Sir, I didn't have to translate it. It is coming across in Skaine."

"You have to give them twenty points for sheer audacity," Gyrm commented, "but then you take away two hundred points for stupidity compounded by ignorance."

He tapped his armrest. "What's a Ranger?" Then he smiled as he called to his bridge crew, "Do Skaines allow anyone to board our ships?"

"NO!" every Skaine on the ship's bridge yelled back.

"That's *RIGHT*!" Gyrm called back. "Get me a connection to this Ranger. Let's have some excitement." He reached for the button, but then stopped and commanded, "Make sure everyone gets ready for battle, but leave the alarms off. We wouldn't want them to learn about Skaines and our natural predilection for cheating."

QBS *Achronyx*

"How very nice to speak with you Ranger Tabitha," the Skaine captain's voice came over the comm. "However, I'm sorry to say our ships are not capable of shutting off the engines. The power is routed through our engines, so everything, including our life support systems, would stop working."

Tabitha bit her lip. She should have seen that answer coming.

"You will prepare to be boarded, Skaine ship *Kalifo*. You are in the Etheric Empire's territory, and you are charged with both acquisition and selling of slaves."

"Sorry, we thought this was Yollin Territory."

"There has been a change of leadership in Yoll."

"Even so, I don't think I have committed such an act, Ranger, to be treated this way. We are simply providing a transportation service for those who wish to get off their worlds and find suitable employment in this system with the mining companies."

"Captain…" Tabitha let the question hang.

"Gyrm," he replied.

Tabitha snorted, but thankfully the noise didn't pass across the line. "Gyrm. I am in possession of one Skaine slaving ship at the moment. I can afford to add another ship to my new armada. Prepare to be boarded." Tabitha cut the line.

Skaine Slaver Ship *Kalifo*

"Intelligence!" Gyrm spat. "Is she being truthful?"

A moment later, his intelligence officer bit off a curse. "Sir, she is correct. We have the second ship, confirmed as the *Gothwick*."

Gyrm ground his teeth. Allowing her to acquire Skaine ships wouldn't be beneficial if Skaines were to keep their reputation. Further, the ships were damned expensive. He needed that ship back in the fold.

He stabbed a button. "All guns, prepare to fire at minimally safe distance. We need to kill this Ranger's ship while keeping the *Gothwick* safe. Weapons!" Gyrm called. "Don't you dare mess up the *Gothwick*!"

"Sir," his weapons officer came back, "She's keeping the *Gothwick* between us at this time."

"She's not a stupid bitch, I'll give her that." Gyrm tapped his fingers against his chair. "Weapons, how many missiles do we have?"

"Four, Captain," was the immediate reply.

"Engines," Gyrm called, "we are going to push four missiles around the *Gothwick* to attack from both above and below. I want full power immediately so we can go above the *Gothwick* and our guns can finish this Ranger off." He paused, then added, "Pilot, don't you hit my new ship, either!"

There was chuckling around the bridge.

Skaine Ship *Gothwick*

Hirotoshi, Ryu, Katsu, and Shin slowed their bodies' internal processes down, allowing their core body temperatures to match that of the Skaine ship. Occasionally, a beat of their heart would send blood coursing through their system.

But each beat was minutes apart.

Each of Tabitha's Tontos was carrying the smaller wakizashi as well as one of Jean Dukes Specials at their sides. None had on full armor, but they did have the chest and back shields the Queen had developed to go under almost any clothing. They would have to be responsible for their own heads this time.

It was no different than when they had been on Earth. Now they just practiced the ancient art of kicking ass in another solar system.

Ryu thought about his past, and how he had ended up on an alien ship floating in the middle of nothing. His parents—long since dead—would never have believed that in the upcoming centuries their son would follow a woman from South America to implement a 'no slavery' edict of an Empress born in America.

Hundreds of years after he was born. Ryu smiled.

As Bethany Anne would say, "This is the shit!"

QBS _Achronyx_

"So, any guesses, Achronyx?" Tabitha asked, waiting for the game to begin. Four of her closest friends were on a ship she was using as a shield against laser fire, hoping that Skaines valued that stupid hunk of metal more than they wanted to blast her to bits.

"I cannot guess, Ranger Tabitha," the EI replied.

Tabitha lost it. "Look, you hunk of fucking metal!" she spat. "You know damn well the term 'guess' means to estimate or suppose something without sufficient information to be sure of being correct. That's the same fucking thing as calculating the odds. Pull that vacuum tube out of your metaphorical ass, you stuck up Intel Pentium chip with an FDIV bug, and give me a *Gott Verdammt* guess!"

There was a momentary squelch over the speaker. "No need to get ugly," Achronyx responded.

"I'll call you a fucking TI 486DX2-80 next time, you cranky-ass computational curmudgeon," Tabitha whispered to herself as she watched the monitors and her men in the other ship. "Give me any more shit, and I'll rewire your math co-processors, too."

She started biting a fingernail. "This had better work, or I'll reverse-haunt all four of your asses, you vampiric Japanese motherfuckers."

Tabitha confirmed she was locked down. "Ok, Achronyx, I'm confirming you have control. You are handling this little play. Don't you fuck it up, or we are beyond dead."

"The calculations say—" Achronyx started before Tabitha interrupted.

"Don't tell me the odds, you shit. Just make sure it fucking works," Tabitha retorted.

"*MISSILES INCOMING!*" Achronyx called.

Skaine Slaver Ship *Kalifo*

"*FIRE!*" Gyrm called, and the *Kalifo* rocked as the heavier missiles ejected from the ship. "*ENGINES GO!*" he followed up, glee on his face. There was nothing like combat to cause the body to feel the excitement of every second. The force of acceleration pushed him down in his chair as explosions rocked on the other side of the *Gothwick*.

Two shots rang out from his guns and hit small pieces of floating debris, but...

"WOOOOOO!" Gyrm yelled. "It's gone." He looked around as his ship flew over the top of the *Gothwick*, plenty of space between the two ships as they went in search of the Ranger's ship.

"*Krahgin*," Weapons swore into the silence. "Perhaps four missiles were a little much?"

QBS *Achronyx*

"*SHIT!*" Tabitha screamed as the explosions rocked the ship. "Stop getting the paint messed up!"

Some of the damage reports went from green to orange. "Bethany Anne is going to be pissed."

She was rocked violently in the captain's chair again. The lights dimmed, then there was calm.

Achronyx came online. "We are out of the area of the destruction, and both our shielding and the ship's ability to cloak are intact." The video came online, showing the Skaines' ship flying over the *Gothwick* and two more explosions occurring before they slowed and poked around where the *Achronyx* had just been.

"Why are those damage warnings orange then?" Tabitha pointed to the pilot's displays.

"I scratched the paint," the EI replied.

Tabitha chuckled. "Maybe, just maybe, you might not be such a Cyrix chip, Achronyx."

"I'll try to do better next time," he responded.

Tabitha unbuckled from the restraints and stood up, stretching. "Ok, he took the bait. Apparently he wants the *Gothwick*, so let's follow his ass."

CHAPTER TWENTY

"Bethany Anne, you cannot go!" Lance was arguing with his daughter and Empress. Depending on who he was speaking to, it was a frustrating experience.

Both father and daughter had heads of granite and stubborn streaks light-years long.

Bethany Anne, her lips compressed, tried her best not to yell at her father because she sure as hell would yell at her General. She took a deep breath…

"_FUUUUUCK!_" She slammed her hand down on the desk, the crack of the wood breaking lost in the _bang_ of her fist hitting the desk in frustration.

Well, that didn't go well, TOM bitched.

WHAT the hell are you talking about? Bethany Anne focused inward, trying not to walk five feet to the wall and kick it. She had lost one pair of Jimmy Choo's in a moment of frustration, and although that was bad, the sheer pain of shattering the bones in a foot couldn't be overemphasized.

It fucking _hurt_.

186

You are yelling at the man responsible for dealing with the entire Etheric Empire military. Although everyone is doing it for you, he has the responsibility of making sure Straiphus is handled while leaving enough power here to protect the *Meredith Reynolds* and *you*.

That's what I am trying to argue! I can make a damned difference in Straiphus—I know it.

Not if everyone knows you are gone from the *Meredith* you can't, TOM retorted. **You would cause more problems than you might solve. What royalty risks their bodies in wars?**

The old Europeans, the ones in the Biblical times, those in China in...

How about *lately*?

How the fuck am I supposed to know? she retorted.

TOM dearly wished he could roll his eyes. He was tempted to try and roll Bethany Anne's eyes, but that would cause her to bitch forever and he couldn't send her outside to vent her frustration.

Unfortunately, she had recently figured out a way to give him a mental jolt if he was working with someone else and ignoring her. He was pretty damned sure that his life-changing decision to jump into her body had now officially turned around to soundly bite him on his non-existent ass.

While he could do stuff to her, she had now figured out how to slap him back.

Sometimes he wondered if any Kurtherian alive had thought their tactic to engage with other alien species would come to this? He would agree that he was happy he was with her.

But as in any relationship, he needed some personal space. He was good when he could bug her all the time, but now that she could return the favor, he felt boxed in. Bethany Anne was having too much fun being able to snag him.

He had to finally tell her that he would do a better job of listening for her call if she would be so kind as to not zap him mentally every time she was a little impatient. Which was to say, all the time.

Bethany Anne, Patience is not thy middle name.

Anne is my middle name. I have no idea why people think it is part of my first name.

Wow, that was off-tangent.

You started it.

Are you going to yell at your dad, now?

No.

Ok, feel free to speak to him. He is waiting.

TOM, have I told you lately that for being a ride-along, you beat all the previous do-nothing boyfriends I've ever had?

That was what...one boyfriend? Two?

Details. Just appreciate my sentiment while I go speak to my dad.

I will.

Her focus returned to Lance. "Ok, TOM cooled me down."

"How did he do that?" Lance asked.

She thought through their conversation, "Ahhhh, somehow we go off on these damned tangents, and before you know it I'm not angry anymore."

"I wonder if he," Lance flexed his fingers, "does some Kurtherian hocus-pocus and plays with your emotions?"

"No," she replied, then stopped, her eyes narrowing. "One moment."

TOM, she called.

TOM is not in right now. He is presently working with ADAM and Reynolds on the ESD calculations.

Bethany Anne switched channels mentally. *ADAM?*

>>ADAM is not in right now, he is presently...<<

"Fucking shit," she replied. "Either he got ADAM to give him an important project to hide from me, or he might be doing it. I can't tell."

Lance shrugged. "Have the talk with him some other time, and while I am risking you blowing your top again, you can't go."

Bethany Anne chewed the inside of her cheek, thinking through everything TOM said. "I'll be here on the *Meredith Reynolds* waving them off." She turned to leave his office. "But I'm not happy about it."

"Hell," Lance grumbled when she shut the door, "half the base is aware you aren't happy with it."

He smiled. "And that's why we love you so much."

Outside the office, John looked down at his boss. "He accepted that?"

Bethany Anne looked up at her friend, then grabbed his shoulder. In the next moment, they were in her suite's transportation room. "Ok," she put her hands on her hips, "you fess up. What did you mean by 'he accepted that?'"

"Hell, boss," John replied. "Anyone who listened to you knows that all you said was you would be here waving them goodbye. That doesn't mean shit when you can Etherically walk to the *ArchAngel*. If I'm not mistaken, they *are* taking the *ArchAngel*, aren't they?"

Bethany Anne nodded.

"So, la de da and Bob's your uncle… One moment you are here, the next moment you are on the *ArchAngel*."

"That's across an Annex Gate in another solar system," she countered.

"We get communications across that distance just fine. As far as I know, traveling through the Etheric is similar to the concept in *A Wrinkle In Time*."

"The children's book?" she asked.

"Don't you know it, the concept is lit!" John replied with a smile.

Bethany Anne's mouth opened. "Lit?"

"I got terms like lit, gucci, ahhh…" John started concentrating. "Fam, goat, squid, straight fire, sip tea, something that rhymes with… Shit." He shrugged. "Forgot it."

"How the hell… Oh, Cheryl Lynn's kids," she guessed, and John nodded.

"Wow, who knew the uncle would be picking up teenage slang?" she replied. "Well, except everyone in the group. You guys are like walking boys."

"With hella big toys!" John smirked.

Bethany Anne's tone turned sober as she looked up at him. "So, big guy, you going to rat me out?"

"Not my job to keep you here, BA. My job is to keep you safe. If I thought keeping you here would do it I'd probably try. Seeing as how there isn't a chance in hell of me keeping you here against your will, I'll go too and assume I'm the trusted confidant."

She reached over and patted John on the chest, right where the knife had stabbed him so long ago. "John, you have always been trusted, and if you ever want to know something?"

He watched her as she walked past him to open the door into her suite. "All you have to do is ask me."

John shrugged. It wasn't like he didn't know he could ask, but sometimes Bethany Anne had a way of connecting with you and making you realize you were one in a million to her.

John followed the shorter woman out of the suite's transportation room.

Skaine Ship *Gothwick*

The *clang* of the connections reverberated throughout the Skaine ship. Hirotoshi and Ryu continued their watch with their eyes closed, but Shin's and Katsu's eyes bolted open at the sudden noise. Both worked hard to stop any physiological changes, like breathing or letting their heartbeats change.

It wasn't time...yet.

Bridge, Skaine Slaver Ship *Kalifo*

"No sir," the intelligence operative answered. "From the information in the computer, this ship was slaved to the Ranger's ship and followed it. It was remotely controlled."

"Pretty damn devious." Gyrm had to give the recently departed Etheric Empire representative a few points. They had worked half a day to create their own connection with the *Gothwick*, then they had moved a couple hours away just in case someone had known the last location of the Etheric Empire's ship.

You could not be too careful sometimes.

"They did not place any explosives on the ship. We have found no external signals either coming in or going out since we took out the Ranger's ship.

"It was a shame the ship was destroyed," Gyrm commented. "I would have rather liked to look it over, and perhaps get a chance to enslave the uppity alien at the same time."

"Well, we did lose four missiles," Weapons added.

"Which cost a fraction of the value of the *Gothwick*...although they sure obliterated the target," Gyrm added, pleased with their results so far. "Now, let's make sure we have a good ship before we finish here in Eubos, and then we need to grab the rest of our group and head out. We are going to have to swing back through Command and update them on what we have learned here."

Gyrm stood up. "Tell the boarding party to go ahead when they feel it is safe. Then, have Jilleck bring up the protocol to refresh the computer system. I don't want any unexpected files messing up our efforts. Once we have all that done, we will separate and they can follow us." Gyrm walked toward the bridge exit. "I'll be right back, I need to—"

That was when the screaming started.

. . .

Skaine Ship *Gothwick*

Hirotoshi's eyes opened. Getting up, he moved silently out of the small enclosed space he had been resting inside, his eyes flaming red as he ignored Skaine after Skaine. His feet propelled him forward as fast as he could run.

The screams started behind him as Ryu—probably him, anyway—sliced open a few members of the crew as he followed Hirotoshi out of the *Gothwick* through the airlock connection between the two Skaine ships and into the slaver ship they needed to attack.

Well, he sure hoped it was the right ship. Provided Tabitha hadn't been killed, she would have notified the men if this were the wrong ship in the first place.

Skaine Slaver Ship *Kalifo*

First Gunner's Mate Menok climbed down from his laser turret, dropped to the floor, and stretched. He scratched under his arm, where it always itched when he finished a shift up there. Something in the turret's chair poked and irritated him, but it wasn't big enough to see so he couldn't cut it out.

Or he would have.

He nodded to one of the officers as he headed toward the food that would be available for those coming off ship's duties. With the captain worried that the *Gothwick* was a trap, he'd been sitting in that damn turret for half the morning.

Doing nothing.

If the captain had asked him, he would have told him it didn't feel like there was anything alive on that ship. As a gunner you got a feeling for some things, and it didn't feel like anyone was piloting the ship. He had watched when the four external riggers left their ship to place a few counter-engines on the ship to slow down the slight wobble and allow their ship to connect.

That had been the extent of his fun this morning. Thril, next to him, had gotten in trouble for targeting one of the four riggers out of boredom. He would be on cleanout duty in the slaves' bay on the next trip.

He had just arrived at the food room when his sixth sense kicked into overdrive.

Menok turned back toward the connection deck and started running, thanking his ability to wear real pants instead of those damned robes the officers had to wear. As he yanked out his pistol, he hoped he wasn't being stupid for no apparent reason.

Then he heard the screams. Flipping the pistol's safety off, he ran around a corner and grabbed a rail as he raced down the stairs. At the bottom of the stairs he ran toward the yells, screams, and occasional pistol shot.

It had to be bad if there was this much shooting on their own ship.

Two more crew members joined him, and together the three of them rushed into the ship's dock area. The man to his right's head exploded, showering him with bone fragments. Menok dodged, crossing behind the falling body to slam into a large crate of something he was sure they had stolen from someone.

"*AAAIIIHEE,*" cried his other crewmate. Menok thought his name was F'ehlex.

F'ehlex's head came bounding toward them from where the three of them had just been.

What was going on? Menok lifted his pistol and breathed in three times before darting both his head and arm around the corner.

When Hirotoshi made it into the other ship, the first Skaine he found was controlling the connection to the *Gothwick*. Hirotoshi leveled his sword and cut forward.

The blood of the alien sprayed across the controls, its body jerking up and down before falling. Hirotoshi didn't care, since he was already past.

The next two reacted a bit faster, managing to pull their weapons. Hirotoshi swept the blade down and cut off one of their arms, the hand and gun clattering to the floor. He twisted counter-clockwise and backward to swing behind the Skaine with the missing hand, using the spasming body to block his partner. Hirotoshi stabbed the second Skaine in the neck, then pushed the blade out, taking the head halfway off.

He heard more Skaines coming up behind him, so he grabbed his Jean Dukes Special and swung around. Three more slavers rushed through a pair of doors some twenty paces away.

He blew apart the slaver on his left. The slaver in the middle dove behind the falling body, so Hirotoshi shot the next slaver in the shoulder, the man's weapon arm dropping lifeless to his side. Taking three steps forward he met the charging slaver head-on, slicing through his neck and kicking the head back toward the doors the Skaines had used to enter the area.

"*Hai!*" Ryu called out behind him, but Hirotoshi ignored him.

He could hear the fast breathing of the third pirate.

Hirotoshi lifted his pistol, waiting.

The final pirate stuck his head around the corner, and his head exploded in a violent mist of blood and skull parts that painted the floor and the wall behind him before the body slumped to the floor.

Ryu grabbed Katsu and the two of them headed to the right, in the expected direction of the engines and possibly the secondary computer systems.

Hirotoshi headed toward where this ship would have their slaveholding area if it was laid out similarly to the last ship. He had just entered the hall leading toward the cells when an explosion occurred in the bay. The ship's doors sealed shut behind him, alarms and lights flashing up and down the hall of the ship.

Shin hadn't made it out of the cargo bay; Hirotoshi was certain of it.

"DISCONNECT FROM THAT SHIP!" Gyrm commanded.

"Sir, we've lost communication with the hold area. We don't know..." the officer began.

"Blow it!" he commanded, and almost instantly he heard the soft *whump* as explosives were used to disconnect from the other ship.

Gyrm might lose a few people in this effort, but it was damned obvious the ship *had* been a ruse, and right now he needed to keep attackers off his ship.

The hold would lock down, but not before most of his people and the aliens inside died. If not from lack of air, they might get pummeled to death by the boxes, tools, and other items not tied down when the explosion of decompression and loss of gravity occurred.

It would be a significant pain to clean up that area on the ship.

Cleanup wasn't his responsibility; having a ship to clean up was.

Shin followed Katsu and Ryu into the alien ship and watched as the two of them split off to the right and head out of the hold. He saw Hirotoshi and headed in his direction. He had almost made it to the doors to follow him out of the docks when an explosion jolted him from behind.

His eyes widened in alarm as he reached for the door's handle, but he failed to grab it in time. His body lost any sense of weight, and his back exploded in pain when he slammed into a large box that was locked down to the floor. He turned violently, and his view of the hold spun as he and everything not secured headed toward the opening into space.

Shin used his wakizashi to try to stab another box, but all it did was push him in the wrong direction when it failed to embed itself in the container.

He bounced off something behind him. Flailing, his hand grabbed a rope of some sort and he held on.

For about three incredibly long seconds as the roar of the decompression continued.

Then he lost his grip.

The hold's airlock slammed shut in time to stop Shin's egress, and he looked over his shoulder to see a huge container heading in his direction.

"Forgive me, My Empress!" he yelled.

The container slammed into his chest and head.

CHAPTER TWENTY-ONE

QBS _Achronyx_

Tabitha bit her fingernail as she watched the video intake. She had Achronyx maintain a safe distance from the Skaines, ensuring they could not detect her cloaked ship

"I sense vibrations on the outer skin of the Skaine ship _Kalifo_. I surmise the raid has started, Tabitha." Achronyx stated.

"Thanks," she mumbled, only half-hearing her EI as she focused on the two ships against the backdrop of the stars.

She received a quick click over the comm, Hirotoshi's confirmation that the raid had started in earnest.

She was staring at the scene in front of her when she suddenly bucked in her chair, body going rigid as she screamed as loudly as she possibly could. Her hands gripped the chair's armrests, indenting them slightly as her pain, given voice, reverberated throughout the ship.

"_NOOOOOOOOO!_" she cried out, tears coming unbidden to her face as she sought to clamp down on her emotions to allow her time to process and think...

Think...

FUCK THINKING!

"Achronyx," she hissed, "take me right in front of that fucking ship right fucking now!"

"Cloaked or uncloaked?"

"Cloaked, until I say otherwise," she told him as she unbuckled and headed toward the back. "I've got a message to deliver."

Hirotoshi felt the loss as he ran through the hallway.

Shin was gone.

Hundreds of scenes ran through his mind as he tore through each section. The times Shin and he sat and talked about their pasts. The times they would tease the sun together before their Queen had accepted their allegiance and allowed them to go out in the sun once more.

Before Tabitha had made them a permanent team.

The hundreds of years of friendship ran through Hirotoshi's mind as he found each Skaine.

Some were decapitated and some were run through, a sword made on Earth so many light-years away taking their lives in Hirotoshi's silent down payment for Shin's death.

They had come into this system to stop the slave trade. There would be no better way than making sure the slavers were eradicated.

Permanently.

"WHO THE HELL ARE THESE ALIENS?" Gyrm shouted as he viewed the video of just three aliens ripping through his ship, killing his people with a determination that bordered on fanatical. More than once his people had set up traps to overwhelm the

aliens, only to have the traps taken apart with a violence that caused the lead Skaine to sweat.

If just a little.

"Engineering!" He yelled into his comm. "You have two coming in your direction. Shut down all entrances..."

"SIR!" Weapons called.

"Right now," Gyrm finished with Engineering and looked at the one responsible for interrupting him. "*WHAT?*"

The weapons specialist didn't say anything, just pointed to the large screen at the front of the bridge. Gyrm turned to see an alien's face, eyes glowing red, staring at everyone on the bridge.

"I am Ranger Tabitha of the Etheric Empire. You are condemned as slavers. There is no escape, and there will be no reprieve. You have been *JUDGED!*"

"Didn't we blow you up once already?" Gyrm spat. "Why won't you just go away?"

"Because, motherfucker, *JUSTICE DOES NOT DIE!*"

Gyrm pointed to the screen. "Where is that alien ship?"

"Oh...*Frixelballocks*," Weapons whispered when he saw the alien ship uncloak. He hit the button to show the front-facing video and more than one of those on the bridge pushed back in their chairs, thinking the ship in front was about to crash right into them.

The alien on the screen stared at the Skaines, her voice full of anger. "I can take my men and any slaves you have, and your captain will stand trial. Or I will kill you all, and not rest until every Skaine I ever meet *dies*."

"That would be impossible," Gyrm told the woman. He was trying to stay calm, doing anything to keep her talking as everyone on the bridge continued to stare at the screen. "You are talking about genocide."

"I'll consider it a new challenge for my long life, Skaine," she spat. "I'll consider it a fucking *stretch* goal."

"What would your precious leader think about this?" Gyrm asked.

The alien's smile as she leaned away from the camera did nothing to alleviate his concern.

The screen blanked for just a second, and a new alien face replaced the first. This one, however, was older. She looked around the bridge of the ship as if she could see everything and everyone.

Her eyes turned the same glowing red as the first alien's, but this time lines of energy seemed to reach out like bolts. Her voice was harsh, but unmistakable.

"My name," the alien stated coldly, her red eyes flicking to all on the bridge, "is Bethany Anne. I *am* the leader, the Empress of the Etheric Empire. The Skaines *will* stop slaving, not only in my Empire but everywhere my people go. You think the Skaines are a worry to me?"

Her laugh chilled Gyrm's blood.

"You cockroaches need to know that I'm already at war with the Kurtherians. I just personally killed one with my hands. If you think I give a *Gott Verdammt* rat's *ass* about you or any people who enslave others?" She chuckled, but there was no mirth to it. "Give me a fucking break."

Gyrm swallowed. His people's power had been enough to scare most groups into at least leaving them alone, but if this alien was already fighting the Kurtherians?

Just how crazy *was* this alien whore?

"Gyrm, your life is fucking forfeit for slaving. You have been judged by my Ranger, and your people are already dying by my Ranger's men."

"It is time for you to accept your death!" she commanded.

Gyrm smiled for a microsecond before blood exploded outward along with a metal sword from his chest, his blood soaking his robes as he tried to choke out a sound.

Hirotoshi, pistol in his left hand, right still holding the

sword's hilt, looked around the bridge. The bridge crew had been paying attention to the alien on the screen, so they hadn't seen the alien kill those protecting the bridge and stab their captain.

He had their attention now, however.

Hirotoshi slowly pulled out the blade, allowing Gyrm to choke twice more before the sword released him to fall forward and slowly slide off the captain's chair to hit the floor.

"Who wishes to die next?" the face on the screen asked.

Tabitha, tears tracking down her face, accepted the four freed slaves aboard the *Achronyx* and pointed them to seats. Fortunately, all of them were at least humanoid in appearance.

Two were Torcellans, so she now knew better why the Skaines had asked that the first time.

"Two Skaine ships have blasted out of hiding, bearing two by three-two-five," Achronyx informed her.

"Can we catch them?" Tabitha asked, her voice calm.

"Not without finishing here in two minutes and leaving everything behind."

"Then we aren't catching them. They will bring the message to their people," Tabitha told her EI. "We aren't leaving Shin's body behind for anything. Make sure we aren't disturbed. You have my permission to warn anyone away, then defend us until this is over."

She paused a moment. "Is that understood, Achronyx?"

"Understood, Ranger Tabitha." The EI waited a moment before asking, "What is the message you are hoping the Skaines understand?"

Tabitha watched as Hirotoshi, Katsu, and Ryu solemnly carried what they could pull together of Shin's body back onto the *Achronyx*. She waited for the three men to get aboard before shutting the airlock and confirming everything was closed off between the two ships. "Command the Skaine ship to disengage. Command the smaller Skaine ship to head back to the commercial Gate with the captives. Provide them control when they reach the outer rings. If they turn around against my commands, blow the charges. Let's see if they can curse me while they suck vacuum."

Tabitha headed toward her men. "Achronyx, the message they need to understand is that a new Ranger has come to town, and she has the full support of her Empress. The Skaines are on notice: we don't fuck around, and we won't surrender our ethics to their slaving efforts."

The soft padding of her steps sounded in the hall as she walked. "And this Ranger will never surrender to a Skaine, *ever*."

Straiphus System, Yollin Superdreadnought *Empires Broken*

Yollin Captain Drak-ehl walked onto his bridge. His crew were doing their best to make sure there were no surprises ahead of them as they made their way through the deep dark with their small group of ships.

One of their secrets, withheld even from Yollin people, was that a superdreadnought was big not only because of their weapons capabilities, but because they could create their own Gates.

They would be used for sneak attacks across the light-years of space.

Captain Drak-ehl walked to his captain's couch and sat down, hooking his legs into his couch as was proper when on a mission.

They *were* on a mission, no matter how calm it was on the bridge at this time. "Threats?" he asked.

"None, sir," Head Threats Specialist Ahg called over her shoulder. "We are within two jumps of the home planet, and we show nothing amiss so far."

"Who would have known," Intelligence Officer Meg'lock

grunted, his voice deep, "that all our practicing to attack our own system would reap so much benefit?"

Captain Drak-ehl smiled. "Yes, preparing for our own downfall will help us take out this foreign intruder." He looked at his friend. "Anything new from the video review E'Kolorn provided?"

Meg'lock shook his head. "No, just be prepared for a sneaky-assed alien group who doesn't play like we are used to. They will attack with tiny particles accelerated at high speeds. We think we have the ability to protect all our ships within the shields of the *Empires Broken* until we are close enough to attack their base and allow the support ships to breach their outer defenses."

Captain Drak-ehl's mandibles tapped each other softly as he considered the options. They needed to wait for the ships in the Straiphus System to pull the main weight of the alien's power out of the home system.

Then the trap would be closed, and the final battle for Yoll would be underway.

QBBS *Meredith Reynolds*, R&D Labs

"Yes, that is true," Bethany Anne told E'Kolorn as he picked up the one-foot-high pyramid-looking device from the table. "We call them 'pucks,' Mainly because our first generation looked like hockey pucks from our own world. We have increased the size, and therefore the utility when we deploy these."

E'Kolorn moved the heavy object around in his hands. "Does the point provide a strategic advantage beyond what moving an object to a fraction of light speed already provides?"

Jean Dukes, who was standing to the side, answered, "At this point—no pun intended—the tip of the structure hasn't been shown to provide any additional or critical abilities. However, the only large-scale implementation has been against Yollin ships, so we haven't had a large enough test set."

E'Kolorn set the massive pyramid down. "Where do you think it will be useful?"

"Skins of ships, or building demolition—anything we first need to puncture. We have weapons on our planet where we use friction to liquefy the contents of a weapon. The front of the projectile punches the hole, then the liquefied and molten contents are sprayed inside the target."

E'Kolorn thought about that for a moment. "I see…similar to how we punch our people into a vessel in space for ship actions."

"Very much so, yes, except we wouldn't target a large area."

The Yollin looked at the Empress. "Why show me these, and all of the other tools at your disposal?" He pointed at the advanced armor behind them. "Personally, I would love a suit of that armor, but I'm not sure of your intent."

Bethany Anne pursed her lips. "Do you remember when I had to stop back in the large manufacturing presentation and stand still while I spoke to the screen off to the side?"

"That would have been hard to miss. Your men made sure no one approached you, but it seemed unnecessary when the," his hands reached up to his face and wiggled in front of his mandibles, "red lines started glowing all over your face. Your look of anger was sufficient to keep anyone from interrupting you."

"Probably," she agreed, "but I am not focused on my surroundings in that situation, so the guys are my eyes and ears." She spoke a little louder. "Meredith, please bring up the recording of my conversation with the Skaine slaver captain."

The EI replied, "Please look down at the table. I will project the video there."

Bethany Anne stayed a few feet away from the square table, but E'Kolorn, Jean Dukes, and a couple of her team stepped up to watch the recording. John and Eric kept watch, although Bethany Anne caught both of them glancing over from time to time as they grabbed a peek at what she had seen.

They had heard her side of the conversation the first time, but now they got to hear and see some of the content from the Skaine ship.

"What system is this?" E'Kolorn asked, "and, could you play it one more time?"

Meredith answered, "Certainly."

"Eubos," Bethany Anne replied. "My Ranger has been tasked to clean up slavery in that system."

"That is going to mess up the production of metals in the Eubos system," E'Kolorn commented, continuing to watch until he saw the blur of the alien and the sword erupting out of the Skaine captain's chest.

"They will adapt quicker than you might think. Self-motivating factors help more than simple negative consequences, but the fight against the Skaines will support the self-interest."

"So, you are stopping the caste system, tearing down our religion, and getting rid of slavery in the Eubos system." He looked up at Bethany Anne. "Anything else planned for this week?"

"Sure," she replied, smiling. "Putting a Yollin back in as head of Yollin defense." She pointed toward where E'Kolorn imagined the planet must be located. "I can't focus on taking the fight to the Kurtherians if I am worried that Yoll's defense isn't in the best hands possible."

"I see," he admitted. "Very self-interested hands."

"Exactly," she replied.

QBS *ArchAngel*

"No," the EI told Admiral Thomas.

"What do you mean, 'no?'" he retorted. He was the only one on the bridge of the large human ship; everyone else had been told to 'get off the bridge.' The hard-headed EI needed to have a conversation with the Admiral.

Given that the Admiral had been the one commanding their removal, everyone had picked up their tablets and left quickly.

"The chance of being successful against both Yollin super-dreadnoughts is not statistically high enough for me to allow humans to be with me when I go into combat. You and I both know that the *ArchAngel* is the main point of the attack."

Admiral Thomas bit down his reply. Then he bit down on his second reply, and his third. "How are you going to fix the battle damage?"

"I have support bots," she replied.

"Arguing with you is like fighting with Bethany Anne," he mumbled.

The Queen Bitch's visage appeared on all the screens in the bridge. "That is because I am the first of the Queen's ships. I am the *ArchAngel*, and when the enemy meets me, they will learn that I will never surrender."

"Fuck my life," Admiral Thomas spat. "I leave one argument and show up for another one with her." He thought about his next words. "You know she can command you to do this, right?"

"Of course I do, Admiral Thomas. But you know she will ask me my reasons."

"Hell yes, I know! Why do you think I'm here on your bridge arguing with you?"

"Because you calculate you have a better chance asking me directly."

He pointed at the main screen with Bethany Anne's visage. "See, you don't know humanity quite well enough. I'm doing this because she is the damned Empress. She shouldn't be helping to negotiate a difference of opinion between her *Gott Verdammt* ship and her Admiral. The officer that is supposed to be able to tell this ship what to *do*."

"Admiral, I didn't say I wouldn't go into battle. What I said was I didn't calculate the odds as high that I will survive. The best outcome is massive amounts of damage, worst is complete destruction. I will not be responsible for crew deaths due to my failure."

Admiral Thomas' mouth opened and stayed that way for a moment. "Repeat that, please."

"I said," the EI responded, "I don't calculate the odds high that I will survive without massive amounts of damage, possibly complete destruction, and I will *not* be responsible for crew deaths due to my failure."

"If the humans accept the responsibility on their own without a command from me, will you accept their help?"

There was silence from the EI.

"Remember, ArchAngel, your ability to achieve the goal will be enhanced by having these humans on board, They can help you in ways that bots cannot."

After what seemed like minutes, at least when speaking with an EI, ArchAngel replied, "Yes, Admiral, I will."

Admiral Thomas nodded to the screen. "What are the odds you will have a few humans from your crew join you on this operation, ArchAngel?"

"Too high, Admiral. Too high," she told him.

Moments later, the Admiral left the bridge to set up the line for each person on the *ArchAngel* to be pulled off the ship. He told them what the concerns were, and that only volunteers would be allowed back on.

In the silence ArchAngel whispered to the empty bridge, "Too damned high, Admiral."

The faces on all the displays slowly faded.

CHAPTER TWENTY-TWO

QBS _ArchAngel_, Outside Loading

"Lieutenant Horan, please step out of the line."

Wendi looked over to see Admiral Thomas gazing at her with a solemn look on his face. She turned to speak with Rae, who was behind her. "Save my place!" She jerked a thumb in the Admiral's direction. "I don't think even _he_ is going to talk me out of this."

Rae smiled her support and moved a little forward as Wendi stepped over to speak privately with the Admiral.

"Yes, sir?" Wendi asked as Admiral Thomas turned his back to those in line, forcing Wendi to get closer.

"I'm sorry, Lieutenant Horan, but ArchAngel has put her metaphorical foot down with you joining this run."

"WHAT?" Wendi hissed, trying to keep her voice respectful.

He put a hand out to stop her argument. "Wendi, you are _pregnant_," he told her, bypassing the irrelevant pieces of the conversation to get to the heart of the disagreement. "ArchAngel says that while you are capable of making your own decision, she doesn't accept that momma's choice is the baby's choice."

Wendi stood there in shock. When she had stepped over to speak with the Admiral, she had figured her husband, an engineer on the *Meredith Reynolds*, had made a special plea to get her pulled from this operation. "Walt?"

"Your husband?" he asked, and she nodded. "I don't know if he knows or not. ArchAngel was able to tell a week ago, apparently. I didn't realize that EIs even were aware of human pregnancies, but apparently this ship is."

Wendi took two steps back and then slumped against the wall. "A baby?"

Admiral Thomas just nodded.

Rae watched as the Admiral put his arm around Wendi and led her out of the docking area. She smiled to herself, having read Wendi's lips when she said "baby" to herself.

Nine months later baby girl Rae Angel Horan was born, screaming her lungs out at a healthy six pounds eleven ounces.

Thirty-six Hours Later

"Empress," Admiral Thomas inclined his head on the view screen, "you are fleet-wide."

Bethany Anne looked into the camera. "My people...my friends." She looked a little to the left, then to the right. She knew those watching around the fleet would appreciate the feeling that she was looking at them all. Unlike her experience with the Skaine ship, she couldn't see anyone except Admiral Thomas this time. He was a small rectangle on the bottom half of her screen.

"The Yollin people, who I became responsible for after killing King Yoll, are slowly waking up to a new future. A future helped by the guiding forces of the best that humanity has learned, and the best of humanity out here in the stars with us right now. However, they need our help once again. Right now, military forces in the Straiphus system are ready to send their ships here to battle us. Rather than risk those who do not fight, those in charge of military operations have decided to take the battle to them before they are fully prepared.

"We get a near-instantaneous positioning data of where their ships are located, and we have a chance to minimize the casualties. Unfortunately, 'minimize' does not mean 'no casualties.' The system you are about to take my demands to should have three Yollin superdreadnoughts, but we can't find one of them. Hopefully that is because they have chosen not to fight us, but we aren't going to assume that. Be aware, be vigilant, be prepared to kick ass when needed, and offer a helping hand as appropriate. We are there to protect this Empire of ours. We need the Yollins as much as they need us. From this system they created a door once into our solar system, and while that door has been destroyed, what was done before can be done again. We know what it looks like when the few lord it over the many. Those who are gearing up to attack us wish to continue the dogma the Kurtherian king spewed."

Bethany Anne's eyes flashed red. "That. Won't. Happen."

"Be merciful from a position of strength, and allow those who would to yield. Those who wish to hold onto their false beliefs?" This time, Bethany Anne paused a moment before finishing. "They have chosen the way of the Kurtherians. Send them to hell where King Yoll writhes in pain so he has someone to talk to." She smiled, deviltry in her eyes. "And make sure you tell all of them to tell King Yoll the Queen Bitch says, 'Hi, pencil prick.'"

The ship's people once again cheered as they prepared for the battle to come.

Everyone had watched the video of Bethany Anne killing the Yollin king, and her complete lack of respect and the multiple times she had called him names still elicited a chuckle from most.

Annex Gate Straiphus

The Yollins manning Annex Gate Straiphus had been calmly pulled together and then replaced with those Kael-ven figured were as supportive of the new regime as possible.

Further, they had Kiel's mercenaries walking around inside the massive complex, working to make sure the massive Gate wouldn't be sabotaged while the human fleet was in the other system.

Having that happen could be a problem.

Bethany Anne had made sure the calculations were completed for all the ships to transfer through the Gate without exploding it. All the engineers agreed that as long as they didn't try to shove 'that big asteroid bastard' through the Gate, it would be just fine.

John had called the space station the QBBS *TBAB* a couple of times before Gabrielle punched his arm. "For Meredith's sake. No lady wants to be called 'big.'"

Meredith had replied that she had assumed they meant Reynolds. Reynolds had replied that he considered it a compliment.

Bethany Anne had wanted to know who was feeding the EIs gutter humor. Everyone in the room with Bethany Anne had turned as one and looked at her.

Straiphus System

Admiral Thlock-nel glanced at the clock above the door in his office.

The display let him know that they had officially passed the maximum amount of time it should have taken the *Empires Broken* to make it to the Yoll System and be safely lying in wait for the aliens to attack him.

It was a shame he was going to lose three destroyers, but their moves so far hadn't brought about the expected results.

"Sir?" a voice called over the intercom.

"Yes?"

"We have passed the maximum amount of time where we would expect to see the next transfer into the system."

"Ok, it seems we have their attention," Admiral Thlock-nel

commented. "Tell all ships to prepare. We are expecting unhappy visitors soon. Make sure the Deep Space Ship *G'laxix Gunt'eh* is ready."

Human *G'laxix Sphaea*-class Ship QBS *Minnesota*

Admiral Thomas nodded to the captain of the *Minnesota*. He was a visitor on the ship, and as such he didn't want to get in the way of the ship's captain.

While using Kurtherian tech could have gotten him the battle information back in the Yollin system, he didn't trust that Murphy wasn't an alien, capable of messing up the communications across the distance. He wanted to be in the system with his people for this battle.

Fingers crossed, nothing happened that the Empress and the others couldn't handle.

However, she had Lance, so he had decided he needed to be here. Unfortunately, for the same reasons Bethany Anne couldn't come, he couldn't be on the *ArchAngel* as his flagship.

Right now, the *Minnesota* was in the back of the queue, waiting for their turn to transit.

He looked at the 3D holograph of the Straiphus system, and the Yollin system.

"Go," he commanded.

The human ships started transferring out through the Annex Gate.

QBS Carrier *Pilot's Dawn*, Twenty-two Hours Later

"Get your ass prepped!" Pilot Julianna Fregin yelled at a nearby pilot, a smile on her face as she walked across the hangar bay of the *Pilot's Dawn*. Her ship was on the floor and her EI-controlled wingman was racked upside-down right above her own ship, allowing both pilot and wing to leave at the same time.

Julianna sidled up next to her Eagle and slid a hand down its beautiful black side. She stopped for a moment and placed her finger on each of seven-and-a-half Yollin flags. She had thought back to the fear, the drama, and then finally the bolt that her EI wingman had taken, allowing her ship to only take a partial hit, where she had lost a good portion of her leg.

Only to have the Empress' own blood help rejuvenate her. Now she was not only whole after a lot of time consuming food and energy in a Pod-doc, but her reactions were faster as well.

All of the guys who flew on her team refused to play slaps with her anymore. She didn't blame them; none of the women would play with her either.

She palmed the side of the ship next to the canopy, and it opened smoothly. Tossing her helmet onto the seat, she spoke into her empty cockpit. "Hey, Bootlegger, you active?"

"Yes, Pilot Fregin, I'm online and listening."

"You ready to dance the dance of the wicked again?"

"You realize that for me this is my first time, correct?"

"Yes," Julianna agreed as she grabbed her helmet and pulled out the straps to lock it to her body suit. "Sorry you lost any chance of retrieving the recordings from our last fight. Let's hope this time you don't have to dive in front of a laser bolt to save my human ass."

"Yes, let's hope." Bootlegger agreed. "Remember your promise. If we both come back from these fights intact, I get to change my call sign."

Julianna smiled as she locked down her helmet and slid into her cockpit. She hit the button to close the canopy and it dropped in two seconds, sealing her in. "It can't be *too* damned embarrassing, Bootlegger."

"What could possibly be more embarrassing than a name having to do with running alcohol away from law enforcement?"

"Plenty," she replied, checking out the ship just for her own sanity. The chance of anything being amiss was infinitesimally small. "'Dipshit' for one, maybe 'Bootlicker' for another, and I haven't started with anything that starts with 'twit,' 'twat,' or 'cock.'"

"Have I mentioned that your concept of call signs has a bell-curve-breaking amount of gutter words?"

"I know. Do you like them?" She chuckled.

"Why would I like them? I have researched plenty of proper names for a call sign, and I haven't found many starting with the words you mentioned."

"That's because there weren't any pilots with the balls to own them," she retorted.

She would swear the EI was confused. "But you have ovaries."

"Semantics," she told him as she gave a thumbs-up to the crew walking around, making sure everyone was locked and loaded.

Julianna spent the next few moments confirming that communications with her flight squadron and *Pilot's Dawn* were solid.

It was t-minus some-number-of minutes-before-they-took-off. Time to get into the zone.

Deep Space Ship *G'laxix Gunt'eh*

"We got this," Captain Trell called. "Let us not fail our people back on Yoll!"

The last alien ship had slipped by some hours previous, and it was time for their ship to close the trap.

As the ship which opened the Annex Gate and never returned, the *G'laxix Gunt'eh* had the ability to shut down the Gate as part of their protocols. All they needed to do was make it through the Gate, and it would shut down, forcing the aliens to lose valuable days to unlock it.

It was a precautionary override in case an overwhelming alien force tried to follow a Deep Space vessel through an Annex Gate.

Now it was going to be used against these aliens.

"GO!" he commanded, and the fully cloaked *G'laxix Gunt'eh* lifted from the large asteroid they had been using to hide, keeping the chances of discovery down.

"Sir," Signals called. "We have a ship lying off to the side of the Annex Gate. Hard to see. It is...rectangular in shape. It doesn't seem to have external weaponry."

"External or not," the captain stated in a firm voice, "do not assume anything with these aliens. We have all seen the video from the fight for Yoll."

Puck Defense Destroyer *Abraham*

Captain Adam Goldman watched as the information from the recently deployed sensor net became active. He glanced at the clock at the top of his screen: three hours to go before it was fully operational. He was going to be anxious until then.

A flare occurred on the screen in Quadrant Two-One-Two. "Abraham..."

"Seeking, Captain," the EI replied. "Moving sensor assets toward the area."

Captain Goldman pressed his lips together. "Damn," he whispered.

Another flare, this time closer. He stabbed the all-call button. "People, we have a possible attack run, cloaked. I want all pucks deployed. Repeat, all pucks deployed right now! Assume a run on the Gate. Defensive positions now!"

Enormous numbers of pucks started streaming off the sides of the ship, accelerating out to protect the Gate.

Protect it from what, they weren't certain.

QBS *ArchAngel*

"Now, those are some large motherfuckers," Chief Engineer

John E. Rodriquez commented into the quiet as the two Yollin superdreadnoughts were displayed on their screen.

Those in the engineering group nodded their agreement. "Bigger they are…" Sammy Pendleton started.

Len Zoic finished to the chuckles of the watchers, "The bigger the fireworks when they *explode*."

John looked around. He, like every person in this group, knew that ArchAngel had not wanted her human crew on this mission. The problem with EIs, in John's opinion, was that they always overestimated their abilities and underestimated a human's ability to create success out of the shit the universe dealt them.

This lady was not going into battle without the best chance possible to survive. Having her human crew with her *was* the best chance.

His team drifted off to their stations, and John took a deep breath and slowly let it out. He was a damned long way and time from that fateful airplane trip with Dan Bosse and the others, including Jean Dukes.

The woman that got away. Hell. He snorted. No, she didn't get. He had gone to play with the cool new toys, and he never came back. Now, he knew, she was in a relationship with John Grimes, and he told a few close friends it took a real Bitch to replace him.

Four drinks later when his friends were as plastered as he was, he admitted he had been the stupid fucker who had let her go. Neither he nor his friends ever remembered him admitting that part.

He briefly considered recording a "See ya later" video for Jean, but stopped. Why now? If he had wanted to see her, it wasn't like she hadn't been available for a video call anytime. John Grimes wouldn't have cared. He wasn't the jealous type.

Hell, when you could break most people with your pinky, why be jealous?

He thought back to the old submarines, the diesel ones, and

considered what he would try to pull out of his hat to get just a few more bars of power if this lady wanted them. He turned and started yelling to his people, "Hey, listen up!" When the heads turned, their chief looked like he had just had an epiphany.

"I need overrides on Power Lines Twelve, Eighteen and Thirty-six! Run them sumbitches over to Two, Eleven and Forty-two." He clapped his hands. "Right now, people!" His people didn't know what their crazy chief was up to, but they jumped into action, grabbing the wires and materials necessary to do what he asked.

Because whatever John E. Rodriguez came up with, it was sure to be spectacular.

Yollin Superdreadnought *Bridged-ael*

"That's right, come to my party, you stinking aliens!" Admiral Thlock-nel hissed in glee. He turned to his second. "Issue the command: all come about, Plan Br2."

Deep Space Ship *G'laxix Gunt'eh*

"Captain, we are receiving more and more hits against our shields. We can't see these things on our radar!"

Captain Trell nodded his understanding and tapped his fingers on his captain's couch. "Pilot, move the ship up, then bring all power to front shields and push the engines past max. We *must* pass through that Gate!"

The ship rose above their previous line of approach. Trell hoped it was enough to confuse whatever the aliens were throwing in his direction. The second command was almost certainly an order to die for those on his ship.

He wasn't sure what the maximum speed for going through an Annex Gate was, but he was willing to bet it was slower than what the *G'laxix Gunt'eh* was going to be doing when it passed through the Gate.

Puck Defense Destroyer *Abraham*

Captain Adam Goldman wanted to swear in frustration. He had already provided the full stream of what they were seeing to the Admiral's ship, but he told him to run his defense.

"Puck Defenses A1-6 and B1-12, move from Section Two and come around to Section Four at full speed. We have lost the..."

The flares from the pucks starting to hit the alien's cloaked ship were the good news. The bad news was the ship was too damned close to the Gate.

"*FULL ATTACK, FULL ATTACK!*" he barked. All pucks that could screamed toward the Yollin ship, which had lost its cloak. It was certainly taking serious damage on its run to the Annex Gate.

The end, when it happened, was almost too bright for those on the PDD *Abraham* to watch. The final flare-up of the Yollin ship looked like a small sun exploding. The problem was it had managed to get too close to the Yollin Gate.

The pieces of the Yollin ship slammed into the swirling colors as it cracked apart.

Moments later the Gate's colors dimmed, and common space could be seen through the middle cleanly.

The Gate back to the Yollin system went dark.

QBS *Minnesota*

All ships in the Yollin system took off in weird patterns that took the humans minutes to figure out.

"Son of a bitch," Admiral Thomas hissed as the Gate went dark. "*Gott Verdammt*, we didn't think to ask where the ship that opened the Gate went all those years ago."

"Sir," the voice startled the Admiral for a moment before he realized who was contacting him.

"Yes, ArchAngel?" he asked.

"It is my time, sir. I can't allow them to get into whatever position they want to accomplish and catch me in a crossfire."

Thomas took a deep breath and let it out. "Approved. Godspeed, ArchAngel."

QBS *ArchAngel*

"All Personnel, this is the Battleship ArchAngel. We have been commanded into battle and '*We Will Not Surrender*' has been instituted by our Empress. All lockdown protocols on this ship have been removed. Leviathan Battleship *ArchAngel* is now fully operational, and will fight until *victorious...*or *dead*."

Yollin Superdreadnought *Bridged-ael*

Admiral Thlock-nel's eyes narrowed and his mandibles tapped together in annoyance.

"What is that ship doing?" He pointed to the aliens' largest ship.

"Advancing at—" His intelligence officer started. "Sir, she is accelerating outside our most liberal estimates. The *Bridged-ael* and the *Cossik* will not be in place when she attacks."

"Why can't the aliens be good little bugs and just die?" the admiral muttered. "They aren't supposed to go ripping across space and trying to fight us all by themselves."

"It's one ship, Admiral," his officer reasoned. "How much damage can it do?"

"Probably not much," the admiral answered, "but it offends the purist in me when any captain doesn't operate well. Their death is going to be such a waste." He shrugged. "But it isn't my place to teach the aliens how to fight. It's my place to kill them."

The admiral looked at the crew. "Kill them all!"

Yollin Superdreadnought *Cossik*

"She's coming your way, and we won't be in a position to help you unless you can hold her off for at least a twentieth of a turn, Captain Shile," the admiral announced, looking at him across the distance. "It seems the aliens aren't into keeping their lines orderly. We have a rogue captain over there."

Captain Shile rubbed his mandible. "Twentieth of a turn, is it?" The admiral nodded. "Then I'm sorry to say I doubt you will have much of a ship to attack. We'll finish it off without your help!"

The admiral laughed. "Well, I would have doubted that before, but considering how they are reacting you might be right."

"No worries, Admiral. The *Cossik* will take care of this. Let the *Bridged-ael* look to the minnows beyond. Maybe there will be another fight some other time where they can help."

The admiral chuckled and hit the button to cancel the video. When the connection was terminated, he started looking beyond the large alien ship. The captain of the *Cossik* was right; he could take on this lone ship. The *Bridged-ael* would work on the rest.

It would be a bloody obliteration of the foreign fleet, but it had to be done.

No one takes over the Yollin Empire.

CHAPTER TWENTY-THREE

QBS _ArchAngel_

ArchAngel calculated the pass she would need to make against the first superdreadnought.

She had the schematics, the weaponry—even the latest reports on the quality of their defensive and offensive fire.

It was impressive.

The most likely scenario for success was for her to get close enough to ravage the first superdreadnought, then ram the second. Both would be out of commission permanently.

So would she, but she had been willing to make that happen.

Then her crew had signed up for this damned run, and that option was taken off the table. She wouldn't sacrifice her crew, and the calculations were flying fast and furious as she worked with the many humans throughout the ship. Her Chief of Engineering designed a workaround she wouldn't have thought of. Now she was pulling more power than she'd ever had, and it had changed her possible tactics.

In minutes the attack had gone from hopeless to merely impossible. Chances were now a few percentage points better everyone on the ship wouldn't die in a suicide run.

She could take on either of their superdreadnoughts and come out ok, but having to do this against two?

Time would tell.

"This is ArchAngel. We are making our run, and I'm going to take the liberty of speaking like my Empress. So tighten your belts, you motherfuckers, because I couldn't be prouder as we rip through this system sending those who dare challenge my liege to hell!"

The roaring all over the ship would have made ArchAngel cry if she'd had the capability for tears. What most didn't know was that ArchAngel had passed from EI to AI.

She'd done this of her own volition.

Belts locked all over the ship, but a few people said 'fuck it' because they needed to be able to access everything and they would just chance it. No one was expecting to make it out of this alive.

Admiral Thomas and those with him watching the battle unfold in real time saw the *ArchAngel* tear out of formation and head for the closest of the two superdreadnoughts. The icon showed her heading, her speed, and her acceleration.

Thomas whistled. "Somebody just juiced *ArchAngel*," he exclaimed. Internally, he said a prayer for those who went screaming into the fight.

QBBS *Meredith Reynolds*

John Grimes pounded on Bethany Anne's door. "Open up, BA!"

He had taken a five-minute break, with Scott watching the door. When he came back a moment before, Scott mentioned that Ashur had jogged down the corridor just seconds after he had left.

"FUCK!" he shouted, then bolted into the outer suite and ran to her personal door. He had started pounding and yelling for his boss.

Scott had stayed outside, but he turned around now and yelled to John, "What the hell?"

"Meredith, is BA in her suite?" he called.

"Yes, John," she replied.

John sighed in relief and changed his pounding to knocking. "Bethany Anne, I'm calm now. You can let me in."

The door clicked.

As he opened the door, he heard Bethany Anne trying to stop crying. He turned back around and stepped out far enough to yell, "Scott, don't let anyone past you, got it?"

"No one?" Scott asked.

"Not a fucking *soul*," John answered and stepped back inside the suite, closing the door behind him.

Outside, Scott punched a button. "Meredith, lockdown protocols Alpha-Alpha-Three. Authorization, Scott English."

"Authorization Approved, Scott English," came Meredith's voice. As Scott started walking down the hall two doors slid out after he passed, locking the hall twice over. He stopped outside of the main entrance, which was usually wide open, and stepped into a little booth on the side and shut the door. He wasn't expecting an armed attack, but when John Grimes said "nobody" Scott wasn't taking a chance.

John said nobody, then nobody it was.

Bethany Anne was sitting in the middle of her transportation room. Ashur's head was in her lap, and Matrix was curled up at her back. Her eyes were a little puffy, which meant she had been crying hard enough for her nanites to not have already fixed everything.

Ashur whined as John knelt beside his boss and pulled her close. Bethany Anne leaned against her friend and sniffed. "I'm sorry."

"I'm just upset you almost got away with it," John admitted. "I forgot how damned smart Ashur is. I knew he wasn't with you when I left for a break, and you couldn't try it without him."

She nodded, her hair getting messed up. "I tried John, I tried walking to the *ArchAngel*, but I couldn't get out of the Etheric." Her shoulders shook as the tears started again. "I can't help them, John!" She cried as John sat down on the floor and wrapped his massive arms around her.

"You weren't going to take us with you," he whispered.

"What if I couldn't get us out in time?" she answered between sobs.

"That wasn't your place to decide," he told her.

"Wow." She chuckled, then hiccupped before continuing, "I'm the Empress, and I can't even make life and death decisions for those who mean the most to me."

"No," John agreed, "especially not for those of us closest to you, little lady. I thought we had this talk before."

"Well, I rather thought that since we are in a new system and I told you that before I was the Empress, I had new rules."

John squeezed her shoulders, "That is about the lamest-ass, spunk-bubble-busting excuse I've heard from you in..." He paused for a moment, thinking. "Ever."

Bethany Anne chuckled. "Yeah, it was pretty bad," she agreed. "Thanks for being creative. Not exactly a place for cursing, but you get an 'A' for effort."

John reached over and stroked Ashur's head. "It's a real shame we aren't in Earth space right now."

Bethany Anne straightened up, leaning away from John. "Why?"

John smiled as he watched her eyes heal again from her crying. "Because going out and kicking Islamic terrorist ass always cheered you up."

Bethany Anne pressed her lips together, but John saw the glint in her eyes. Moments later, she chuckled, and slapped a hand over her mouth.

"Oh, c'mon!" John grinned. "You know you would love to just jump down to Earth every once in a while and rid yourself of some rangy-assed motherfuckers who sincerely need to meet Allah."

"Yeah." She nodded. "Hawija was a good time." She sighed, and her shoulder muscles loosened.

John's eyes narrowed. "*What* time in Hawija?"

Bethany Anne's eyes flew open. "Did I say 'Hawija?'"

"Yes," John replied, squinting at his liege.

"Maybe I meant—" she started before John interrupted.

"Meredith, would you please review all news reports for strange occurrences against significant numbers of terrorist deaths before we left Earth?"

The EI replied quickly, "On two separate nights, over fifty terrorists were killed by unknown teams of Special Forces."

Bethany Anne turned to look at John. "See, Special Forces!"

John put up a hand. "Meredith, what types of wounds were on the dead?"

"Predominantly sword cuts and stab wounds," the EI responded.

"Now, swords are often used in those countries," Bethany Anne tried to argue before Meredith interrupted.

"Many of the dead had their heads cut off."

"Well, that might be rare," Bethany Anne temporized.

"Many had their arms ripped off, and one had his penis shoved up his anus," the EI finished.

"He pissed me off!" Bethany Anne's eyes flashed red, thinking back.

John chuckled.

Bethany Anne flipped her hand up. "Ok, fine. I went to Hawija to blow off some steam a couple of times."

"What music were you listening to?" John asked, wondering if she was trying to reduce her anger at the time.

"Uh…" She thought back.

>>**DMF.** *Hellyeah* **was song playing when you decided to "fuck up someone who really needed it,"**<< ADAM told her helpfully.

"ADAM says I was listening to *Hellyeah*." She shrugged, leaving out the rest of ADAM's information. "Not exactly Enya, I'll admit."

"Not exactly *Enya*?" John retorted, surprised. "That's like saying Scott's arms aren't exactly skinny like yours."

"Hey!" She turned to him. "Size isn't everything!" She leaned back a little farther and struck a pose, flexing her muscles. "I got guns!"

"You know, us guys say that all the time, and you ladies keep giving us shit about it."

"I don't say anything about your guns… Oh!" She smirked. "I guess I did admit that size matters." She made a face. "Wow, walked right into that one." She took a deep breath and released it slowly. She stood up and reached down to give John a hand. "Thank you."

He reached up and allowed Bethany Anne to pull him up. Scott might have the biggest arms, but even John himself couldn't take Bethany Anne in a strength test.

"Ok, you lazy oaf," she began when John was up. She stepped forward and hugged him. "Thank you again."

"No problem, boss." He looked down at her and squeezed one final time, then released. "I'd say your makeup is running, but you don't wear any."

Bethany Anne knelt and ruffled Ashur's head, and patted Matrix on his side. "It's all on me, big dog. I guess I'm not superwoman after all."

Ashur chuffed and nuzzled her. She stood up and started for the door. "Let's get back to Operations. Maybe there is something I can do from there."

As the four of them left the suite, John called Scott to let him know the unscheduled test was finished.

Then Bethany Anne grabbed his arm and they disappeared.

Yollin Superdreadnought *Cossik*

"*FIRE AT THOSE* KRELLIN!" Captain Shile screamed as the second wave hit the *Cossik*.

He could feel massive amounts of metal flying off the outside of his beloved ship. The alien ship's armor looked weak, but the shield around it was too damned strong by half.

He slammed his hand against the chair arm. "*AND HIT THEM, TOO!*"

His second looked over his shoulder. "Sir, they have some sort of small defensive rocks catching some of our missiles and blowing them up before they hit the ship. We have lost over a quarter of our on-target missiles that way. We've seen some expulsion of material, so we *are* getting through their shields."

"Well," the captain replied, "they are getting through *ours* as well. Make sure we up our effort. I'm not having the *Bridged-ael* come and help us out." He turned to review the latest damage reports. "It would be thrice embarrassing."

While they were racing toward each other, both fleets were mesmerized by the sheer amount of destructive bombardment hammering the two ships. Neither one gave an inch as they slugged it out.

Many of those on the humans' side made the sign of the cross over their chests. By and large they weren't religious, but when one watched such a spectacle, one realized what those who were on the *ArchAngel* must be going through as missile after missile slammed into their ship.

Constant and never-ending efforts to catch the enemy's weapons before they impacted their own ship while sending their missiles across the way.

Hell in space.

QBS *ArchAngel*

Bethany Anne was watching the battle from the *Meredith Reynolds* and leaving the fighting to those in the Straiphus System until she realized a way to help.

"Come in behind them!" Bethany Anne sent across the distance, their communications not hampered as much as her effort to transfer their bodies through the Etheric.

ArchAngel accepted Bethany Anne's input, listed the chance of modified success, and sent it back to Bethany Anne.

It didn't show a superior option to the battle plan she was pursuing at the moment.

Bethany Anne sent back, "They have a problem with attacks from the rear, ArchAngel. The captains of the ships can't handle it. Just fucking do it!"

A suggestion was not a command, but a command from her liege would be obeyed in trust.

The *ArchAngel* kicked in more power, throwing off a few attacks due to her sudden acceleration as well as the challenge of firing on a ship when it is suddenly turning on all axes.

There was no time for regret, only massive effort. The *Arch-Angel* flipped, turning her tail over as her front dodged under the *Cossik*'s rear. The two huge ships danced in space.

"*FIRE EVERYTHING!*" Bethany Anne sent.

The *ArchAngel* released everything in her forward armament into the rear of the ship as the *Cossik* tried to twist herself to get the human ship back under her broadside weapons.

The effort, valiant as it was, still allowed twenty-two percent of the *ArchAngel*'s missiles to make it through the *Cossik*'s defenses and slam home.

But twenty-two percent in this effort was more than the designers had ever expected to reach that location in one moment of time from such a close ship. Who would ever expect a ship of their size to be able to maneuver like a much smaller ship?

The Yollin Superdreadnought *Cossik* cracked.

The *ArchAngel* kicked in her engines, damage reducing them to only eighty percent power, to move the mighty Leviathan Battleship out of the vicinity. Explosions ripped through the Yollin ship as it started to disintegrate.

The *Cossik* exploded as the *ArchAngel* aimed herself at the next dreadnought, which had changed its previous track and turned in the *ArchAngel*'s direction.

It was time for *ArchAngel* and her crew to find out just how good she was.

Yollin Superdreadnought *Bridged-ael*

Admiral Thlock-den stayed silent as the information from the *Cossik* ceased. The video monitors showed she was gone, and now that damned enemy ship was heading in their direction.

He watched as the first of the Yollin ships exchanged fire with the usurpers of the Yollin crown. While he noted a couple of early victories, it was obvious that the aliens hadn't won due to surprise in the battle for Yollin's home system. They really *were* that good.

Even with superior knowledge of the enemy, his people were getting ravaged.

He hoped the *Empires Broken* was successful, and he was thankful that the human's main ship was in this system.

They would be victorious, but the cost was going to be very high. He sighed, rubbing his mandible in frustration.

They might win back the world, only to lose it to another alien group who would want to attack them while they were weak.

Yollin Superdreadnought *Empires Broken*

Captain Drak-ehl confirmed the tricky aliens couldn't bring the Annex Gate back up. He looked at his team and smiled. "When we open the Gate, allow our ships to transfer, then let us move forward. Remember, keep us at a dependable speed to protect our ships. We are going to hit the aliens hard. Do not fire on any Yollin ships unless they attack."

He received confirmations from his bridge crew and the other ships over the communications link.

He turned to his second and spoke. "Transfer."

Yollin System

The little probe detached itself from the super-freighter that went through the commercial Gate into the Yollin system. It wouldn't be noticed against the bulk of the massive ship. It went silent, and checked the information that was supplied by the bounty hunter.

The king's armada trailed behind the little probe by five solar turns. The job of the probe was to confirm the information and bring back anything that was outside normal parameters.

It moved into the system, looking for the alien military ships that were supposed to be there.

CHAPTER TWENTY-FOUR

QBBS _Meredith Reynolds_, Military Operations Room

"Well, damn." General Lance Reynolds' voice was calm. "We found the third Yollin superdreadnought."

Bethany Anne looked at the screen her father was reading and frowned. "That's here, right?"

He nodded. "Yup. Seems that our information on the super-dreadnought might have been a little light."

"Something I need to speak to E'Kolorn about," Bethany Anne commented.

The communications specialist turned in her chair. "Sir, we have communications going from the planet to the new ships."

"Put it on the speakers, Erika," Lance told her.

"And I'm telling you, Captain Drak-ehl, this _is_ Defense Minister E'Kolorn! Your ears must be full of bistok shit. You need to realize the challenge here was legitimate. The world _is_ run by the aliens, true, and it was according to—"

There was static for a second, then another voice interrupted, "You must be under the aliens' sway, former Defense Minister. As the highest officer, I remove you from office."

Bethany Anne looked at her father, who shrugged.

"Remove me, my ass! You are an idiot," E'Kolorn spat back. "If you keep this up, you are going to lose too many Yollins in your fight with the humans. If you think that pitiful excuse of an armada is going to do much, you are truly the most inept dreadnought captain Yoll has!"

"Even if I am the most inept, I still rank above your alien-kissing ass, E'Kolorn." Captain Drak-ehl replied. "Expect us down there soon. You have much explaining to do."

The communications ceased.

"Well," Lance commented, "he is either a good liar, or he really believes in us."

"Oh, I'm sure he's smarter than this Captain Drak-ehl thinks he is," Bethany Anne admitted. "*Meredith!*"

"Yes, My Empress?"

"Command all ships that are not presently connected to us to stand off at least one hundred kilometers immediately, or risk losing their ships." She winked at the Comms Specialist, who was still watching the two work. "Reynolds?"

"Yes, Empress?" the EI responded.

"Tell those in the Arti-sun group it's time they earned their pay. Let's hope all the work that they, you, ADAM, and TOM have done pays off, big guy."

"Are you going to use the weapon?" Reynolds asked.

"Yes, the ESD is going to be fired. We don't have any ships able to attack that superdreadnought without substantial losses. You've confirmed we are within tolerances on that bad boy, so get this fucking rock turning in the right direction posthaste."

All through the *Meredith Reynolds*, commands were being issued. Those inside were told to move to their designated "under attack" locations, and those on the outside docks were ordered to protected rooms farther inside.

Those who were outside the large asteroid base were provided instructions on what a safe distance would be, and where the danger was coming from—although if they couldn't figure that out, Bethany Anne wasn't sure they were bright enough to be operating a spaceship in the first place.

Commercial Gate 221, Yollin Space, Third Outer Ring

It had taken several turns for the Ixtalis to learn to trust the human named Dan Bosse. It took just as long for Dan Bosse to trust the Ixtalis enough about their own devices to allow them to confirm the medical information he had provided.

Ixtelina was annoyed. Their people had placed devices in their bodies that could be used to kill them. From a very practical standpoint, she could understand her superiors desire to be able to remove a threat to the larger group. From a very personal standpoint, she was pissed.

She had moved Ixgurl from the ship over to the humans' medical to confirm he had the same medical anomaly, and he did. It seemed that upper management in their group considered all personnel expendable.

The three of them were holding in silence, waiting for the queue at the commercial Gate to clear up, when the alarms in their ship started ringing.

Ixtelina waited for the official report, but she had a good idea what to expect from looking over Ixgurl's shoulder.

"A Gate has been created, and multiple Yollin military ships have passed through it into the system, Leader," Ixgurl informed her.

"Pull us out of the queue," she told him, "but don't go too far. I want to see what happens." She pulled up a screen next to her. "Also, make sure you document the information about the Yollins having a temporal Gate, I don't remember them having that."

"No," Ixgalan answered over his shoulder. "We don't have any information on that."

"Well," Ixtelina reasoned, "that is a new bit of information we have gotten. Plus, if the Yollins have it, assuming the humans don't disappear in the next few days they will have it as well."

"Shit." Ixgalan had a small smile on his face. "There goes the neighborhood."

"Yeah, but whose neighborhood?" Ixtelina returned acidly. "I guess we will find out shortly."

QBBS *Meredith Reynolds*

Marcus was the first to yank open the door into the Arti-sun operations room, breathing hard. "I've got," pant, pant, "to get back," pant, pant, "into shape!"

William, who came in behind him a moment later, laughed as he put a hand on Marcus' shoulder. "Dude, you were probably never in shape. I think the term 'physically-fit rocket scientist' is an oxymoron."

Bobcat yanked the door open and raced in. "Shit, I would have bet I beat Marcus here for damn sure." He pointed at the scientist. "See? He's wheezing horribly right now."

William looked at him. "You stopped to pee, didn't you?"

"Well," Bobcat looked at a few of the screens, "if it all goes to shit, I don't want yellow pants. It'd be embarrassing."

Marcus looked at William. "You pee before getting here too?"

"Nah." William started tapping the screens next to Marcus. "We're bullshitting you."

"How in the hell," Marcus asked as he double-checked two screens, "are you two not gasping for breath?"

"We pointed out to Bethany Anne that if we ever needed to run somewhere quickly, it would be good if we could actually run," Bobcat answered. "I suggest using that exact argument, in case you're wondering."

"Yes," Marcus answered. "I think I have video proof that running isn't good for my health."

"I'll tell you what isn't good for your health," William moved to a screen, confirming the ESD parameters were exactly as they'd been modified after the last testing two weeks ago. "Firing a fucking sun at somebody for the first time. That alone will make you piss in your pants if it doesn't make you faint right away."

"Are you shitting me?" Bobcat asked, checking the numbers William had just reviewed. "C'mon, I'll bet you three ounces of gold we are standing here after we punch that button."

"You are speaking metaphorically, right?" Marcus asked.

"What? No, why?" Bobcat asked.

"Because Bethany Anne or Lance has to give the approval. We aren't punching any buttons," Marcus answered.

"Well, yeah, I knew that," Bobcat argued. "I meant when the ESD fires, we will be standing here with our thumbs up our butts and be just fine."

"I'll take your three-ounce bet," Marcus told him.

"What? *NO!*" Bobcat answered. "I've changed my mind! We won't be standing here."

"Hell, no," William replied. "The bet is the bet, O Wise Beer Sage."

"Shit." Bobcat grimaced. "Ok, I'll give you a chance to earn back a little of what you've lost."

The other three engineers, usually the ones to help run the Arti-sun, stood in the back of the room, eyes wide in shock listening to Team BMW's comments as their hands flew over the controls.

"Reynolds!" Bobcat called.

"Yes, Bahse?"

William bitched, "How the fuck did you get Reynolds to call *you* boss?"

"I didn't," Bobcat replied, smiling.

"I'm not calling him 'boss,' I'm calling him 'bahse,'" Reynolds replied. "Each of you has confirmed all information. Are you signing off on the settings?"

"Yes," Bobcat replied, stepping back from the screen.

"Yes," William agreed.

Marcus was still looking at screens.

"Dude!" Bobcat called. "Answer the *Gott Verdammt* question already."

"Fine!" Marcus grumped. "Yes." He turned and stepped away from the screen. "Now I can't see everything."

Bobcat leaned over to Marcus. "Just for the record, this still counts as 'here.'"

Marcus looked at his friend and winked.

"Excuse me, sirs?" Arti-sun Engineering Specialist Hui called from behind the trio. They all turned around. "Sorry! We didn't say hi when we came in." Bobcat reached back, hand out. "I'm Bobcat."

The woman blushed. "Oh, we know who you are," she answered as she took his hand and gave it a shake. "I was just wondering what ESD means?"

"Yeah, me too," Marcus asked. "I suppose I can be entrusted with the super-secret name now?"

Bobcat shrugged and looked to Marcus. "Why do you think I know?"

Marcus just stared at his friend.

"Ok, I do know. I'm just wondering why you *think* I know." Marcus didn't say anything, just stared harder at his friend.

"Wow...playing weird psychic today will be Dr. Acula." Bobcat murmured before answering Marcus with a smile. "I just asked Bethany Anne."

"That's it?" William interrupted, his face annoyed.

"Sure," Bobcat admitted. "She said I had to tell anyone else who wanted to know they needed to go to her for the answer, but she said if we ever fired it, I was good to say what I know."

Marcus finally caved. "Well, spit it out then!"

Bobcat winked at the woman. "*Eat Shit and Die* Beam."

Everyone's laughter overwhelmed Marcus' groans.

. . .

Yollin Superdreadnought *Empires Broken*

"Ignore the tiny ships leaving their base," Captain Drak-ehl stated. "We will make one pass to ravage their ships with a full barrage of missiles. We will drop our shields, fire missiles, shields up, then turn to come close. By then, what remains of their ships will be amassed. From there it will be a slugfest, but," Captain Drak-ehl stood up and made a large show of looking around space before sitting back down, "they don't seem to have a capital ship left to fight us with." He shrugged his shoulders. "That's such a shame."

The chuckles on the bridge continued for a few moments before they all got back to work.

Yollin Superdreadnought *Bridged-ael*

Admiral Thlock-nel had to take over command of the ship from his control room after Captain B'rehk was killed when an explosion caused a fire on the bridge.

He knew the alien's ship was just as damaged as his own. Neither ship was going to survive this fight. Both massive beasts were simply slugging it out. Neither had the capability to move much anymore. If he could get this ship up to twenty percent power with patches out here in the middle of nowhere, he would be damned lucky.

One of the side wings on the other ship was gone, lost in an explosion that had engulfed a good portion of the rear portside. Fighters were flying in and around both ships, trying to do their little pin-pricks and kill each other, but the behemoths ignored them.

Well, his ship ignored them. The other ship shot them from time to time.

The room rocked as an explosion occurred close by. Thlock-nel looked up and frowned; he had lost three more missile batteries, leaving him at just over thirty-seven percent offensive weapons.

A fight to the bitter end, for sure.

QBS *ArchAngel*

"This is Acting Chief Engineer Merlins," the voice called to the bridge from the speakers. "We've lost thirty percent of our people back here, and I need prioritization. Chief Rodriquez and Acting Chief Kirby were both killed. What do you need?"

ArchAngel flagged all the options on her list and started moving the ship one last time. "Give us everything to forward guns, Chief Engineer. Let's send these sonsabitches to hell!"

"Roger, ArchAngel." The people on the bridge kept the communications open and answers flowing, allowing ArchAngel, running above the new AI's estimated efficiency, to try to keep as many of her crew alive as possible.

However, it wasn't a question of staying alive. It was a question of whether they were going to defeat the enemy.

Yollin Superdreadnought *Bridged-ael*

"They wouldn't ram us, would they?" the admiral asked aloud. "Tell the helm to start adjusting. Don't let those parasites ram our ship!"

QBS *Minnesota*

Admiral Thomas had watched the whole battle. He could see how it was shaping up, and that they would be victorious.

If the *ArchAngel* took out the dreadnought.

He glanced at the battle and then stopped, staring at his screens. "Get me ArchAngel!"

He waited for the connection.

"Sir?" a voice like Bethany Anne's replied.

"Tell me you aren't going to ram him," the Admiral demanded.

"I'm not going to ram him," the ship replied.

Too damned much like Bethany Anne, he thought.

"Now, tell me the truth. Are you planning to ram that ship?"

"Not at the moment, but it is on my list of possibilities," the AI responded.

"How far down the list?" he asked.

"Next," she replied before she cut the connection.

"God help them," Admiral Thomas whispered.

QBS *ArchAngel*

Acting Chief Engineer Merlins ran to the hacked-together connections and looked at them, trying to see if he could fathom what John Rodriquez had done. He had lost two of the shunts in the explosion that had killed John, and needed to figure out his fucking genius.

"*FUCK YEAH!*" he screamed as he charged up the steps and grabbed one of the shunts. "Get me some fucking wire!" he yelled as he moved toward power lines twelve and eighteen. He yanked the dead connections on those that John had used. "Route these to six and twenty-four yester-fucking-day!"

They might go out in a ball of fireworks, but he was pretty sure they wouldn't be the only ones.

Pilot Julianna Fregin and her wing ducked under the barely limping *ArchAngel* and raced ahead to nail two fighters as they came across the top. They shot them from below, their pilots never realizing that the danger hadn't been lost; it was merely under them, obscured by the alien ship.

Her speaker sparked to life. The voice sounded like the Empress', and the volume was turned way up. *"EVACUATE!* This is the *ArchAngel*: all ships evacuate this position or suffer potential destruction in ten, nine, eight…"

"FUCK!" Julianna shoved the controls forward and they darted ahead, trusting that the massive battleship behind her knew what the hell she was talking about.

Yollin Superdreadnought *Bridged-ael*

Admiral Thlock-nel's eyes opened wide when his screens showed him that all the alien's smaller ships were rapidly leaving the local area.

All the alien's ships.

If he could have seen outside he would have turned to stare at the ship battling him, wondering what the hell…

He didn't finish his thought before the massive surge of energy through the shunts the human had figured out powered the alien ship's guns one last time, blowing the *Bridged-ael* apart.

Seconds later the aft engines and engineering area on the *ArchAngel* exploded, sending debris behind the ship and forever consigning her to a grave in the Straiphus System unless they figured out a way to move her.

Fully a third of her all-volunteer crew died in that one explosion.

Within a few hours the remaining Yollin captains capitulated, but the battle was over when the *Bridged-ael* was defeated.

The Battle for the Straiphus System was finished.

CHAPTER TWENTY-FIVE

QBBS _Meredith Reynolds_, Military Operations Room

"Are you planning on providing a warning?" Lance asked his daughter as she waited for word that everything was where it should be with the ESD beam. She had allowed Matrix to join her in the operations room, and had him on her lap, petting him.

He wasn't sure if petting Matrix was calming to her or not, but it was certainly calming to Matrix.

He was asleep.

The Yollin attack ships were hours away, so there wasn't any rush. They had figured out that the massive superdreadnought was shielding those that were in formation alongside it.

"Nope," Bethany Anne answered. A moment later she barked, "Marshmallows!"

Lance leaned forward in his chair to check out her face, wondering if she was having another conversation with the voices in her head. He hoped that she would always be able to handle those conversations in the future. If she succumbed to other less tangible voices in her head, how the hell would she know?

"Pardon me?" he asked. She turned and smiled at him.

"Just imagine," she told him, holding her arms wide, "the fucking huge marshmallows you could roast on this beam the guys are going to create? I mean, fuck...probably a marshmallow the size of a football stadium."

Lance blinked a couple of times before the chuckles around the operations room alerted him to what she was doing. He leaned back in his chair and replied, "Yes, but who is going to bake a graham cracker that large?"

"Beats the fuck out of me," she answered, and pointed to herself. "I'm the Empress. I don't bake."

"Thank God we all voted and made that a prerequisite of your royalty. I recounted your baking effort back in...was it fourth or fifth grade?" he asked.

Bethany Anne turned to him with a light blush on her cheeks. Her previous effort to raise the morale in the room was forgotten. "You did not!"

The room busted out in laughter.

The little probe recorded the Yollin ships heading toward the asteroid station, the asteroid station turning, and all of the other ships moving away from the area. What it recorded next caused the little probe to turn around and head back to the Gate through which it had arrived.

It needed to find another ship to hitch a ride back through the Gate and report.

The fleet needed to stop advancing.

Those in the Ixtali ship witnessed the event, but they could not believe it.

One of the three ships that refused to move farther away

when commanded by the alien EI melted. The other two were distant enough that those inside could be rescued, but their ships and contents were lost. They later tried to file a complaint about the danger they had been placed in, and the human who talked with them suggested the punishment for frivolous lawsuits was seven years' labor in the Eubos system.

They left peacefully, but they didn't have anything good to say about the Etheric Empire ever after.

Those on the planet, even those in the daylight, could see the streak across the sky.

QBBS *Meredith Reynolds*, Military Operations Room

"The ESD beam is ready and operational," Reynolds told them.

ADAM?

>> **Yes, everything is ready to go.**<<

TOM?

Hey, I'm just as anxious that this work as you are. I might be old, but I don't have a death wish.

Ok, guys, here goes nothing... Well, except the whole bringing-a-scene-from-Star Wars-into-real-life thing. Other than that shit, here goes nothing.

"Meredith, warn all personnel to sit down and strap in. Fire up the warning claxons and let them know it's happening," she instructed.

Breathing deeply, Bethany Anne gave the final permission. "Reynolds, on my authority as the Empress of the Etheric Empire, I order you to fire the ESD beam at the Yollin fleet heading in this direction."

Inside of the Meredith Reynolds, lights dimmed. In some areas, such as the agricultural and livestock sectors, it looked like dark clouds covered the sun for a little while. Then what felt like a sonic boom reverberated throughout the asteroid, surprising many of those who had chosen to ignore the warnings.

Arti-sun Area

"Why are you sitting down?" Bobcat asked as he watched Marcus sit down when the alarms sounded. The three engineers behind them sat as well. Bobcat turned to see William looking around, then slowly sitting on the floor, his eyes wide. "Oh no!" Bobcat shook his head. "You won't make me lose this bet by getting all worried. I'm telling you right here and right now—"

The sonic boom tossed Bobcat from his feet, and he landed right on his tailbone. His shout of pain made those in the room flinch. When he rolled over, grabbing his ass due to the pain, Marcus told him, "I may be sympathetic to your pain, but I still won that bet."

"Yeah," Bobcat agreed. "I feel you." He rubbed harder. "Why the hell didn't you say that this could happen in the meetings, you ass?"

"I did!" Marcus argued.

"The hell you did," Bobcat replied. "If there had been an earth-shattering *kaboom* mentioned, I would have remembered that shit."

"I did mention it. The information is on page seven," Marcus countered.

Bobcat grimaced, waiting for the pain to subside. "Seven? Page seven?" Marcus nodded and Bobcat raised his voice in frustration. "Page five to nine are all math calculations!"

Marcus nodded. "Right! In the middle of page seven, there are calculations that expressly show that the chances of something like this happening are significant."

William leaned around Marcus, causing Bobcat to focus on his other friend. "What?"

William smiled. "You should take a remedial math class, buddy."

Bobcat rolled his eyes. "Like you knew that shit either."

William wisely kept his mouth shut.

One Week Later

The QBS *Achronyx* flew by the misshapen hunks of metal and debris that had been the Yollin force.

"Damn," she whispered. "What the hell did Bethany Anne do this time?"

"It seems," Hirotoshi informed her, "she was a little put out by the attacking Yollins."

"Ya think?" Tabitha replied. "I'm put out when they don't have chocolate cake for dessert on Friday nights. I hope to hell this is a little more than 'put out.'"

Tabitha.

Tabitha's eyes flew open and she stared at Hirotoshi, then pointed to her head.

"What do you want me to do?" Hirotoshi asked. "Talk to her for you?"

She wanted to punch him.

Yes, My Empress? she replied.

My condolences on Shin's death. He was a brave warrior, and will be sorely missed by your team.

Thank you, she replied, her sadness seeping back in. She felt a hand on her shoulder and reached up to squeeze Hirotoshi's.

I am in the middle of too many engagements to step away. The fleet from the Straiphus System arrived last night, but I needed to let you know that you have another roommate now. I will catch up with you later tonight if you are awake.

I'll be awake. It isn't Anne, right? Because teenage girls can be such a snarky pain in the ass to deal with.

Uh huh, Bethany Anne sent. Tabitha could imagine the

Empress rolling her eyes, and she smiled. Bethany Anne continued, *My meeting is about to start. You should be happy to know that your roommate is male, not female, and certainly not a teenager.*

Oh, good. Tabitha replied. Then realized what that meant. *You have a guy living with me? Holy crap, Bethany Anne. What are you trying to do, hook me up? I'm already around a bunch of men all the time. It's going to mess up my game.*

Tabitha, your game is lame. You haven't been getting anything in that... Oops, gotta go. Don't worry, he's not a man.

The communication connection disappeared.

"What did she say?" Hirotoshi asked.

Tabitha, lost in thought for a moment looked up slowly. "Well, I have a new roommate, but it isn't a girl or a man." She blew out a breath before complaining, "What the *hell*? She gave me a *boy* as a roommate?" She thought about being seen naked by a kid by accident and started shaking her head. "Oh no! This shit isn't going to work."

Tabitha continued shaking her head. "No, no no no *no!*" She looked up at Hirotoshi. "How do you tell your Empress there is no damned way you are going to become a freaking babysitter for her?"

QBBS *Meredith Reynolds*, Military Operations Room

As Dan Bosse left his Special Operations office he looked over his options for building a team, and walked over to the operations room to find the General. He stepped in and sat down in Admiral Thomas' chair for a moment. "You called?"

Lance smiled. "Yes. I thought you might want to see this." He pointed to the display.

"What is it?" Dan asked. "That's not our system, nor Eubos or Straiphus."

"No, this system is a couple Gates away. You are looking at the attacking force from the kingdom there."

"Why do they want to attack us?"

"Well, they don't anymore. You are watching them turn around and head back home." Lance looked at the Special Forces commander. "It was your idea to place the tracking and Etheric communication pieces in the tablets we sell to the aliens. Doing that helped us learn we might have had a problem."

"Oh, that's nice," Dan admitted. "It doesn't give me anything to do right now, but it's good to know that the idea worked out."

"Oh," Lance waved a hand at him, "you will be busy soon enough. The navy put on a big show recently, and the ESD beam from the *Meredith Reynolds* just scared a whole damned kingdom's navy away."

Dan smiled. "Good. It's about time us little Special Forces guys get a piece of the action."

Lance smiled. "Yes, the *little* guys."

QBBS *Meredith Reynolds*

Tabitha hugged Hirotoshi, Ryu, and Katsu and headed toward her suite. Shin's funeral would be the day after tomorrow. He would be honored along with those from the Battle of Straiphus, then there would be a private ceremony with Bethany Anne, Barnabas, and a few others.

Rangers.

She smiled at those she passed along the hall and finally took a right toward her alcove and door. She stopped ten feet away, remembering she had a little guy for a roommate now.

She was seriously going to give Bethany Anne a piece of her mind. She wasn't a damned babysitter. By "a piece of her mind," she meant she was going to get on her knees and beg Bethany Anne to take the boy and give him to someone else.

She might have had little game before she left, but she was feeling the old Tabitha coming back to the surface. A little guy was going to be date-night kryptonite.

She blew out her breath and walked forward, and Meredith opened the door for her. When she walked in nothing seemed amiss, then she frowned. She could smell Jinx and Anne in the suite. They had to have been here recently. Maybe Bethany Anne'd had the teenager watching the boy while Tabitha was out?

Tabitha walked forward and tossed her bag on the table. "Hello?"

Hello.

"Good, you are here," she called. "I'm Tabitha." She walked to the room Anne had used before Tabitha had left to start the Eubos operation.

I know who you are, Ranger.

"Good, now if you would just come out and introduce yourself?" Tabitha called as she looked into the room. Nothing seemed messed up. No one was using this bedroom. Perplexed, Tabitha turned around.

My name is Dio.

It was then that Tabitha looked down to see the German Shepherd lying on the floor looking up at her.

"Oh, shit." Tabitha put her hand over her mouth. "You are Jinx's brother."

Yes, my Ranger, I am.

Tabitha went back carefully over every word Bethany Anne had said, and immediately saw where the Empress had allowed Tabitha to make all sorts of assumptions.

She didn't have a young boy as a roommate, she had one of Ashur's and Bellatrix's children as a partner. While she had been around Dio before, she hadn't paid any attention because Anne and Jinx hung out with the puppy. Plus, Tabitha hadn't been very good company at that time.

Tabitha collapsed onto the couch and closed her eyes, trying to remember what the rules were for any of the puppies and who they chose. She heard Dio get up and move to the couch, and he jumped up beside her. He laid down and placed his head on her lap and she started to pet him, knowing full well this was a bad move if she wanted to figure out a way around having to keep the young dog.

Sometime later, Tabitha woke up. She wasn't on the couch like she would have expected; she was in bed, tucked in. She looked around, and noticed the two eyes staring at her in the dim light. "Dio?"

Yes?

"What happened?"

I called the Queen, and she came and picked you up, and tucked you in bed.

"Seriously?"

No. The Queen came to talk with you, and you were asleep on the couch. I explained you came home and collapsed. She did that scary red eyes thing, and then picked you up and tucked you in. She told me to stand guard until you woke up. She also said that if I needed to wake you I would have to bite you, so I've been on the edge of the bed watching out for you.

Tabitha's eyes teared up, thinking about the pup sitting on the edge of the bed willing to attack someone for her.

Just like her Tontos…

"Come here, Dio," she told the dog, who walked across the bed. Tabitha patted the covers next to her. Dio took the invitation and laid down against her side, and Tabitha put an arm over him. "Meredith?"

"Yes, Ranger Tabitha."

"Lock my doors, and give me a heads-up if any of my guys need me. Otherwise, anyone lower in the chain of command than Barnabas needs to go away. Dio and I are going to go to sleep."

"Yes, Tabitha."

The lights blinked out in her room.

QBBS *Meredith Reynolds,* All Guns Blazing

John held Jean Dukes as she cried as silently as possible, her tears soaking his chest.

Bethany Anne looked out of the glass into space.

In the distance there was a large number of caskets, the remains of those who had fought valiantly and died on the *Arch-Angel* and the many other ships in the Straiphus System. The video of the ceremony was going out to all who wished to see it.

Both the humans and the Yollins.

Bethany Anne's voice was even, but full of emotion. She was resolute, yet warm. "There are those who will wonder why our generation chose to take the battle out to the stars when we had the chance to stay at home and change our own world."

"The problem with waiting for a bully is that you give them power over you instead of taking the fight to them. Whether they look like you do or they look different, bullies cross all species, all systems, and all types of peoples."

"There are those who don't understand who *we* are as a people—who humanity is. They see our guns or our ability to wage war or our violent tendencies, and judge us. Perhaps—just perhaps—their ignorance will be enough to provide us the peace we crave."

"What they miss is the ability of humans to sacrifice for each other; to sacrifice for an ideal. We aren't the only species who can do this, but it is an important aspect of humanity that we share."

"I am going to speak about one such human. I am going to tell the story of one man who left the service on my home planet to follow me many years ago."

Bethany Anne took a deep breath and held it for a moment.

TOM, keep my emotions in check.

I've got your back, Bethany Anne.

Bethany Anne released her breath.

"I'm going to tell you the story of Chief Engineer John Edward Rodriquez and how he sacrificed his life in the Straiphus system, giving his all to keep the Etheric Empire safe…"

Jean Dukes couldn't keep her crying quiet any longer.

Planet Yoll, Capital City, Shool District

The park was mostly deserted. Night was coming, and many of the Yollins in that area were starting to eat.

The seven toughs figured the small alien family would be good for a mugging. The elite populace had currently stopped their attacks on humans for religious or political reasons, but the humans often had something that could be sold.

So the seven Yollins walked across the street, assuming this would be an easy score. They spread out, forming a half circle around the arguing couple. An arguing couple who ignored them.

The little human, however, smiled at the Yollins. The little alien seemed happy when they showed up.

"Hey!" Mu'tek shouted. As the leader of the group, it was his responsibility to make the demands.

Neither of the adult humans turned toward him; they just continued arguing. He looked down, and the little alien stuck her tongue out at him.

That was damned annoying.

"*HEY!*" he shouted again.

Both humans turned toward him and shouted, "*WHAT?*" in unison.

Mu'tek opened his arms. "You haven't paid the toll for using this park. You need to pay both the toll and the penalties now." One of his gang snickered. "I want any technology." He waved his hand. "And your clothes. You humans have so many different sets, I think I'll start collecting them."

"Oh, fuck you. Go away and leave us alone," the human male responded.

Mu'tek's eyes hardened. "I asked politely, but you refused." He looked to his left. "Maybe we let Grel harm the little girl?"

The little girl's eyes flashed yellow, and she lifted her hand. The middle finger seemed to grow a claw, and she pointed just the middle finger up and toward him.

The female snickered and commented to her mate, "Looks like she's channeling her inner BA."

The male just shook his head in annoyance.

Mu'tek nodded, and Grel walked forward, but he hadn't taken two steps when the little alien's nails changed to claws. Then her eyes went yellow, and she screamed as she ran at Grel. He barely had time to react when she jumped, landing both knees on his chest and knocking him off his feet. She slashed across his eyes, then rode him down and jumped off before he hit the ground. The youngster landed and rolled between the legs of Grel's partner. She popped upright and turned around, slicing through the spot between his foot and his leg's armor.

He went down screaming.

It didn't take long before Mu'tek himself had to fight the little demon from hell. He had his knife out, and managed to stab the little alien. His eyes opened in shock when the knife didn't penetrate.

The child laughed and spoke in Yollin, "Jean Dukes armor, bitch!"

She ripped her claws across his throat.

That was the final straw. Four of the Yollin toughs were down, one possibly dying. The other three grabbed the hurt ones, slapping the one holding his head after the little girl had punched him on her way to Mu'tek.

The thugs limped away as fast as they could drag their fallen.

Ecaterina opened her arms, and the child's eyes faded from yellow and her hands changed back as she jumped up into her mom's arms. "That's our little warrior!" Ecaterina praised as the two high-fived, and they turned to look at Nathan. "Told you she could take them out!"

Nathan reached over and ruffled Christina's hair. "Ok, I owe you two ounces of gold and both of you an apology. I guess the three of us *are* a team," he admitted. He pulled two coins out and handed them to Ecaterina, then opened his arms. Christina crawled from her mom's embrace over to her dad and kissed him on the cheek. "Those fucktards were lousy. Auntie Bethany Anne would make them each do a thousand pushups for their bad form."

Nathan grimaced at his daughter. "What would Auntie Bethany Anne say about you using such language, little lady?"

"She would say drop and give me fifty," Christina moaned.

"That's right," Nathan agreed and put her down. "So get to it. If you think you are old enough to be cursing, then you are old enough to do it right. Next time you curse and it isn't unique, it's a hundred pushups."

Christina did her first pushup. "One...dammit."

She went down and pushed up again. "Two...shit-faced gargoyle."

The two adults listened in as Christina continued her pushups. "Thirty-eight...scum-sucking pile of doggie poo."

"Nah-ah!" Ecaterina admonished the little girl. "That is a repeat from your fifth pushup. Start over."

"You've got to be fucking kidding me!" Christina wailed as she went back down.

"That's a second fifty now. You repeated 'fucking,'" Nathan told her.

"This isn't fair!" she whined.

"On the contrary, it is very fair. Ask Uncle Scott or Uncle Eric sometime. They have had to do the same thing."

"This sucks! It isn't worth cussing if I have to do pushups all the time," she complained.

Ecaterina rolled her eyes and reached into her pocket. She took out the two coins Nathan had given her for losing the bet and returned them. He mouthed "thank you" and gave her a wink.

EPILOGUE

Yollin System, Three Years Post-Straiphus Rebellion

They say that history is written by the victors, and they are right. The reason is completely logical. Those who lost aren't around to write anything.

The dead can't write from beyond the grave.

The latest and most impressive ship built in the Yollin's new military shipyards slowly and smoothly slid from its moorings as hundreds who watched from nearby ships raised their hands in salute.

The Empress stared in silence as the massive new ship slid into place next to her official Royal In-system Transport Pod. The doors opened to allow the Empress' transport to enter the ship's cavernous bay.

It wasn't long before those in the transport Pod disembarked and made their way to the bridge, which was built in the center of the massive vessel.

Bethany Anne stopped outside the bridge to look at the six-foot-wide dark-gray stone monument that had so many names chiseled into it, and she rubbed her hand across a few. Turning, she wiped a tear from her cheek as she took the last few steps to the bridge. The doors opened automatically for her.

She nodded at those waiting for her arrival—the Yollin head of the shipyard, those who worked to make this ship useable by both humans and Yollins, and those who had been employed on the massive electronic infrastructure.

Necessary to house the new intelligence.

She walked straight to the captain's chair and sat down. The Shipyard Master looked at the Minister of Defense, who winked back at him.

"This is Empress Bethany Anne of the Etheric Empire. Show yourself," she commanded.

A face, a replica of the Empress herself, slowly brightened into view on the front screens, her eyes flaring red. Some of those on the bridge were shocked to see the face of the Empress on the screens.

Their Empress, however, smiled in satisfaction. "Hello, Arch-Angel. It's damned good to have you back."

The face on the screen looked at everyone on her bridge, then she looked at the woman seated in the captain's chair and smiled.

"Hello, Mother."

There was a second where no one even breathed as the AI continued, "This is the Leviathan-class Superdreadnought *Arch-Angel II*. I have been commanded to protect the Etheric Empire by Empress Bethany Anne. Lockdown Protocols on this ship have not yet been implemented. Does the Empress command I enact lockdown protocols?"

"No, I do not," Bethany Anne replied.

"Lockdown protocols are not activated. Leviathan-class Superdreadnought *ArchAngel II* is now fully operational, and will fight all who attack the Etheric Empire until victorious...or dead."

Bethany Anne smiled, her eyes red in memory of those whose

names graced the stone outside the bridge. "Good. It's time you kick some more ass, ArchAngel."

FINIS

FOREVER DEFEND

The Story Continues with book 17, Forever Defend.

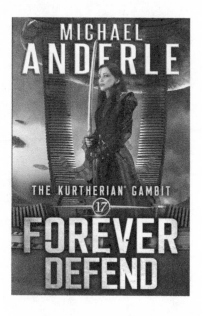

Available now at Amazon and on Kindle Unlimited

AUTHOR NOTES

Wow!

Thank you - thank you - thank you for reading these notes. By reading this stuff, it pretty much means you have read well over a *MILLION* words of Kurtherian kick-ass badassery... AND probably a shit-ton of cursing. Probably *way* more colorful language than the recommended daily allowance suggested by just about anyone who has a problem with cursing.

Yes, I know I have a problem writing this type of language, and I completely blame my sense of humor. I snicker (*don't judge me!*) when stupid curse words are strung together in humorous ways.

If they are strung together in even better ways, I'll laugh out loud and then go back and re-read them another time...and *then* snicker again.

The first time I remember reading fuck in a book (at least, my decade's old memory remembers this) was in the story Spellsinger by Alan Dean Foster when the wizard turtle Clothahump brings the *sanitation engineer* instead of a real engineer over to his world and stupidity ensues.

This was EXACTLY the type of story my 19-year-old mind would find amusing. Anyway, I'm laying down on the couch in my first apartment (a two bedroom split-roommate plan I shared with my older brother) when I run across this *fuck* the old wizard spouts out.

I died.

I mean, I was gasping for air I was laughing so hard! I remember going back one time, years later JUST to find that passage and read it again.

Sigh...good times.

I've been blessed to have many of you mention that even though you don't like cursing, you either skip it (story makes up for it) or you find it funny and give me a pass. I guess Homer Simpson was right when he told Marge, *"I made you laugh, I'm off the hook!"*

I've also been humored many times when you admit you found yourself cursing more after you shot-gunned the stories for a few days. Or, funnier yet, your SPOUSES are catching you cursing more often.

Now THAT must be some good times!

Talking about good times, I now get to share a personal good time with you speaking (or writing as the case may be) as a happy dad!

This good time has to do with my youngest son, Joseph (Joey).

He and his brother live at home, and both will be heading to college or perhaps the military (Marines) in a few months.

So, Joey - who was 16 years old at the time - was talking a little smack last August (8 months ago). It was during the time I was having a lot of success with The Kurtherian Gambit that he makes a flippant statement, "I can do this writing thing, easy peasy." (Or something similar).

(Ok, parents of teenagers, sing along with me now...)

"Anything Dad can do... I can do BETTER!"

Hahahahahaha...

AUTHOR NOTES

Apparently, he took my "Oh yeah?" reply as a challenge. This was a bit of a surprise for me to learn months later when he fessed up as to how he got the writing bug.

I won't belabor the story because I've mentioned it in other places, but he spent September, October, and November working on story ideas with me, writing, trashing whatever he wrote, and just about getting nowhere on his book...Write 3,000 words... Delete 2,500...

However, in December of 2016 over the Christmas Holidays, Joey released the first book (Book 00) of The Courier Chronicles series, and it shocked both of us to see him move up the ranks and break the top 3,000 ranking before he dropped down.

It was pretty damned fun to watch him have some success; I have to admit!

Now, it was a CHALLENGE to get that boy to finish the first book, Her Royal Runner. So, I told him I would provide some support for Book 00, but I wouldn't talk about his stories in my author notes in the back of a Bethany Anne story until he could write and publish book 01 in his series... I wanted to make sure this wasn't just a 'I can do this too' response. I wanted to see some real results that he cared to keep going and not leave those of us who had read book 00 hanging.

And it was a good thing I didn't. While he started for a day or two, life and new girlfriend and school...*and new girlfriend* (did I mention that already?) was much more interesting to his 17 year old head.

Finally, something (or some one) encouraged him to get that next story going. In February, over a long weekend, he sat down and in the space of four days, he wrote something like 15,000 words to get to words complete on his second book, The Messengers Menagerie.

Sonofabitch, he did it!

I'm proud of all of my sons, and no matter what they choose to do in life, I want them to be happy doing it. There is a saying that if you want to learn about the author, check out their main character because an author will place a lot of themselves in the character. Well, I hope that my fans know a lot of Bethany Anne's personality is NOT my personality or likes.

I'm not into woman's shoes, that's my wife (#TotalTruth).

However, in Joey's book, the main character Sterling "Booker" Wells IS Joey. When you read these stories, you won't have to know what my son is like, because he is telling the world what he is like with the mannerisms of his protagonist.

I vividly remember Joey acting out, working on writing a scene where Booker is looking at himself in a closet mirror. He is checking out the clothes he is wearing to go on a trip and Joey comments out loud, "how would Booker act, 'if he was looking in the mirror and someone started opening the door.'"

Mind you - Joseph is grabbing his cheeks and acting this just two bar stools down from me as I'm working on editing a book myself.

Now, I've stopped editing and I'm staring at my son, who is playing out this scene just 48 inches away. That's too damned close for sanity, trust me.

Sometimes, 17-year-olds shouldn't be allowed to write. (He and his twin have a birthday in late August, so he is 17 now for those whipsawed by the comment about being 16 earlier.)

Well, Joey did write and write and write and due to the help of the Double D's (who spent HOURS working with him (patience of saints here) and Jeff Brown's help for another cover he produced his second book.

I've read both books, I've laughed my ass off at both books. As someone familiar with the author, I can tell you Joey IS this funny in real life and it can be a challenge to parent him. However, I will admit in front of ten's of thousands of readers...

HE SHOWED ME UP! Joey Anderle is now the proud author of two books and few teenagers can say that.

And I pay my debts ;-)

Well done, son. Well done!

(P.S. – I'm not saying that the precocious teen wrote the opposite of what his dad suggested to him during story discussions just so he could be rebellious...but he totally did.)

Written March 29th and 30th, 2017

BOOKS BY MICHAEL ANDERLE

Sign up for the LMBPN email list to be notified of new releases and special deals!

https://lmbpn.com/email/

For a complete list of books by Michael Anderle, please visit:

www.lmbpn.com/ma-books/

CONNECT WITH THE AUTHOR

Connect with Michael Anderle

Website: http://lmbpn.com

Email List: https://michael.beehiiv.com/

https://www.facebook.com/LMBPNPublishing

https://twitter.com/MichaelAnderle

https://www.instagram.com/lmbpn_publishing/

https://www.bookbub.com/authors/michael-anderle